THE FLYING BEAV[illegible]
AND THE CRAZY C[illegible]

MAXWELL EATON III

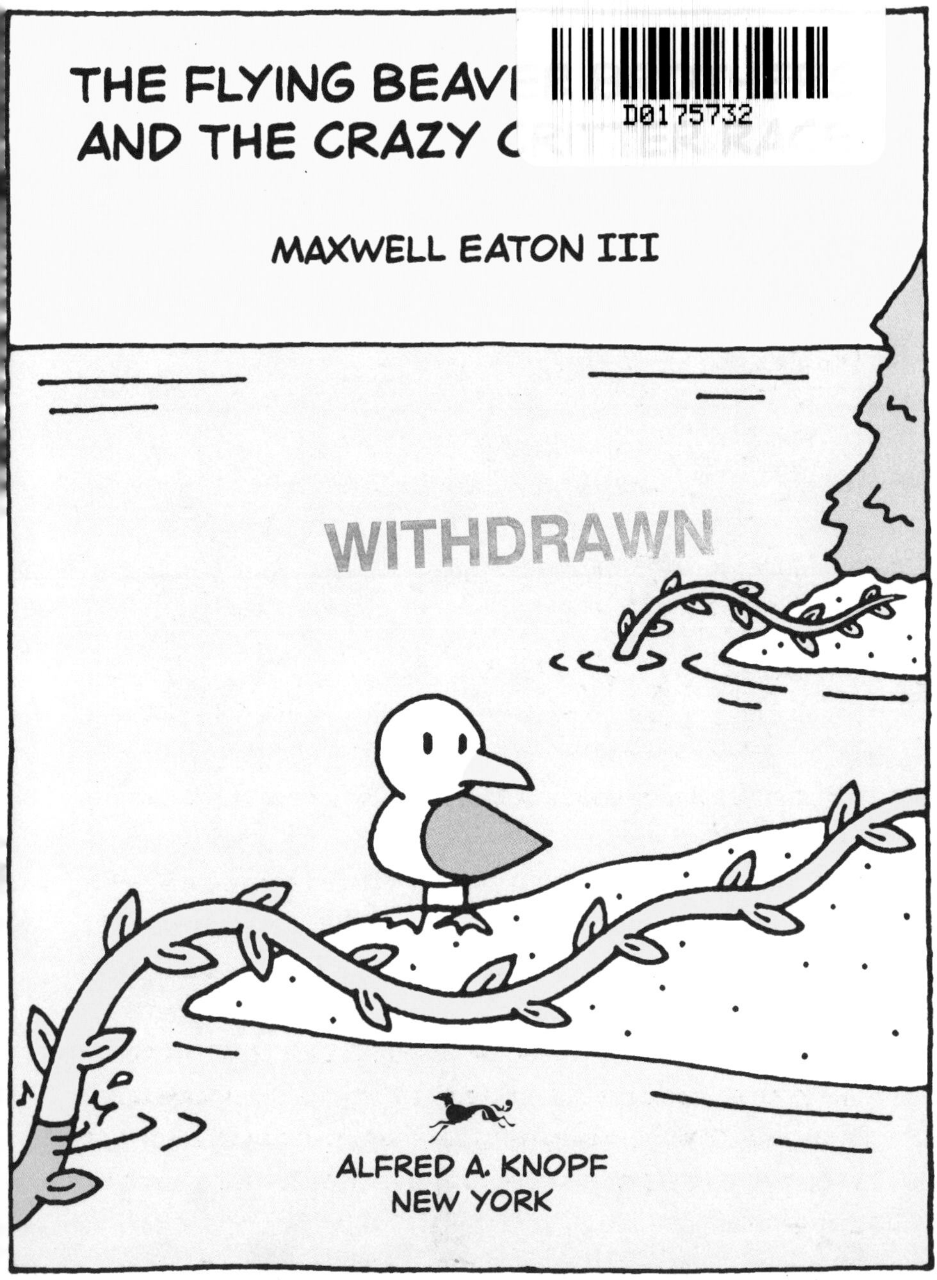

ALFRED A. KNOPF
NEW YORK

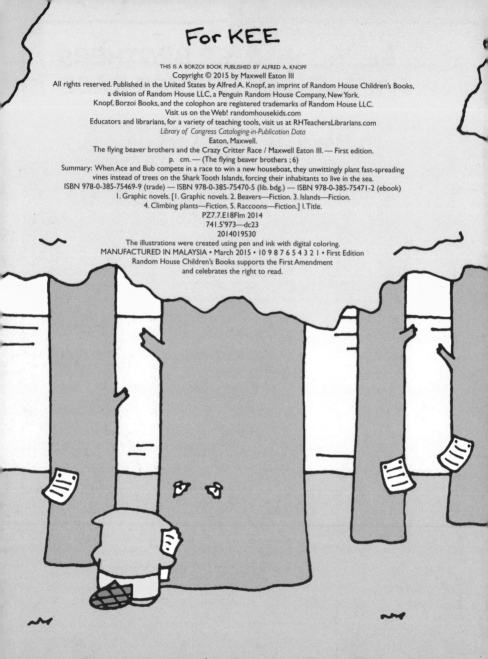

For KEE

THIS IS A BORZOI BOOK PUBLISHED BY ALFRED A. KNOPF

Published in the United States by Alfred A. Knopf, an imprint of Random House Children's Books, a division of Random House LLC, a Penguin Random House Company, New York.
Knopf, Borzoi Books, and the colophon are registered trademarks of Random House LLC.
Visit us on the Web! randomhousekids.com
Educators and librarians, for a variety of teaching tools, visit us at RHTeachersLibrarians.com
Library of Congress Cataloging-in-Publication Data
Eaton, Maxwell.
The flying beaver brothers and the Crazy Critter Race / Maxwell Eaton III. — First edition.
p. cm. — (The flying beaver brothers ; 6)
Summary: When Ace and Bub compete in a race to win a new houseboat, they unwittingly plant fast-spreading vines instead of trees on the Shark Tooth Islands, forcing their inhabitants to live in the sea.
ISBN 978-0-385-75469-9 (trade) — ISBN 978-0-385-75470-5 (lib. bdg.) — ISBN 978-0-385-75471-2 (ebook)
1. Graphic novels. [1. Graphic novels. 2. Beavers—Fiction. 3. Islands—Fiction. 4. Climbing plants—Fiction. 5. Raccoons—Fiction.] I. Title.
PZ7.7.E18Flm 2014
741.5'973—dc23
2014019530
The illustrations were created using pen and ink with digital coloring.
MANUFACTURED IN MALAYSIA • March 2015 • 10 9 8 7 6 5 4 3 2 1 • First Edition
Random House Children's Books supports the First Amendment and celebrates the right to read.

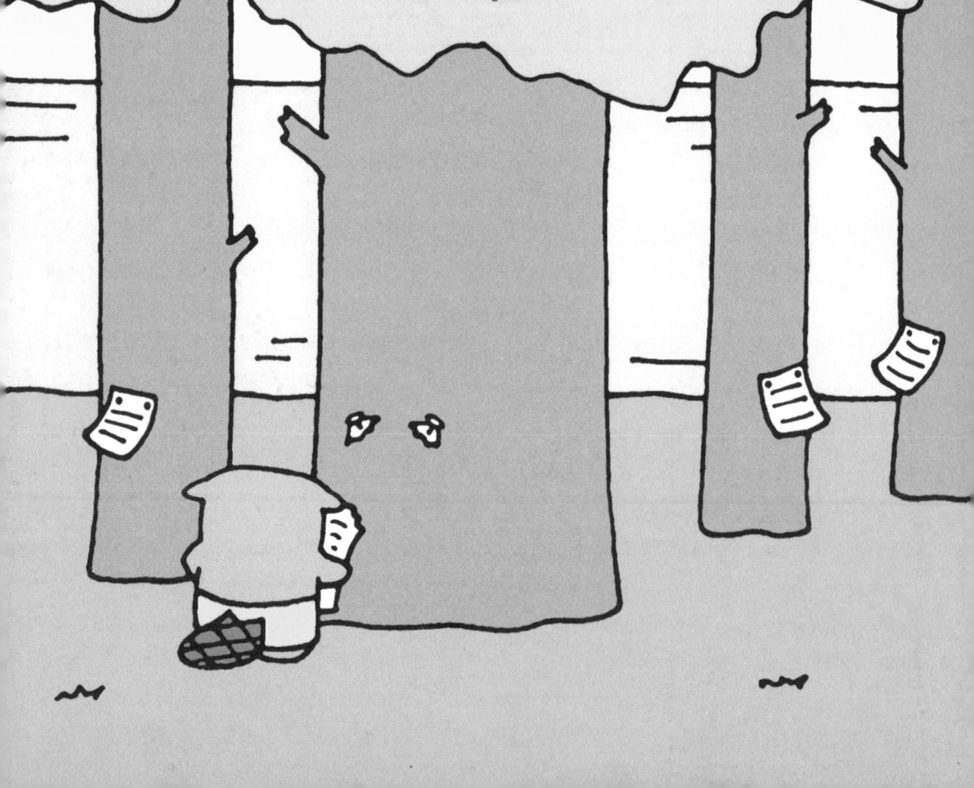

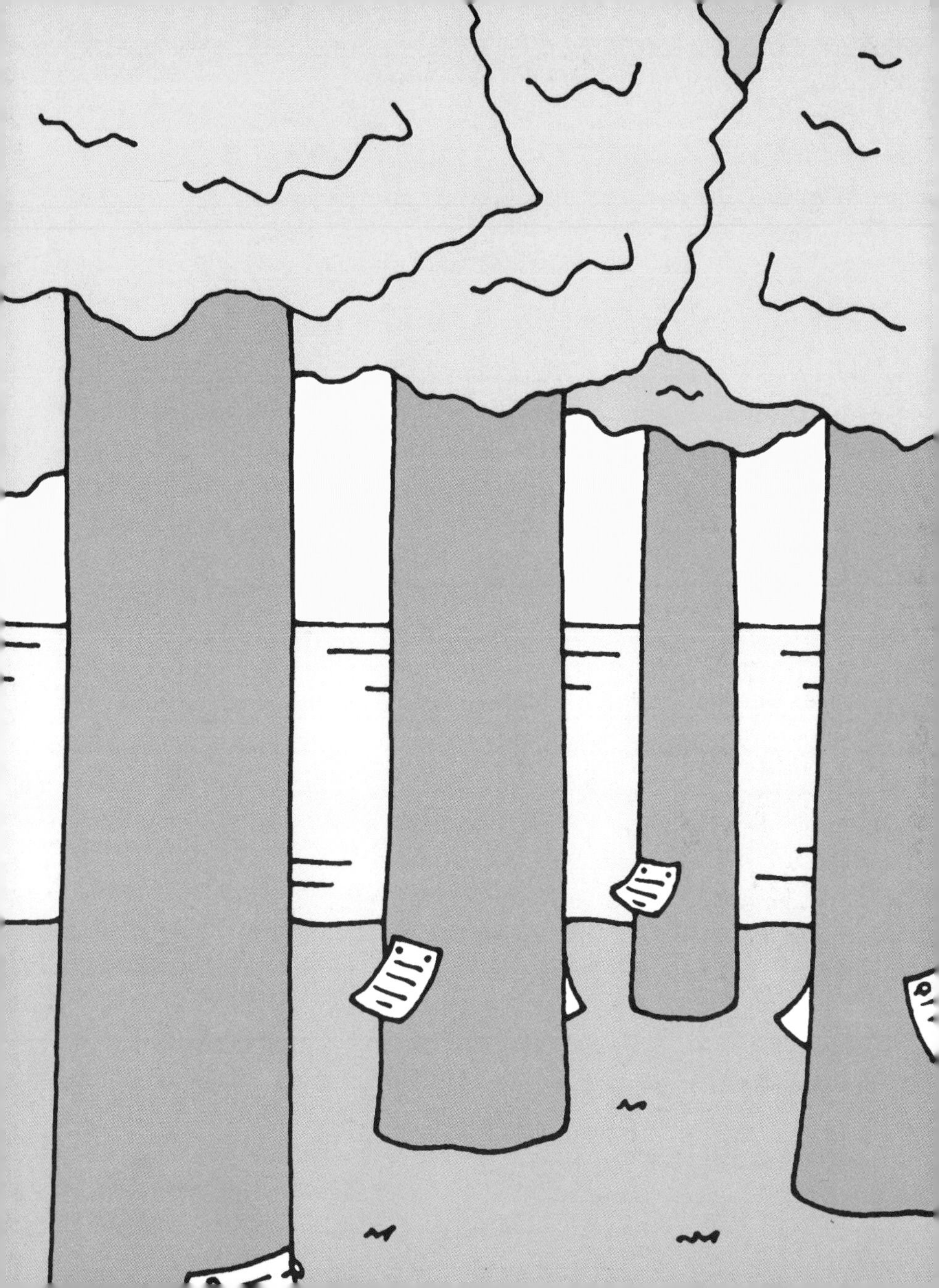

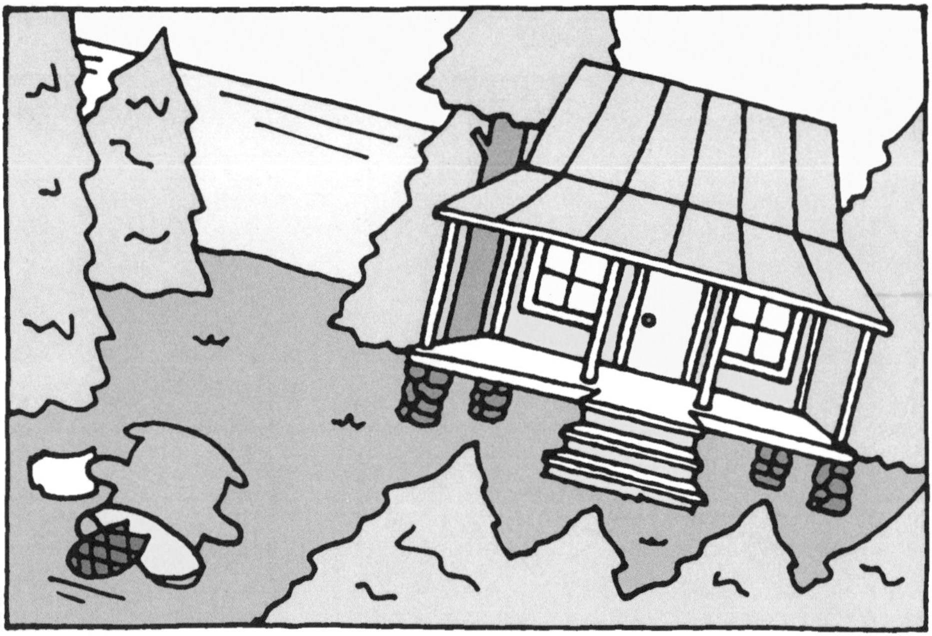

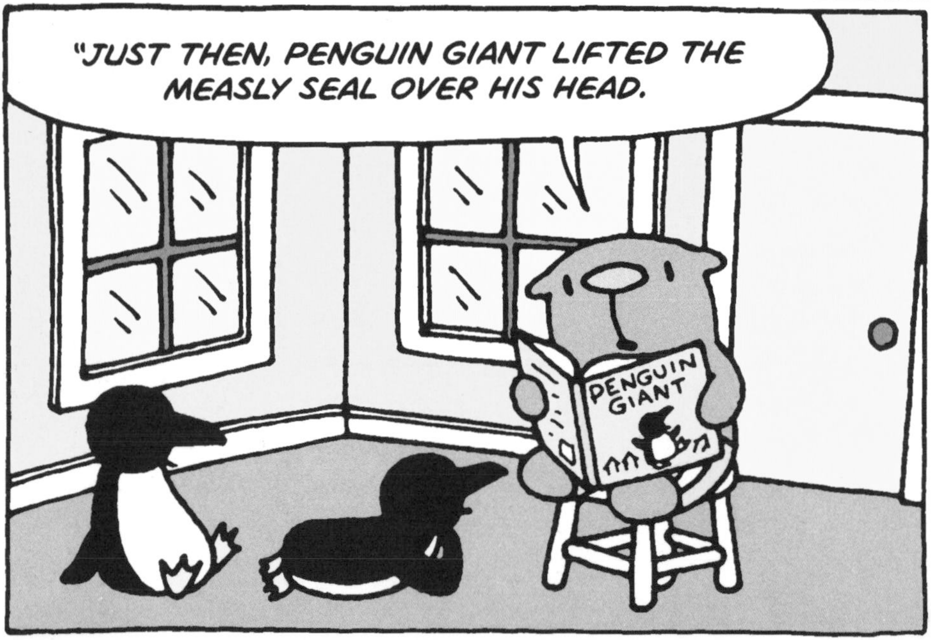
"JUST THEN, PENGUIN GIANT LIFTED THE MEASLY SEAL OVER HIS HEAD.
PENGUIN GIANT

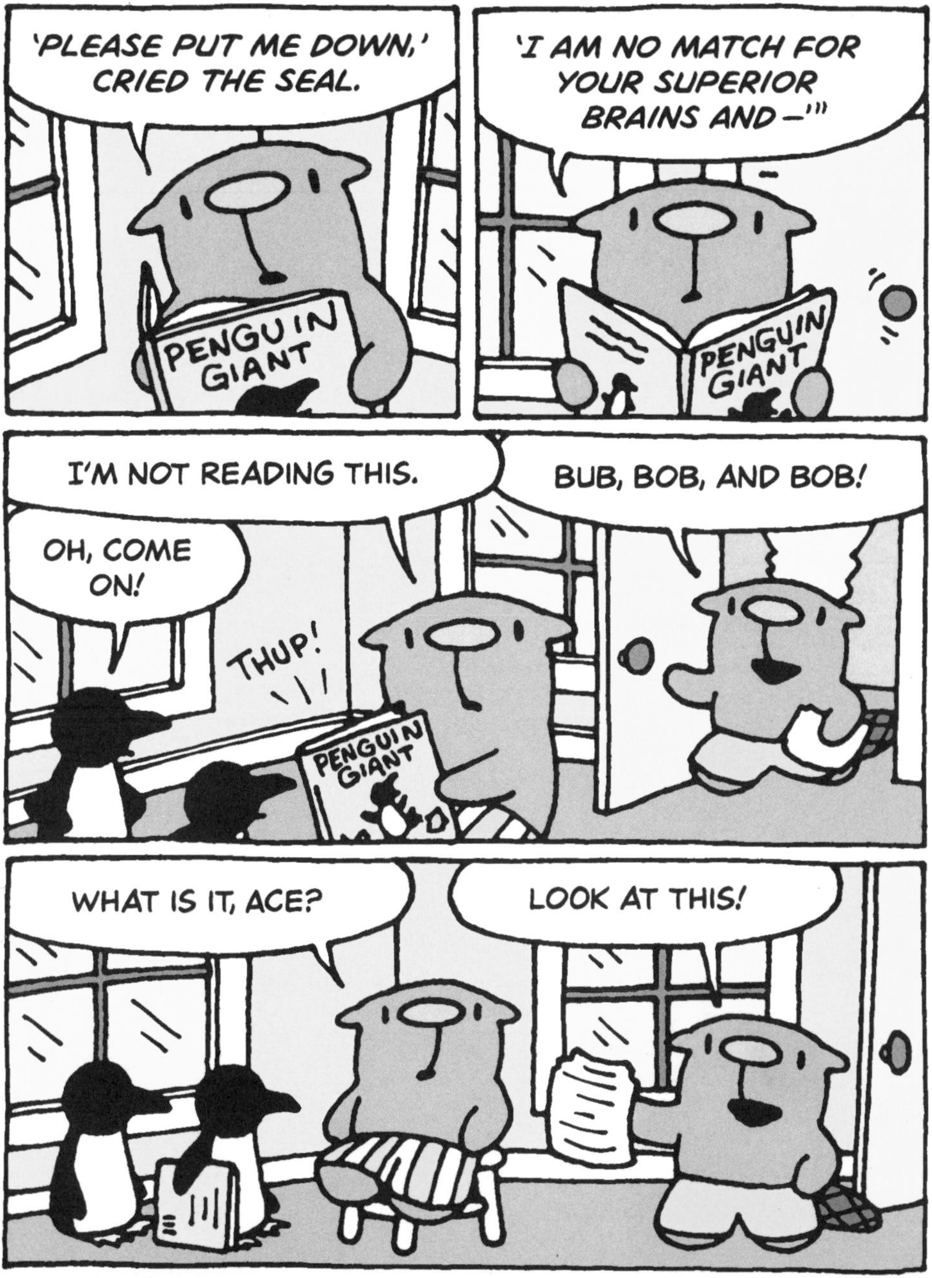
'PLEASE PUT ME DOWN,' CRIED THE SEAL.
PENGUIN GIANT
'I AM NO MATCH FOR YOUR SUPERIOR BRAINS AND—'"
PENGUIN GIANT
I'M NOT READING THIS.
OH, COME ON!
THUP!
PENGUIN GIANT
BUB, BOB, AND BOB!
WHAT IS IT, ACE?
LOOK AT THIS!

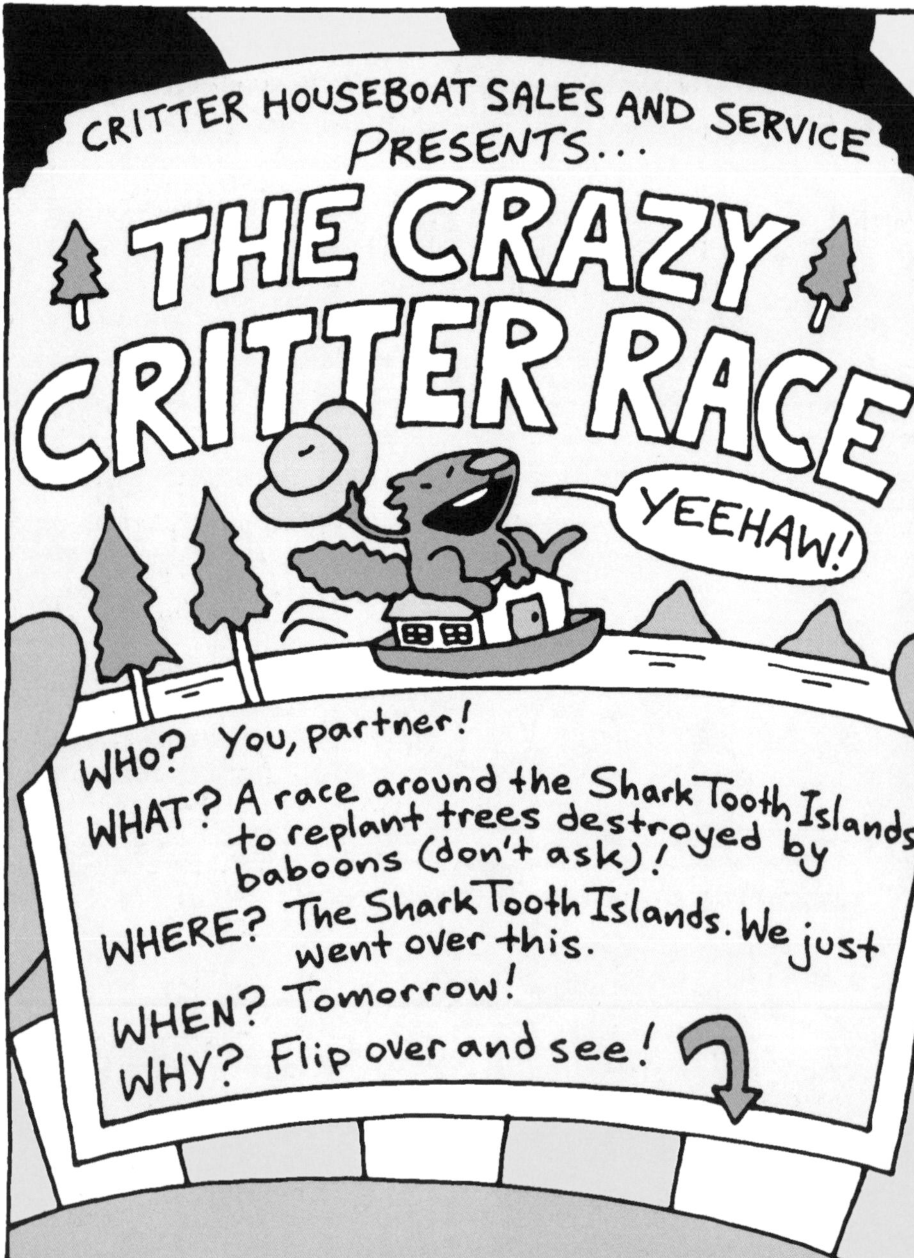
CRITTER HOUSEBOAT SALES AND SERVICE
PRESENTS...
THE CRAZY CRITTER RACE
YEEHAW!
WHO? You, partner!
WHAT? A race around the Shark Tooth Islands to replant trees destroyed by baboons (don't ask)!
WHERE? The Shark Tooth Islands. We just went over this.
WHEN? Tomorrow!
WHY? Flip over and see!

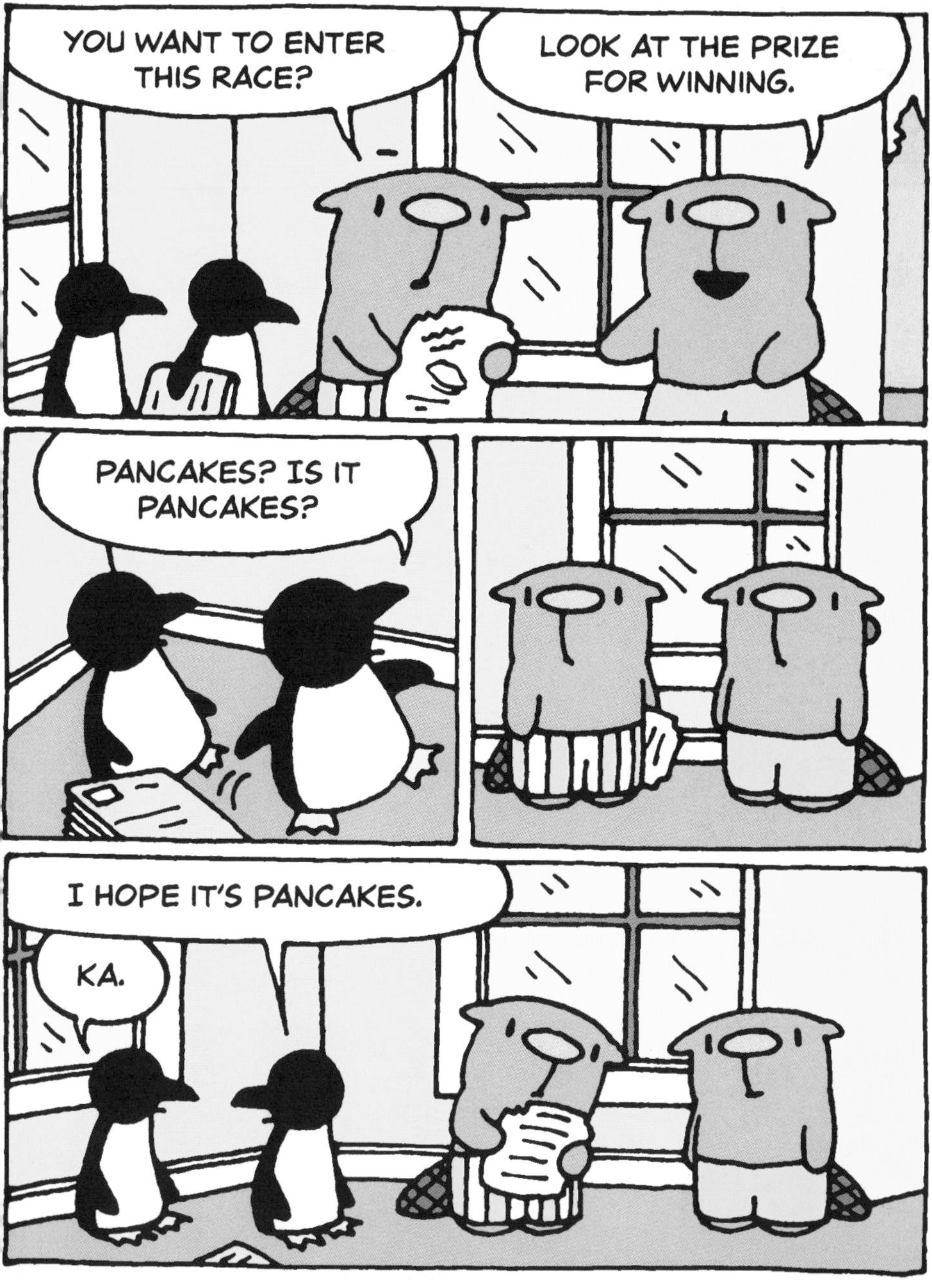
YOU WANT TO ENTER THIS RACE?
LOOK AT THE PRIZE FOR WINNING.
PANCAKES? IS IT PANCAKES?
I HOPE IT'S PANCAKES.
KA.

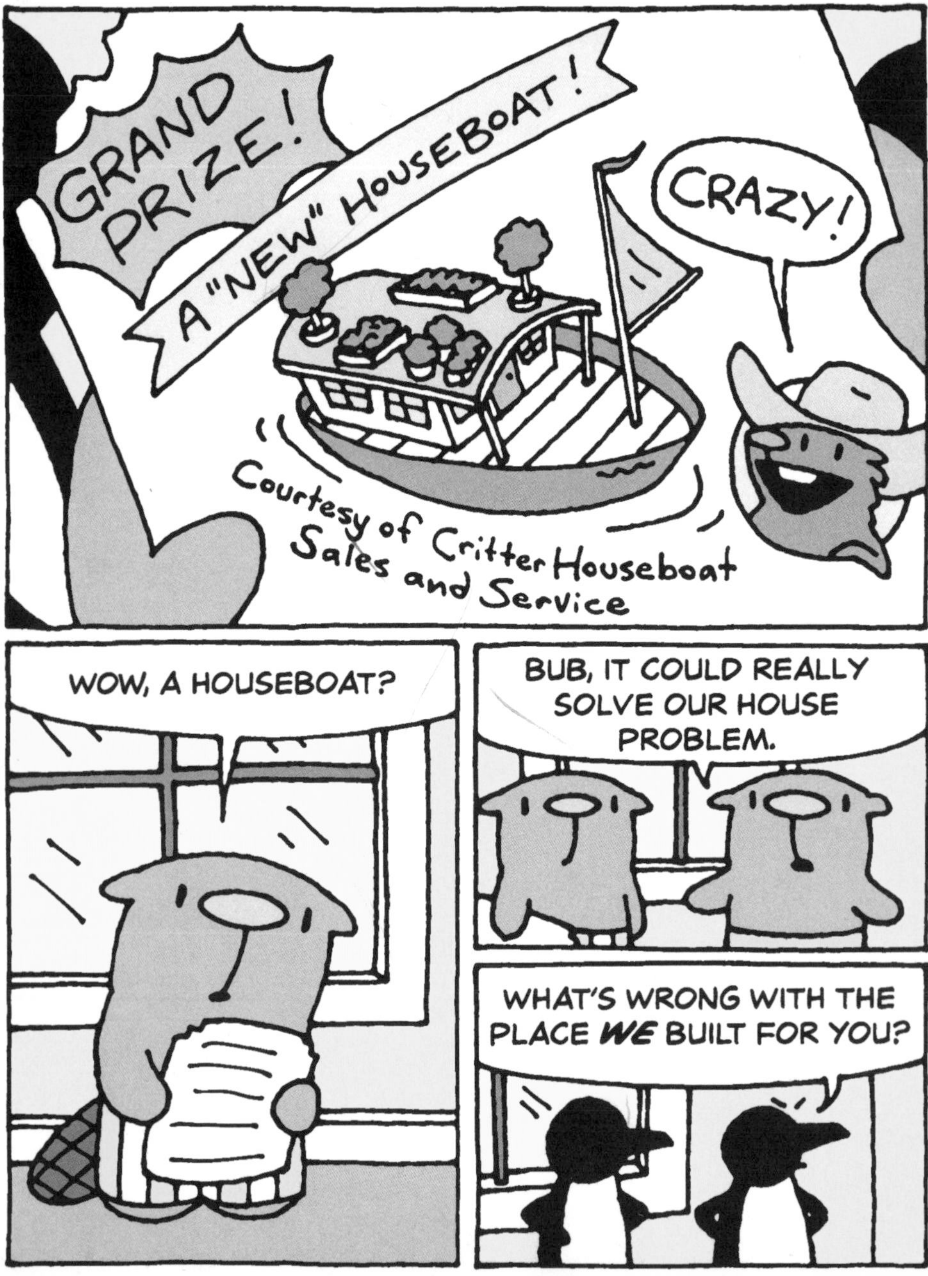
GRAND PRIZE!
A "NEW" HOUSEBOAT!
CRAZY!
Courtesy of Critter Houseboat Sales and Service
WOW, A HOUSEBOAT?
BUB, IT COULD REALLY SOLVE OUR HOUSE PROBLEM.
WHAT'S WRONG WITH THE PLACE WE BUILT FOR YOU?

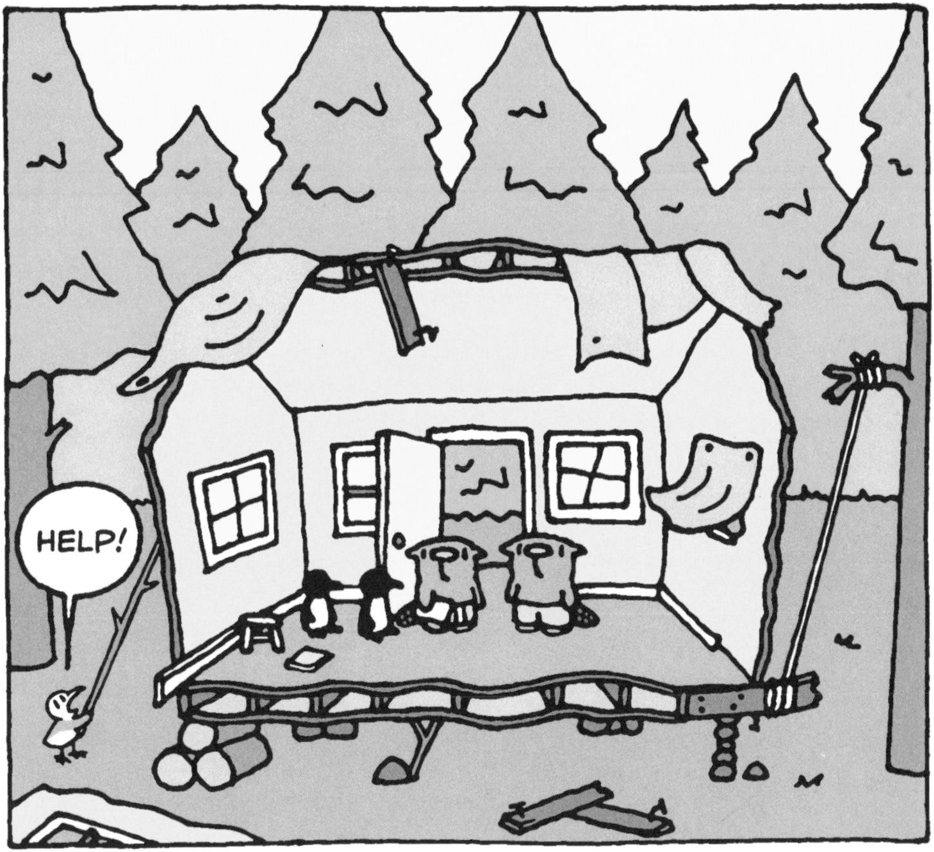
HELP!

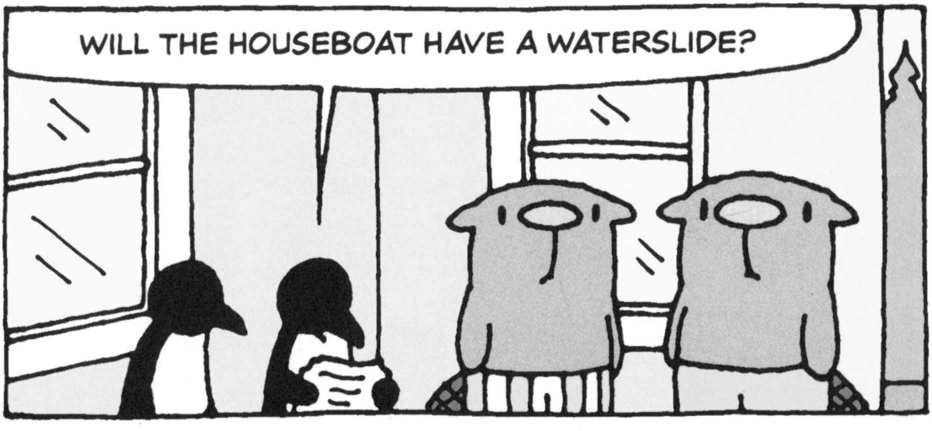
WILL THE HOUSEBOAT HAVE A WATERSLIDE?

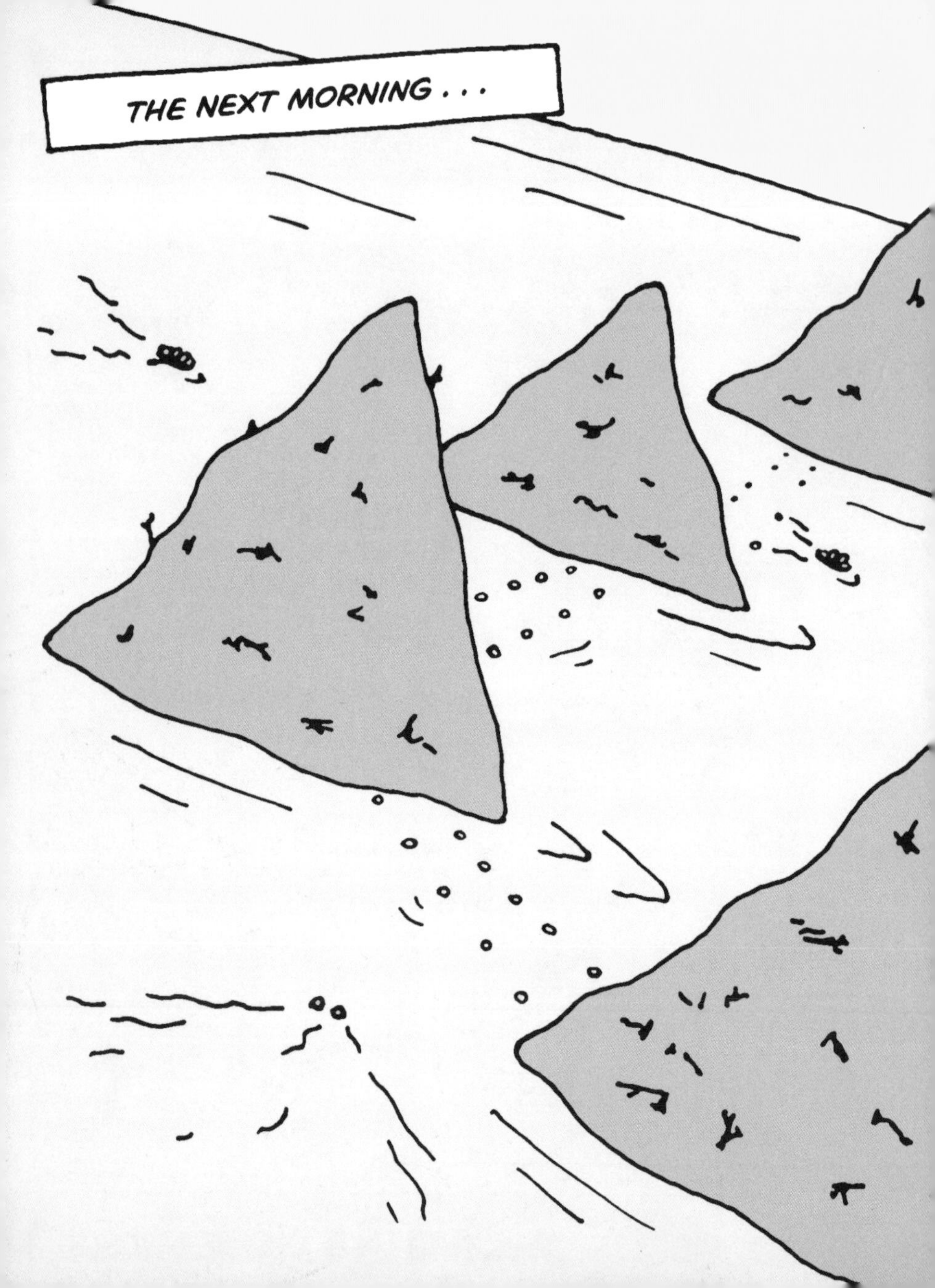
THE NEXT MORNING . . .

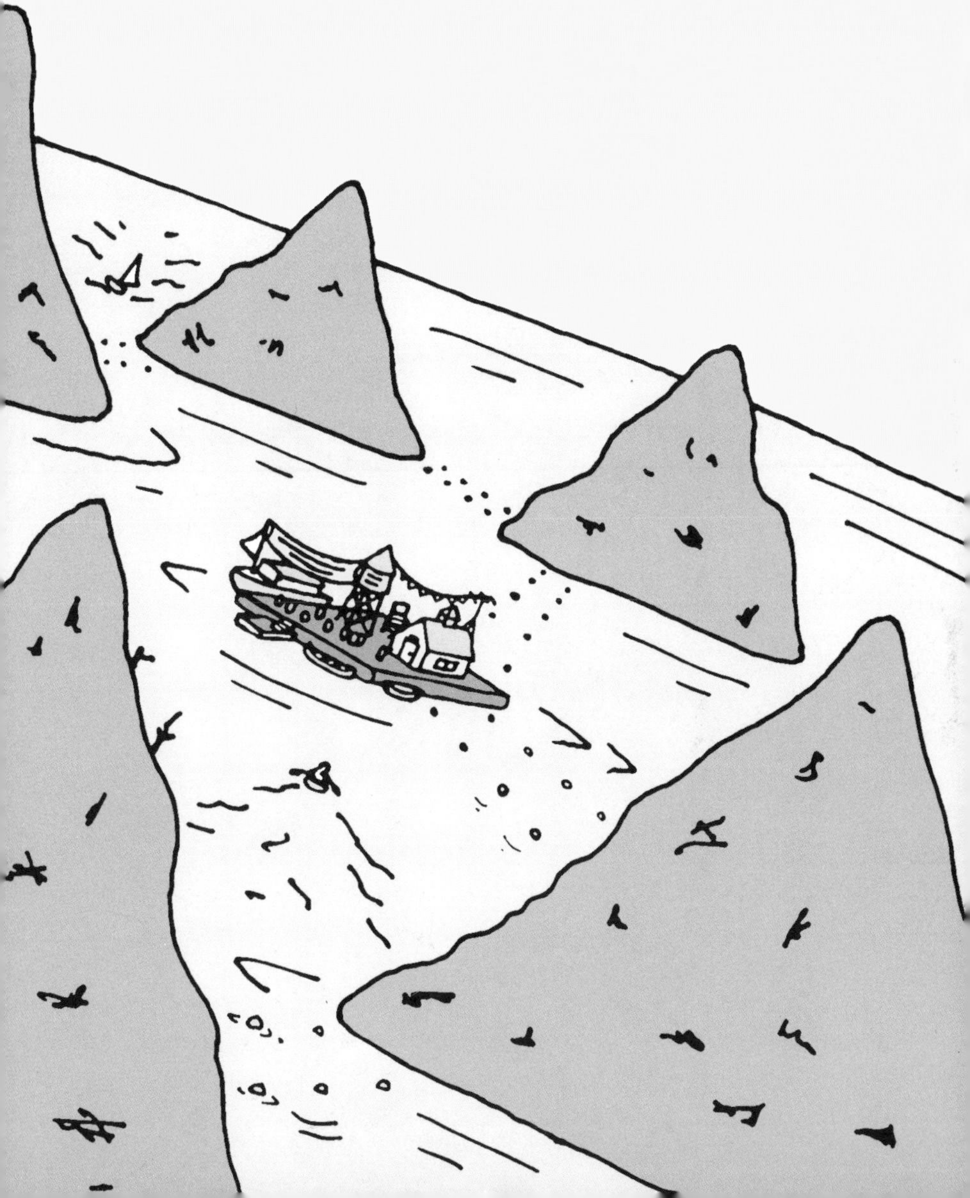

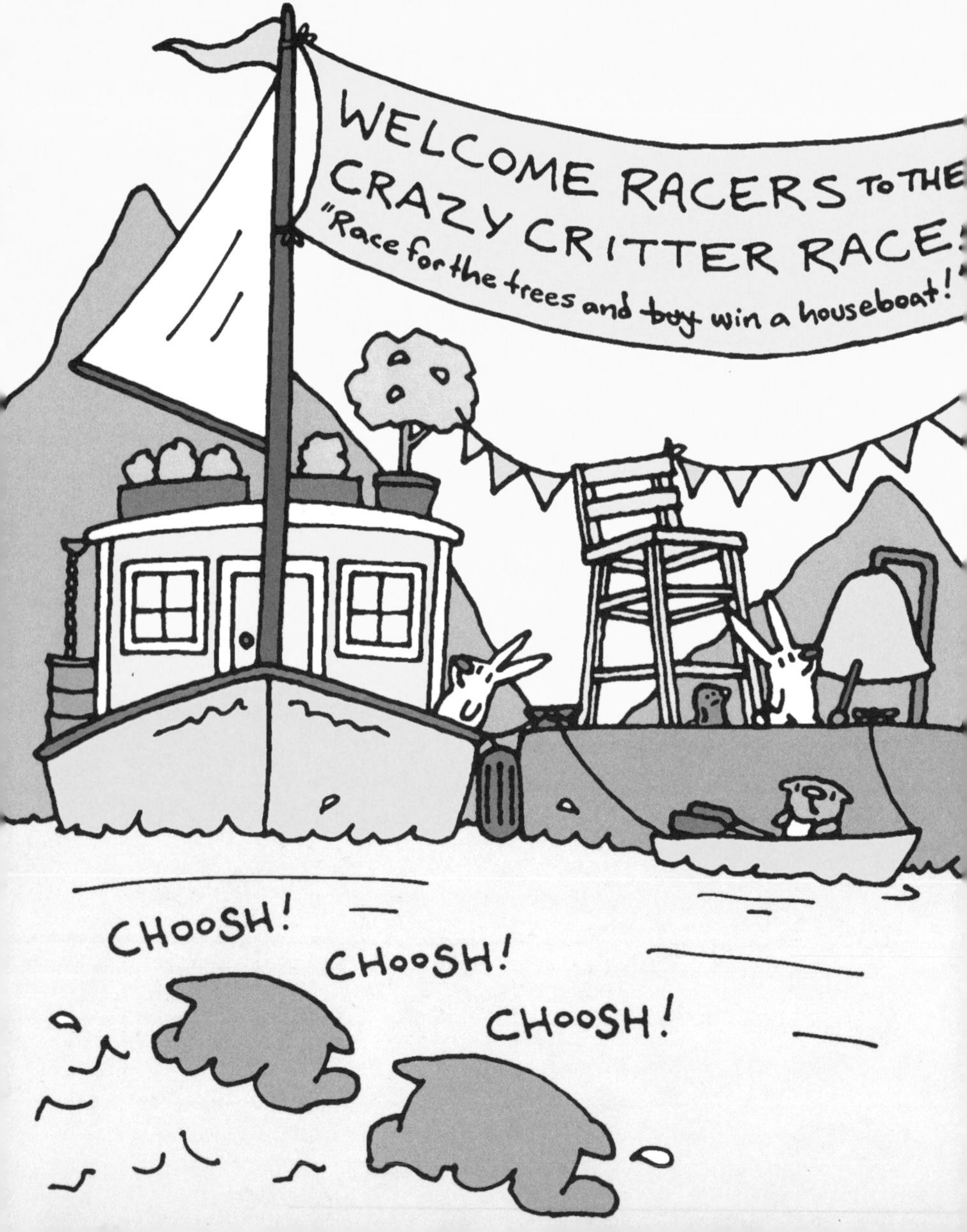
WELCOME RACERS TO THE CRAZY CRITTER RACE!
"Race for the trees and boy win a houseboat!"
CHOOSH!
CHOOSH!
CHOOSH!

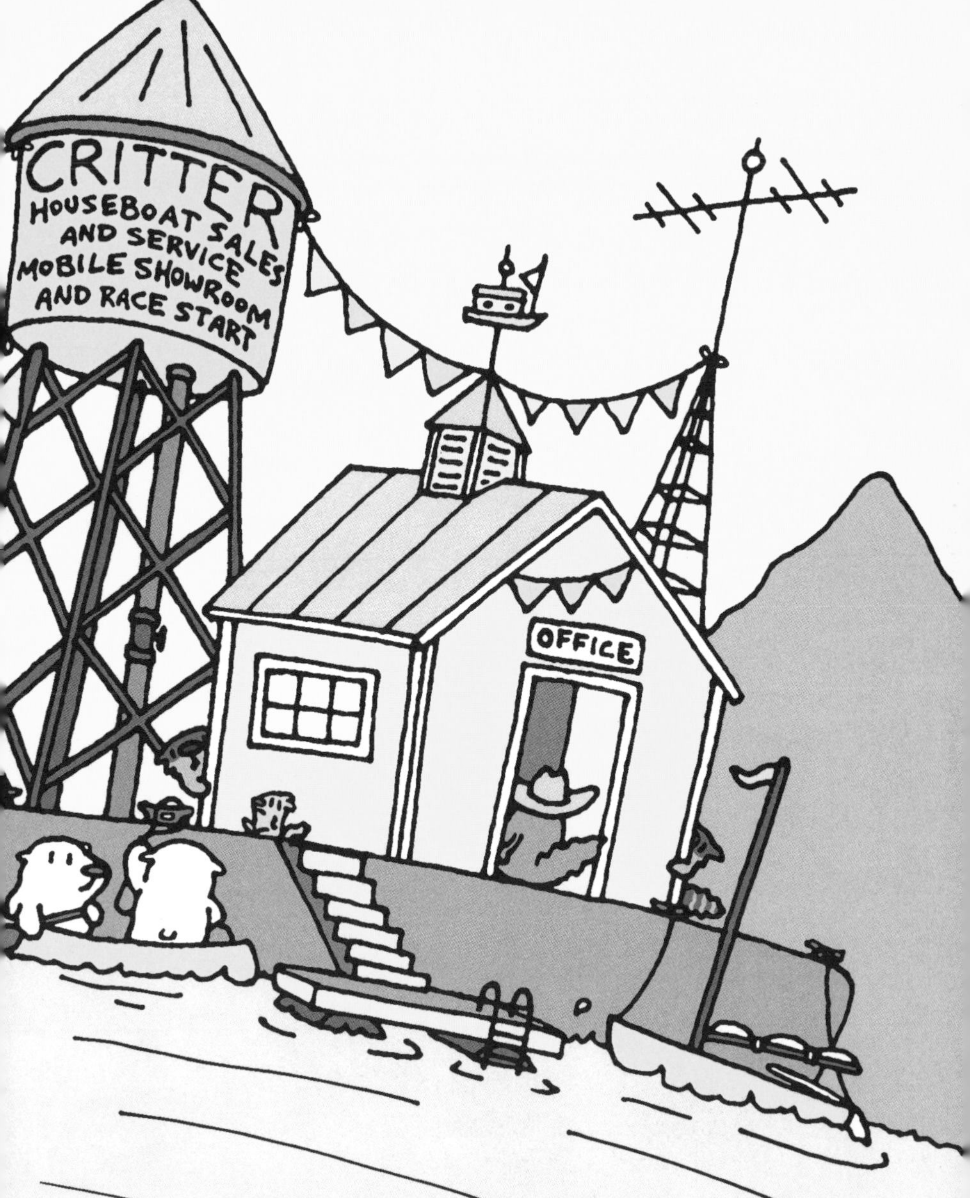
CRITTER
HOUSEBOAT SALES
AND SERVICE
MOBILE SHOWROOM
AND RACE START
OFFICE

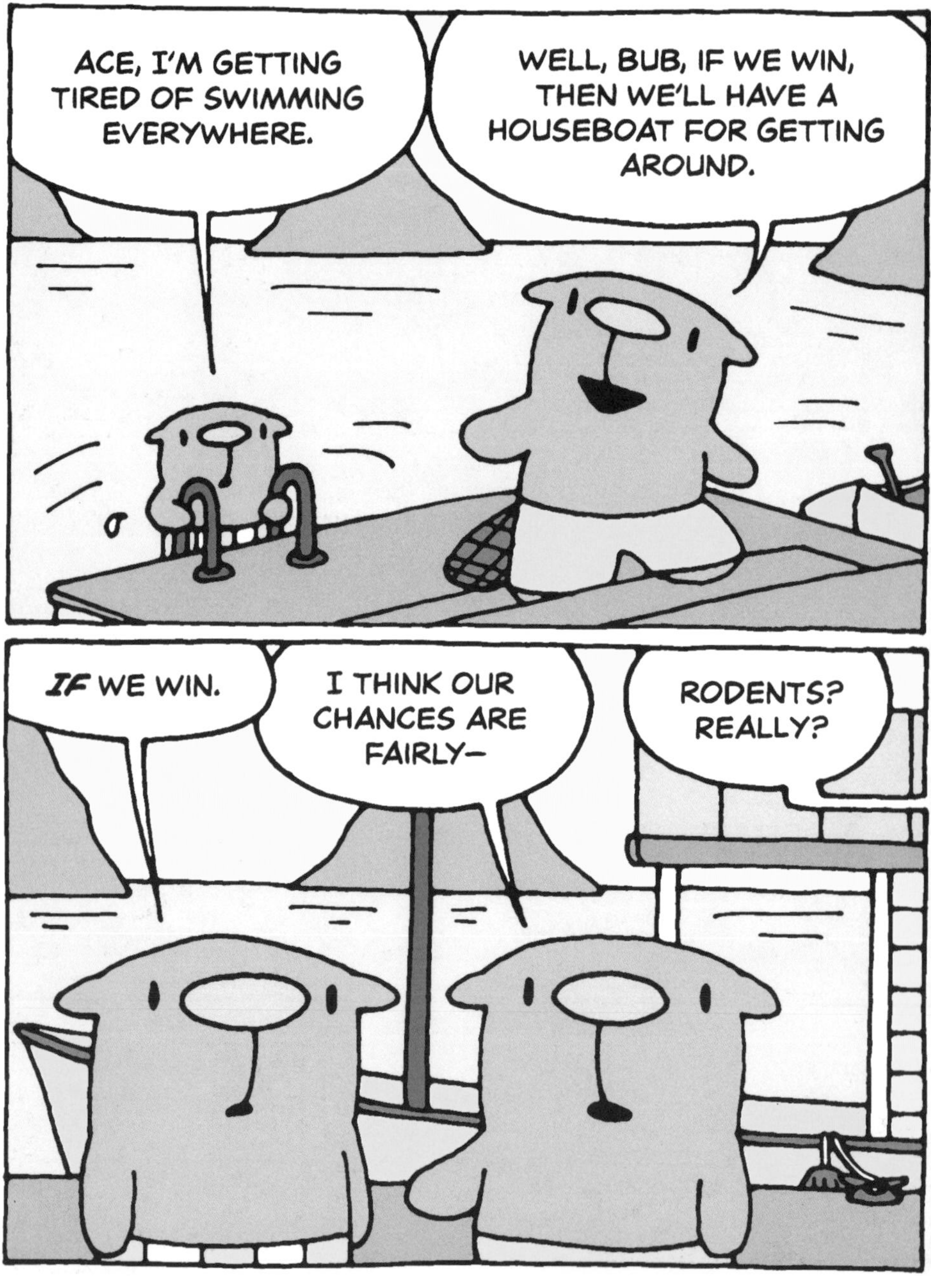
ACE, I'M GETTING TIRED OF SWIMMING EVERYWHERE.
WELL, BUB, IF WE WIN, THEN WE'LL HAVE A HOUSEBOAT FOR GETTING AROUND.
IF WE WIN.
I THINK OUR CHANCES ARE FAIRLY—
RODENTS? REALLY?

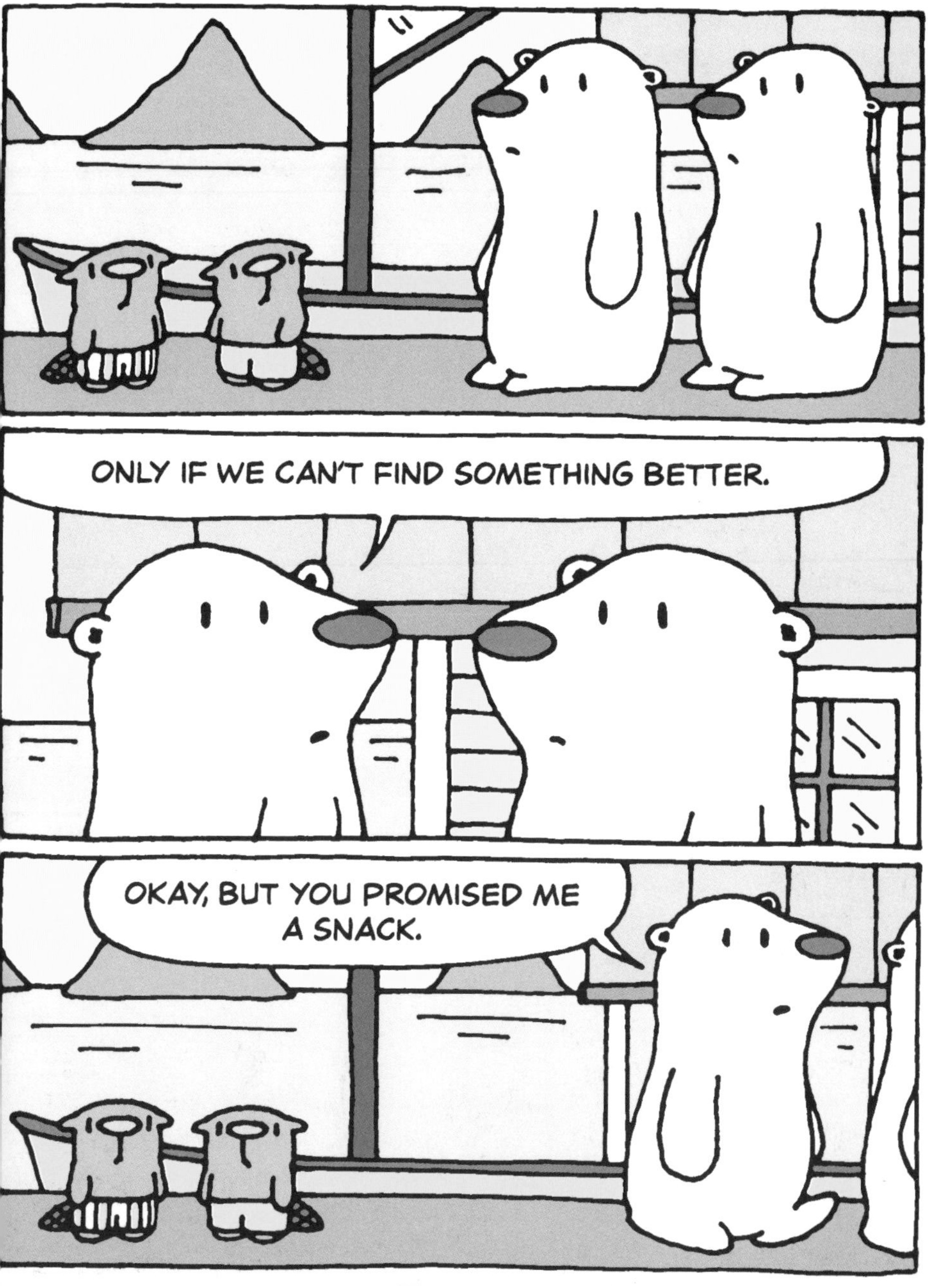
ONLY IF WE CAN'T FIND SOMETHING BETTER.
OKAY, BUT YOU PROMISED ME A SNACK.

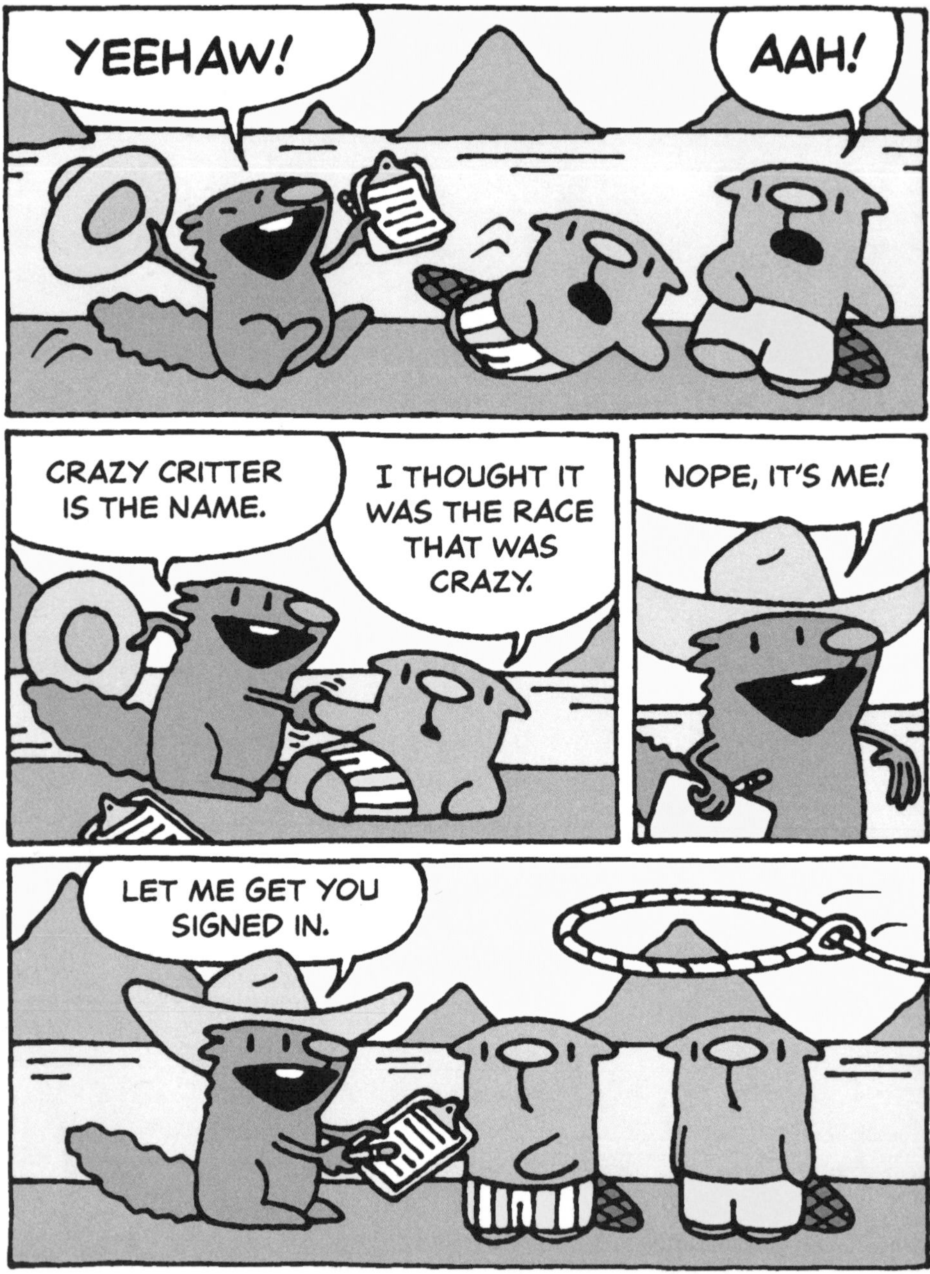
YEEHAW!
AAH!
CRAZY CRITTER IS THE NAME.
I THOUGHT IT WAS THE RACE THAT WAS CRAZY.
NOPE, IT'S ME!
LET ME GET YOU SIGNED IN.

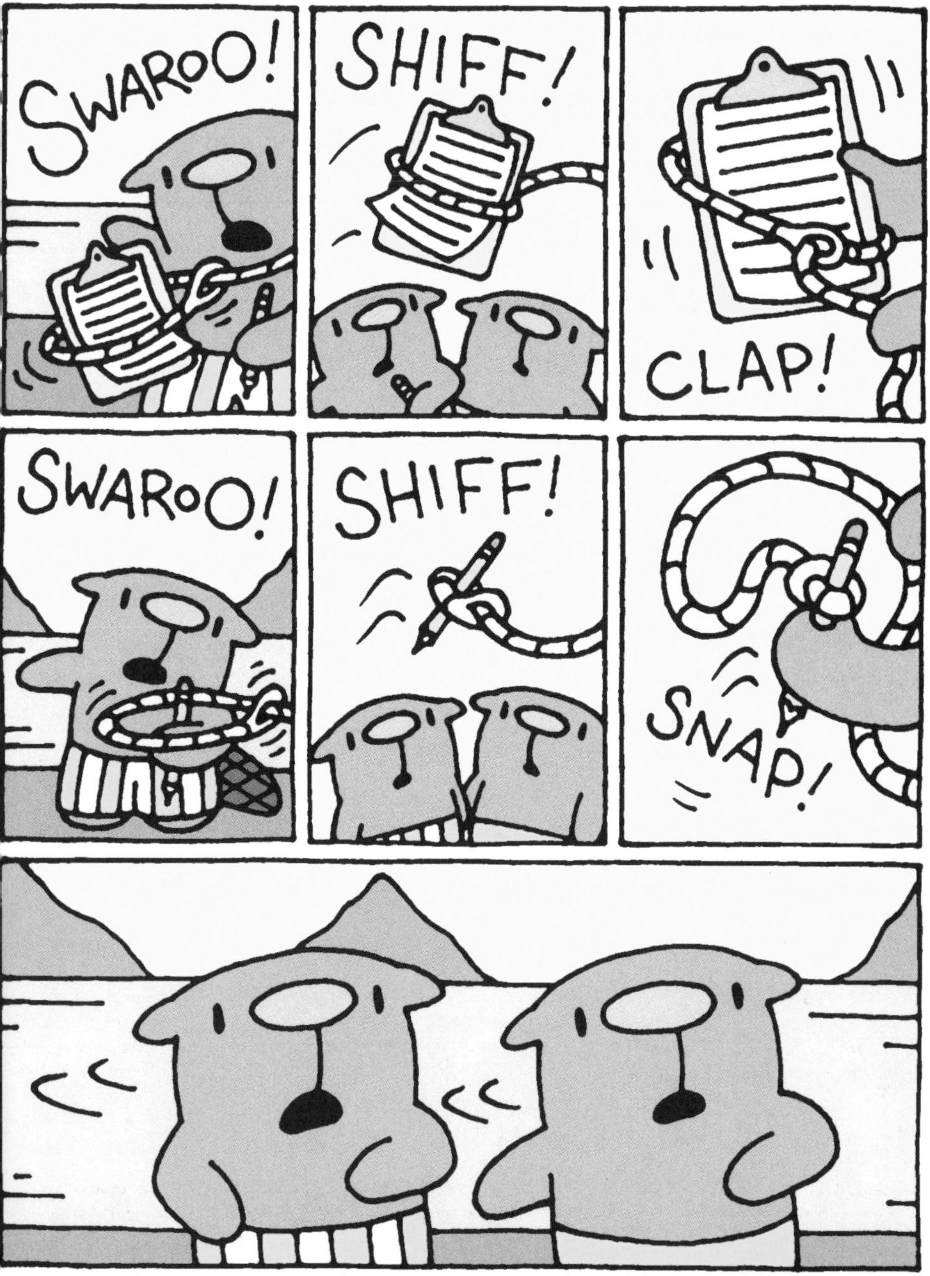
SWAROO!
SHIFF!
CLAP!
SWAROO!
SHIFF!
SNAP!

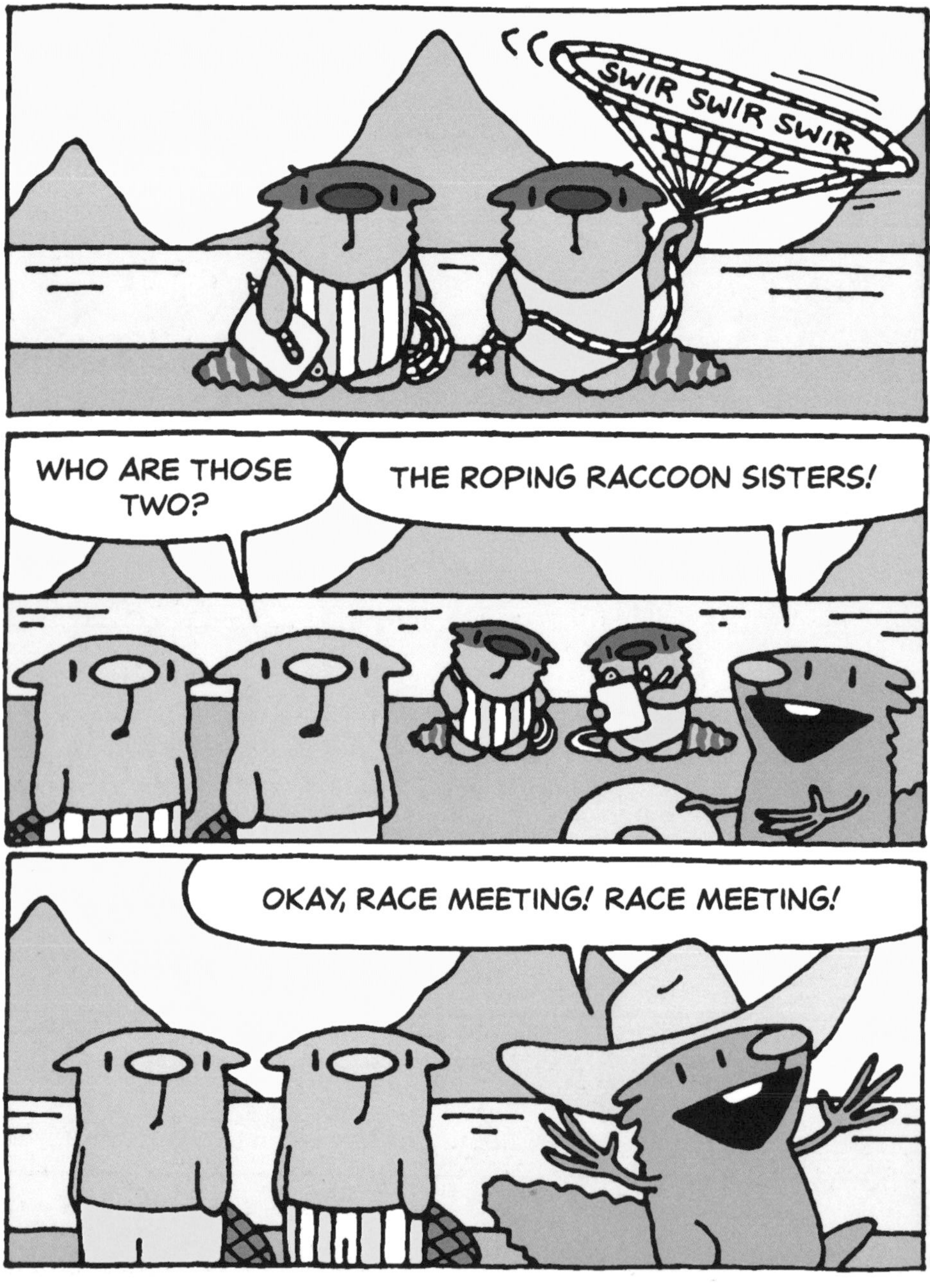
SWIR SWIR SWIR
WHO ARE THOSE TWO?
THE ROPING RACCOON SISTERS!
OKAY, RACE MEETING! RACE MEETING!

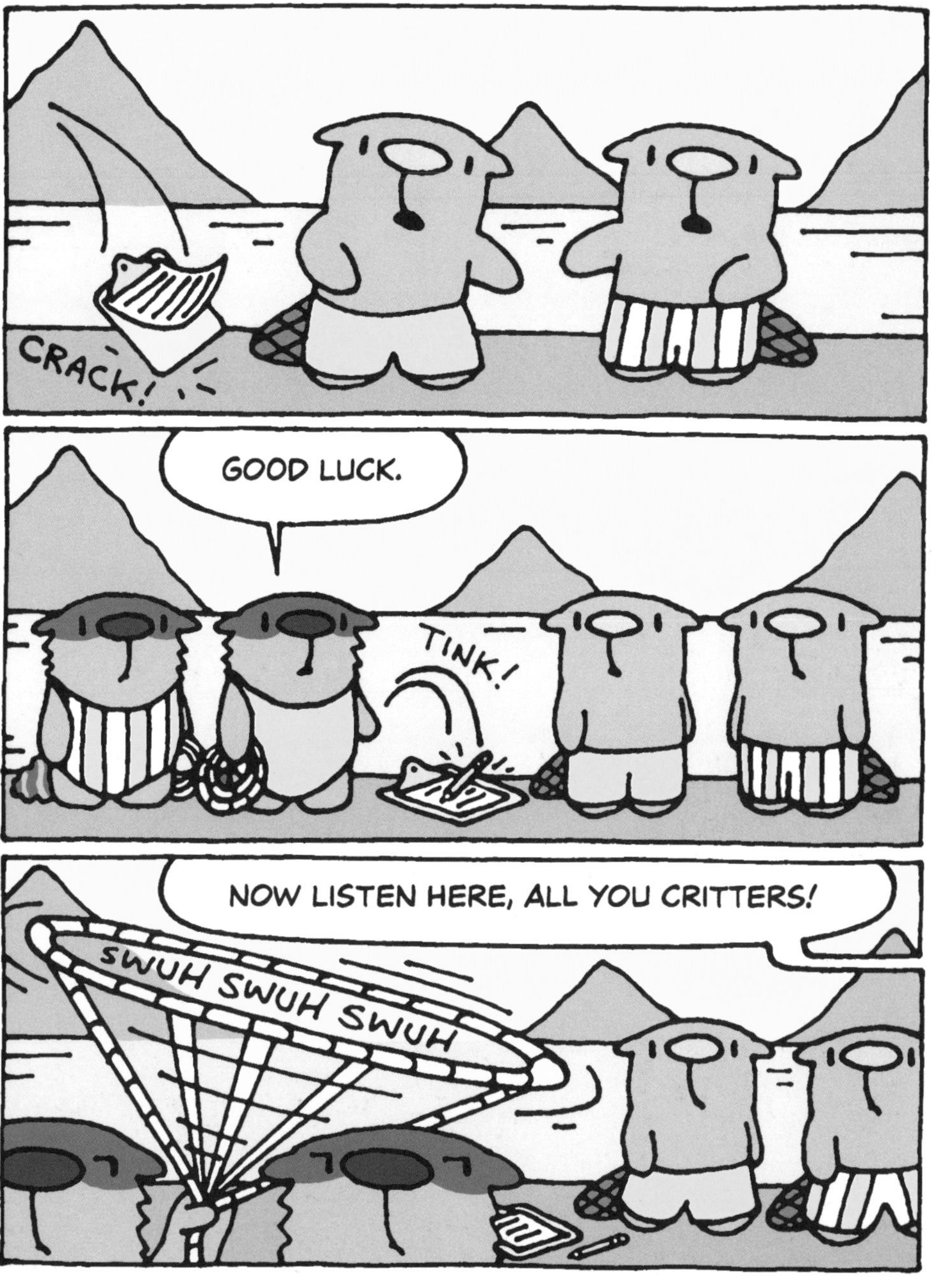
CRACK!
GOOD LUCK.
TINK!
NOW LISTEN HERE, ALL YOU CRITTERS!
SWUH SWUH SWUH

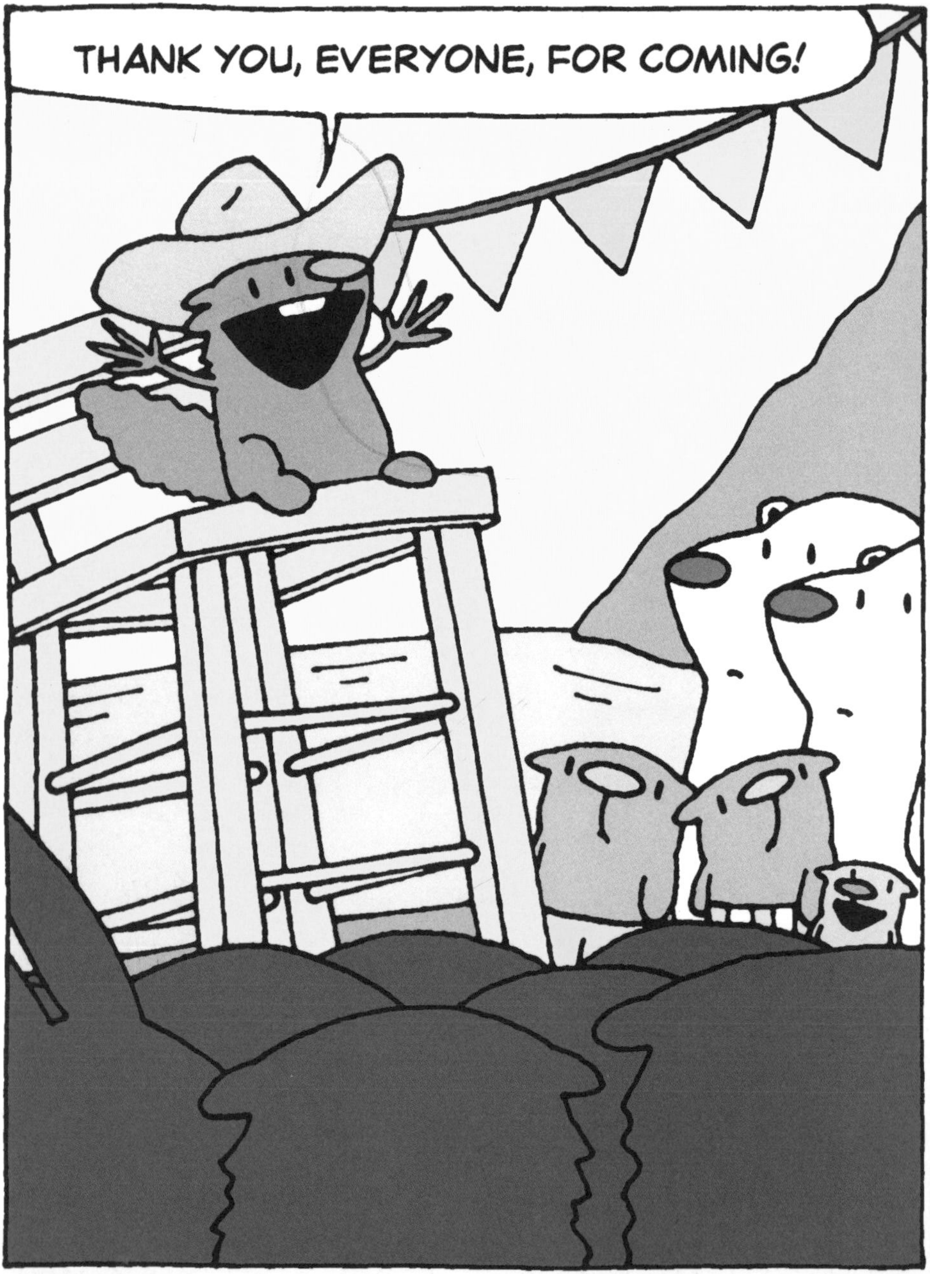
THANK YOU, EVERYONE, FOR COMING!

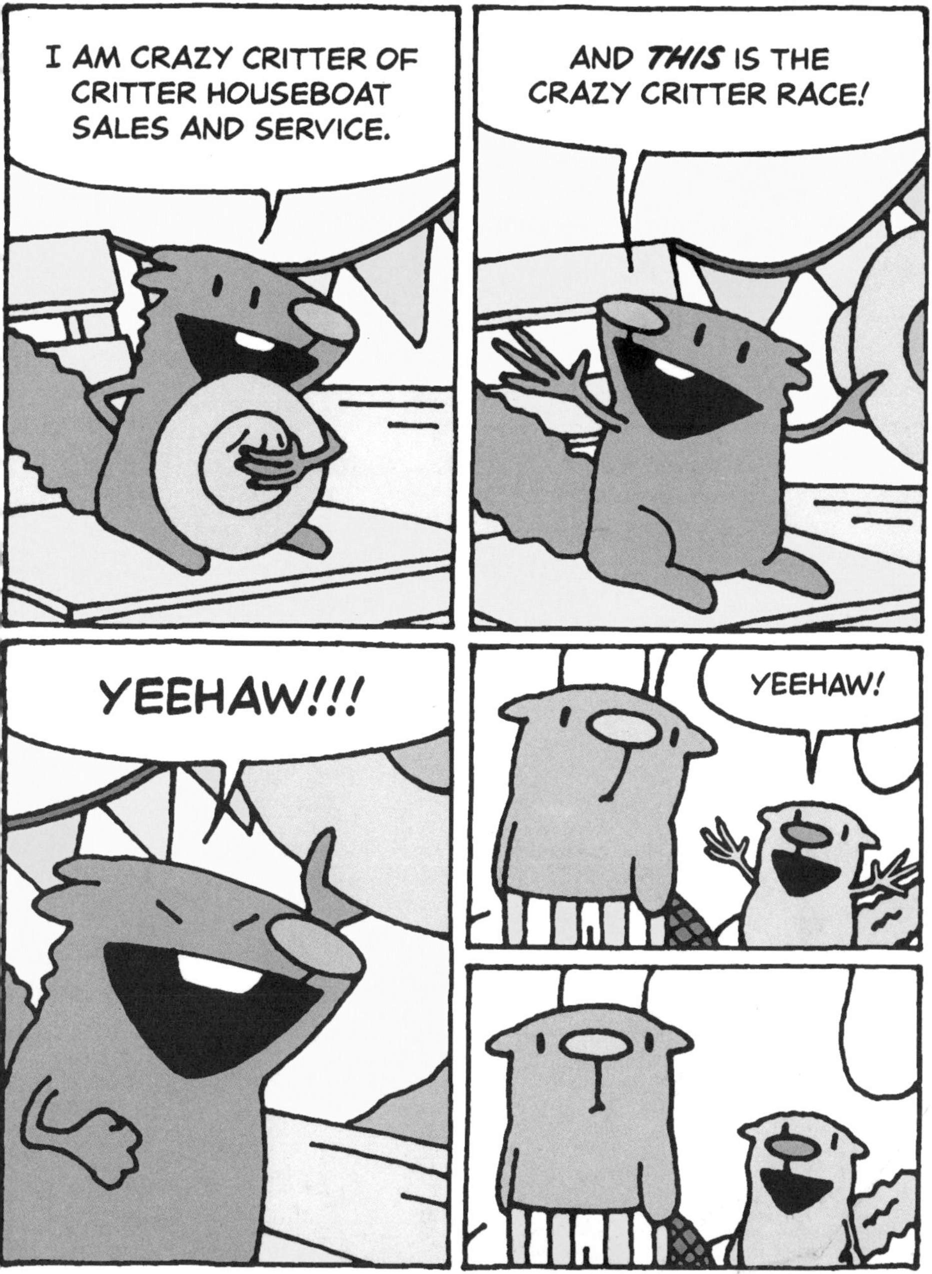
I AM CRAZY CRITTER OF CRITTER HOUSEBOAT SALES AND SERVICE.
AND *THIS* IS THE CRAZY CRITTER RACE!
YEEHAW!!!
YEEHAW!

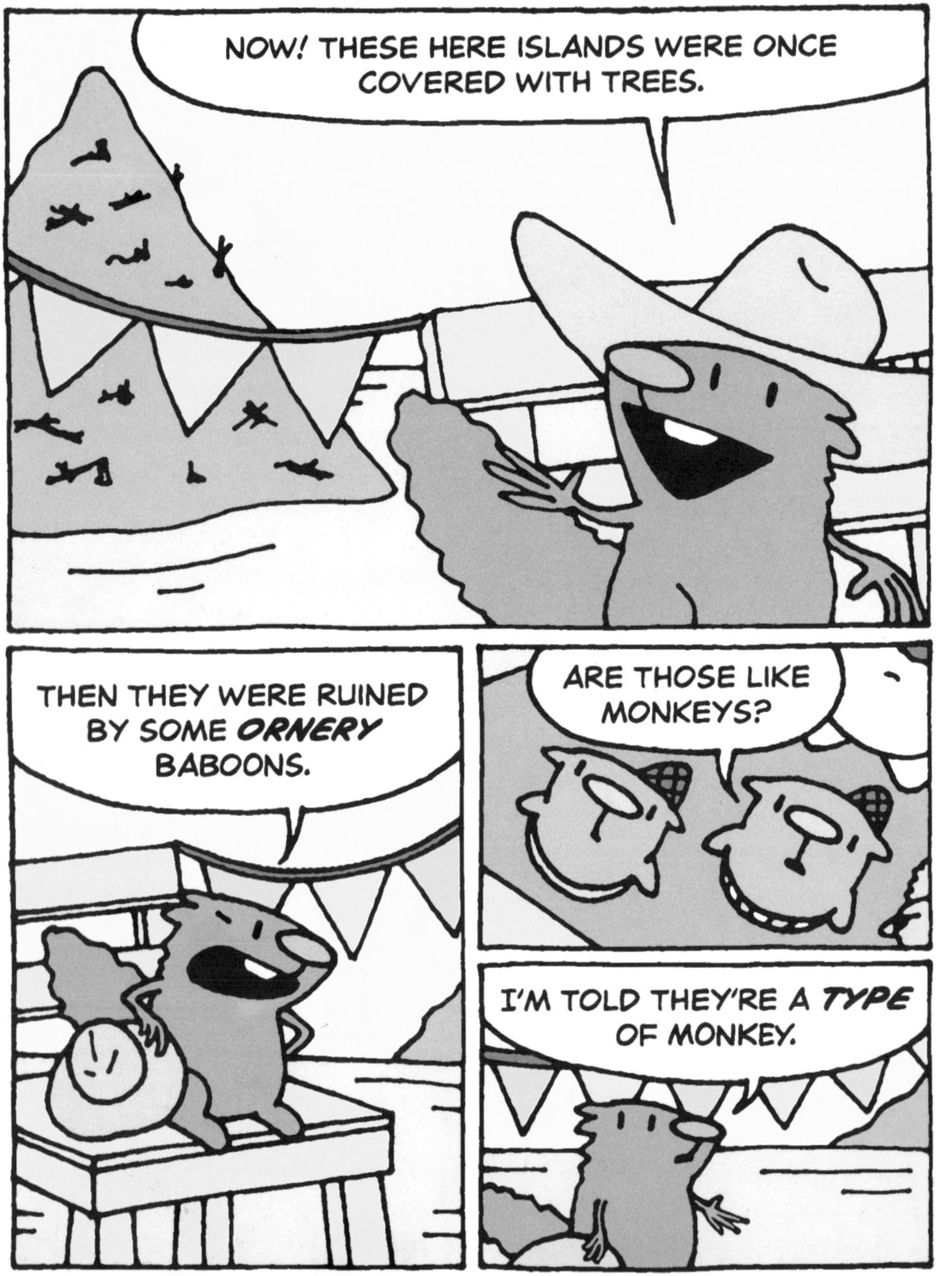
NOW! THESE HERE ISLANDS WERE ONCE COVERED WITH TREES.
THEN THEY WERE RUINED BY SOME *ORNERY* BABOONS.
ARE THOSE LIKE MONKEYS?
I'M TOLD THEY'RE A *TYPE* OF MONKEY.

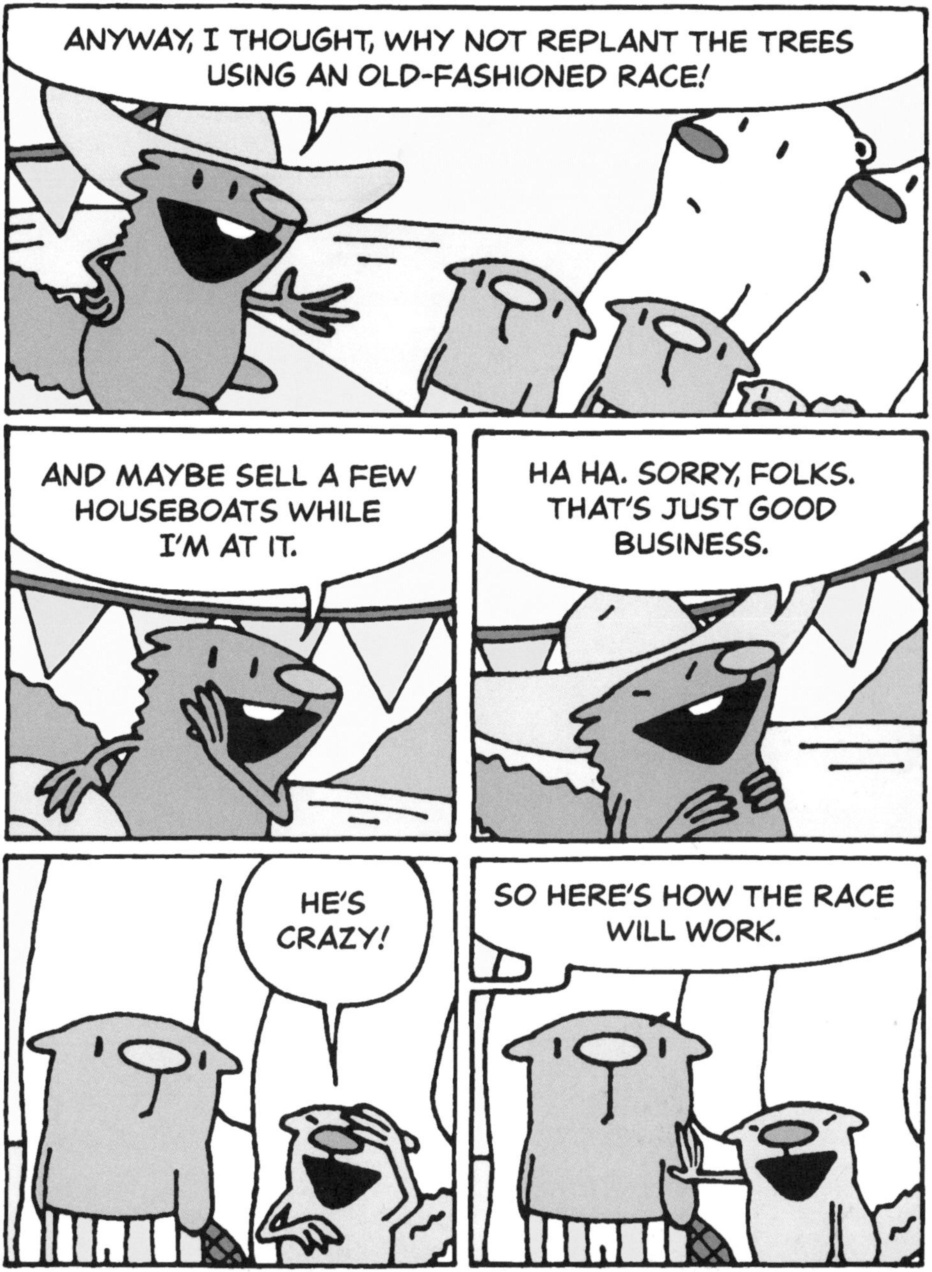
ANYWAY, I THOUGHT, WHY NOT REPLANT THE TREES USING AN OLD-FASHIONED RACE!
AND MAYBE SELL A FEW HOUSEBOATS WHILE I'M AT IT.
HA HA. SORRY, FOLKS. THAT'S JUST GOOD BUSINESS.
HE'S CRAZY!
SO HERE'S HOW THE RACE WILL WORK.

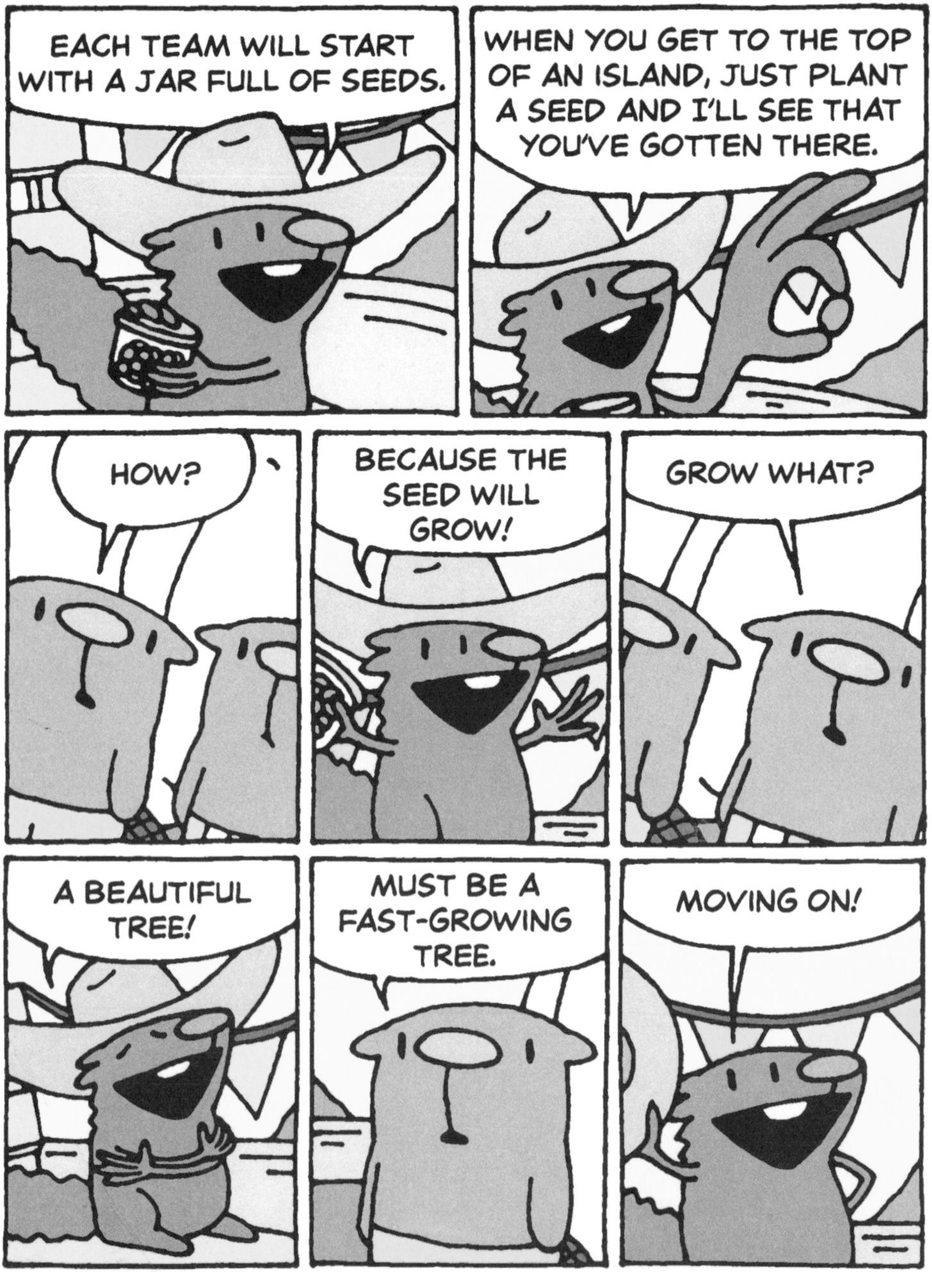
EACH TEAM WILL START WITH A JAR FULL OF SEEDS.
WHEN YOU GET TO THE TOP OF AN ISLAND, JUST PLANT A SEED AND I'LL SEE THAT YOU'VE GOTTEN THERE.
HOW?
BECAUSE THE SEED WILL GROW!
GROW WHAT?
A BEAUTIFUL TREE!
MUST BE A FAST-GROWING TREE.
MOVING ON!

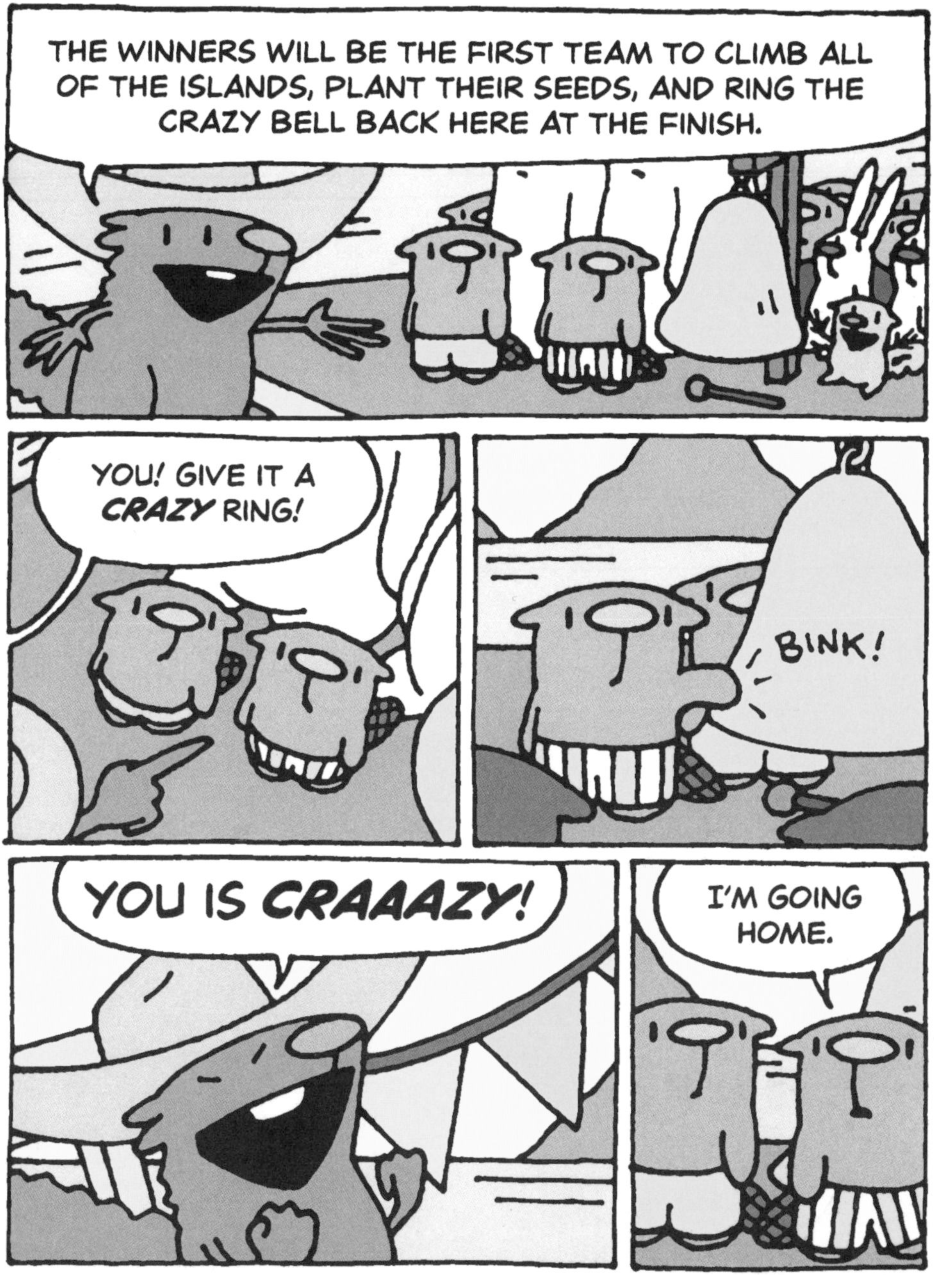
THE WINNERS WILL BE THE FIRST TEAM TO CLIMB ALL OF THE ISLANDS, PLANT THEIR SEEDS, AND RING THE CRAZY BELL BACK HERE AT THE FINISH.
YOU! GIVE IT A *CRAZY* RING!
BINK!
YOU IS *CRAAAZY!*
I'M GOING HOME.

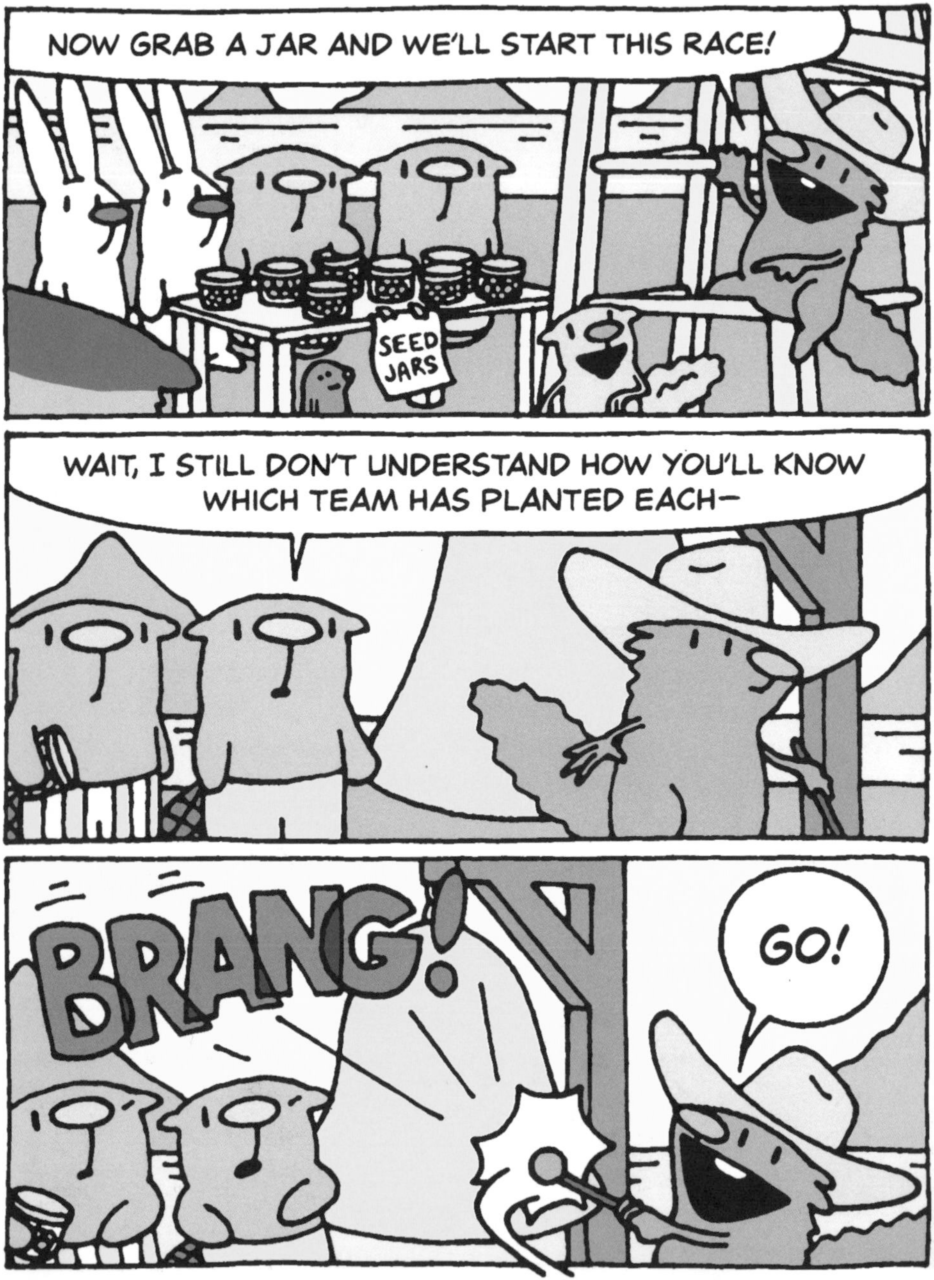
NOW GRAB A JAR AND WE'LL START THIS RACE!
SEED JARS
WAIT, I STILL DON'T UNDERSTAND HOW YOU'LL KNOW WHICH TEAM HAS PLANTED EACH—
BRANG!
GO!

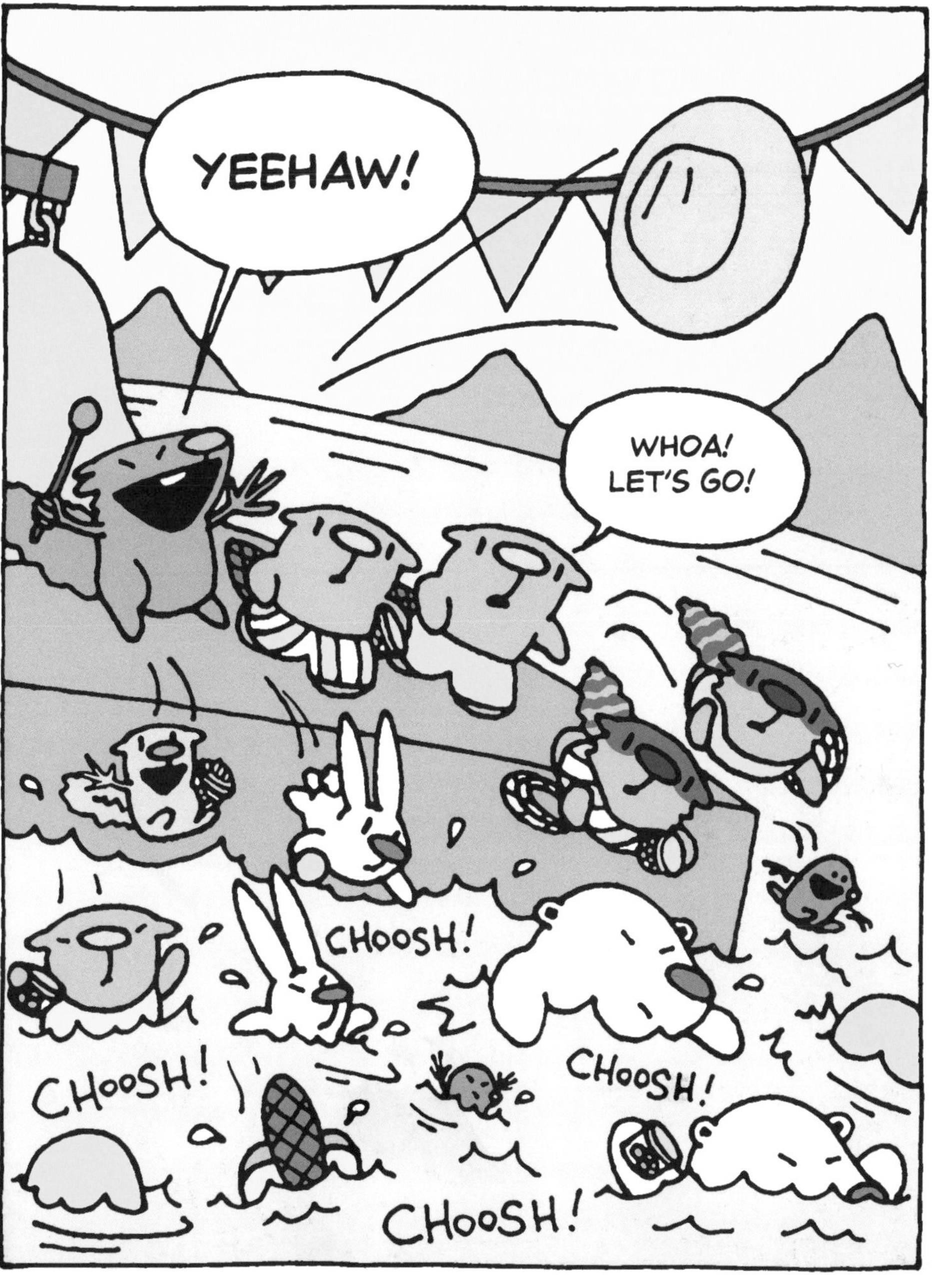
YEEHAW!
WHOA! LET'S GO!
CHOOSH!
CHOOSH!
CHOOSH!
CHOOSH!

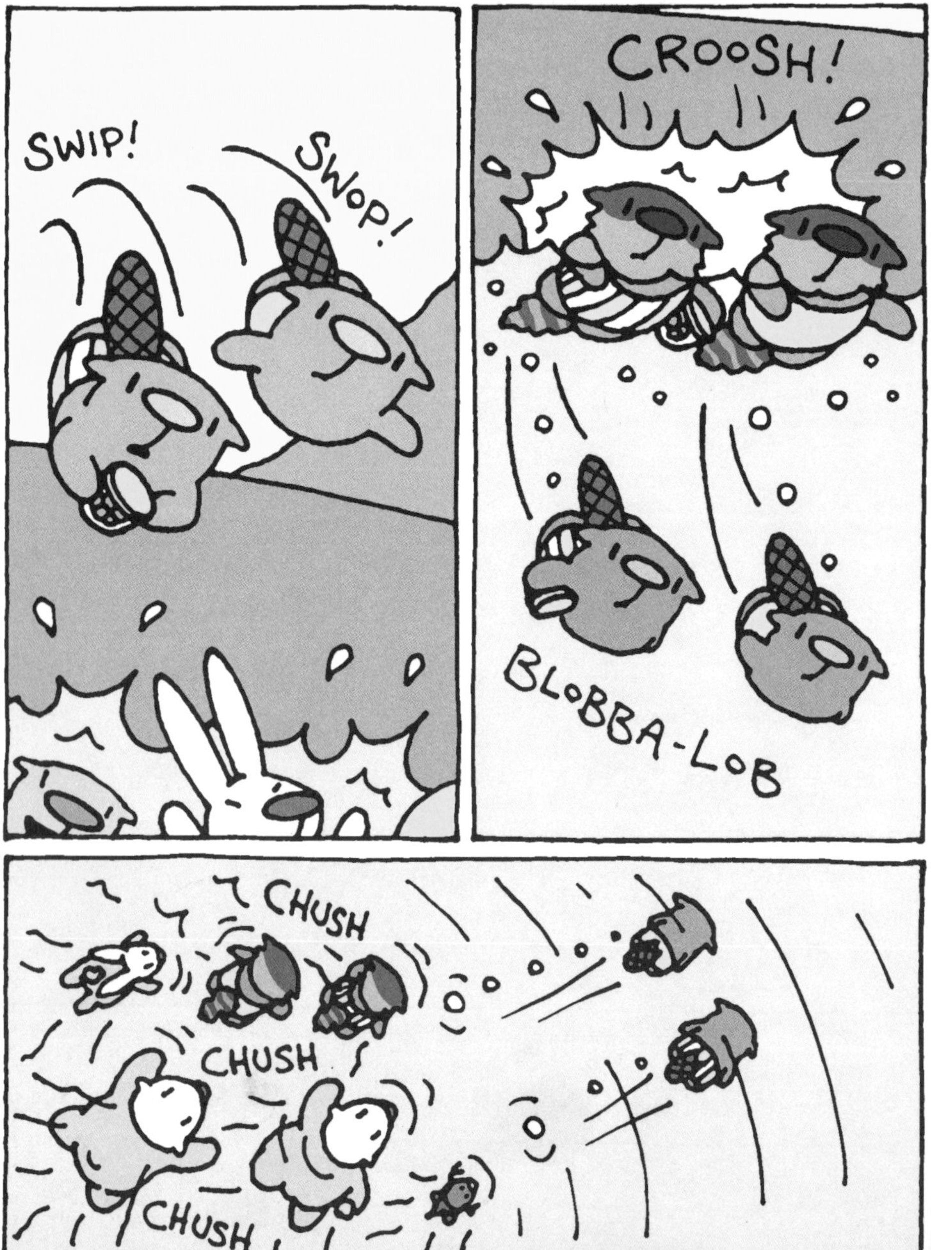
SWIP!
SWOP!
CROOSH!
BLOBBA-LOB
CHUSH
CHUSH
CHUSH

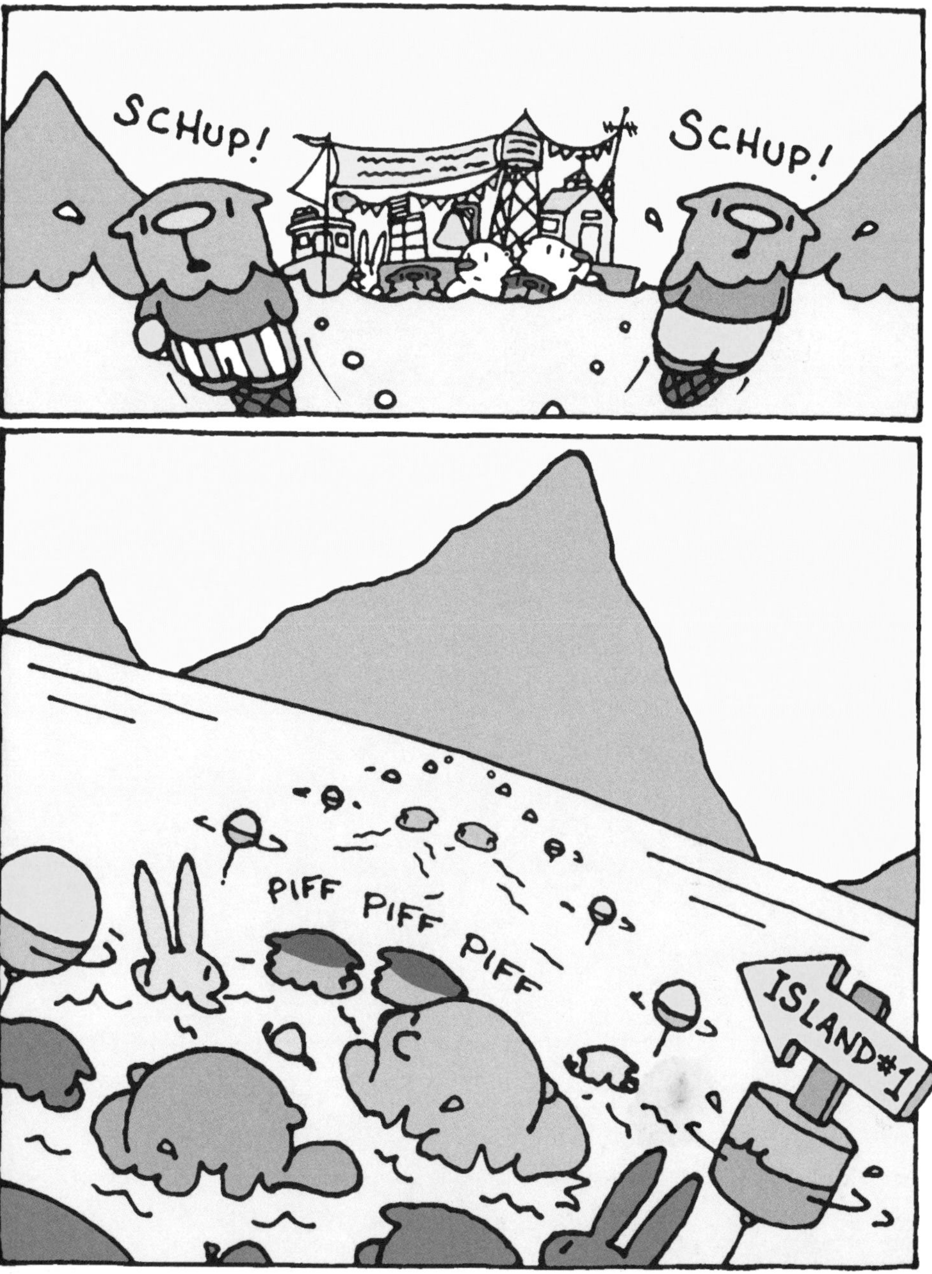
SCHUP!
SCHUP!
PIFF
PIFF
PIFF
ISLAND #1

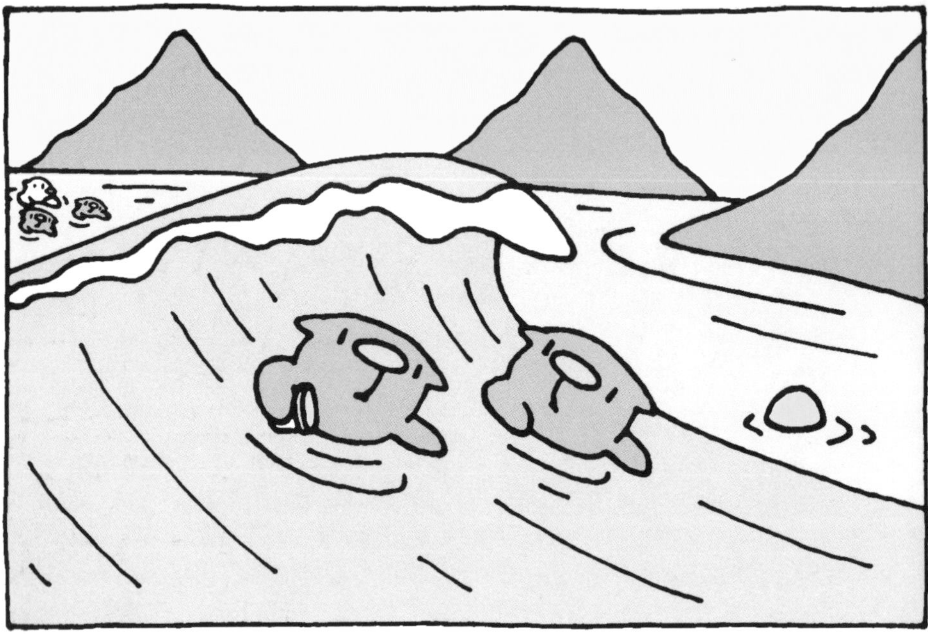

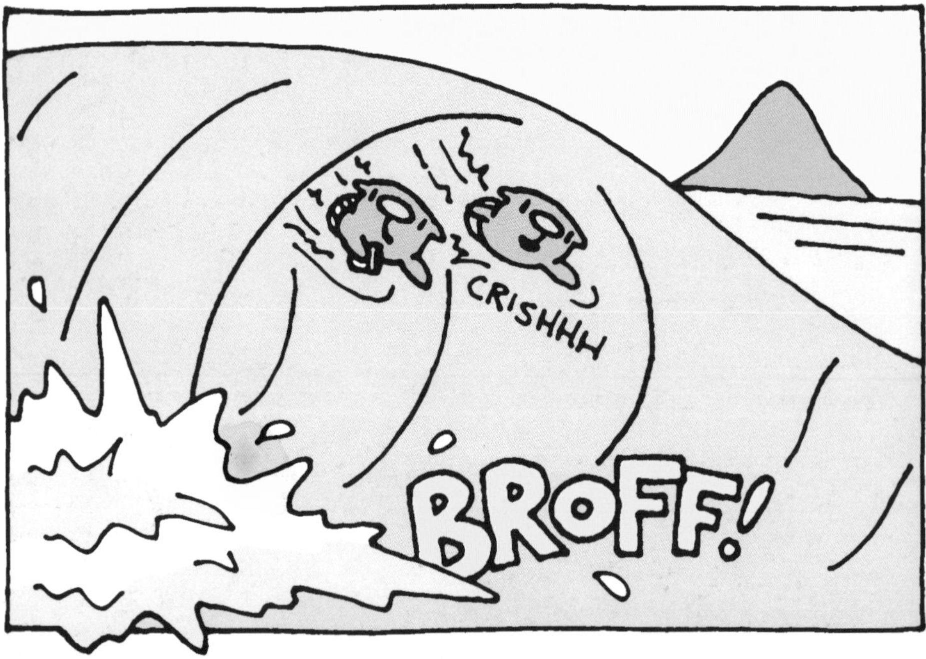
CRISHHH
BROFF!

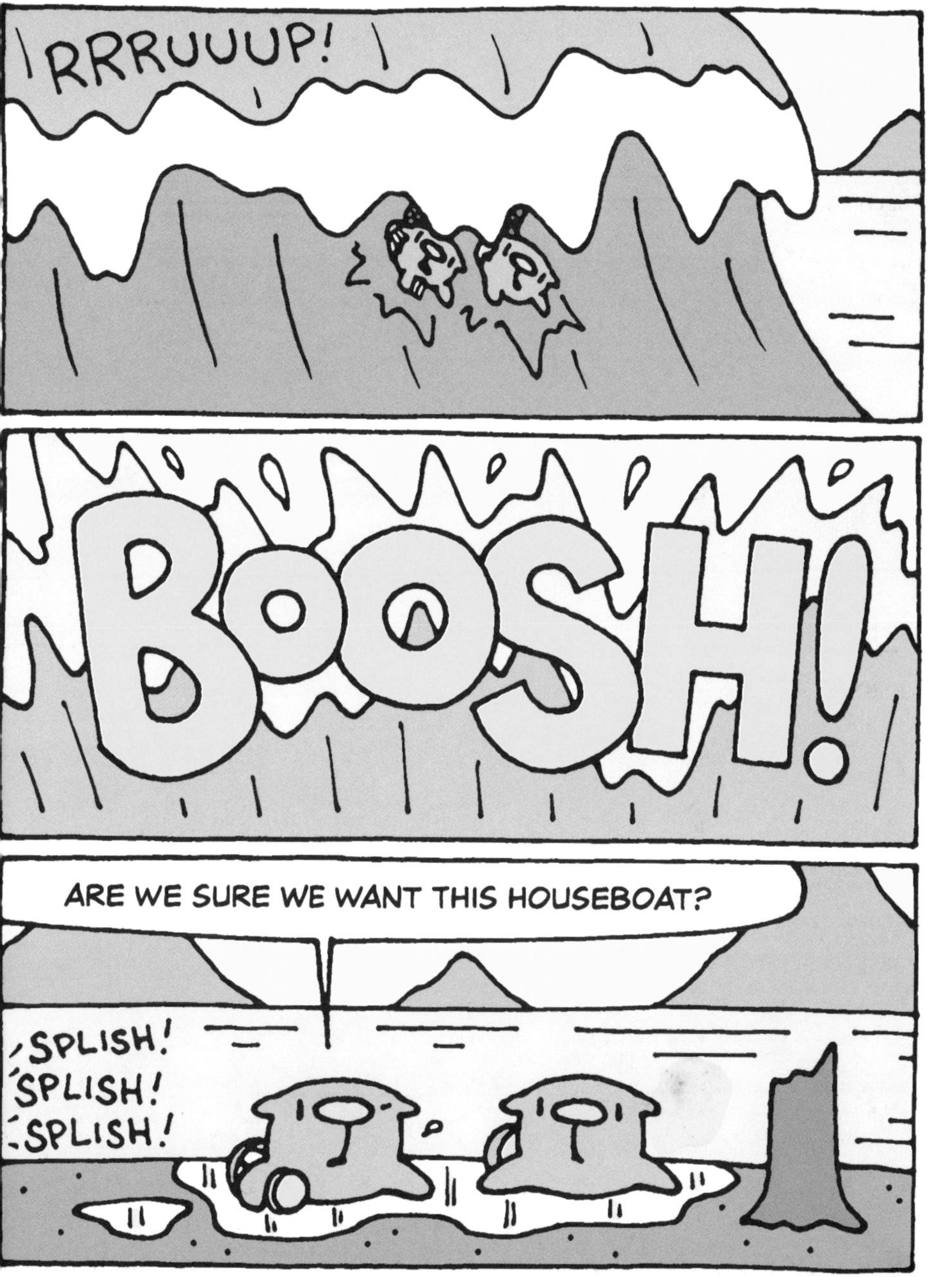
RRRUUUP!
BOOSH!
ARE WE SURE WE WANT THIS HOUSEBOAT?
SPLISH!
SPLISH!
SPLISH!

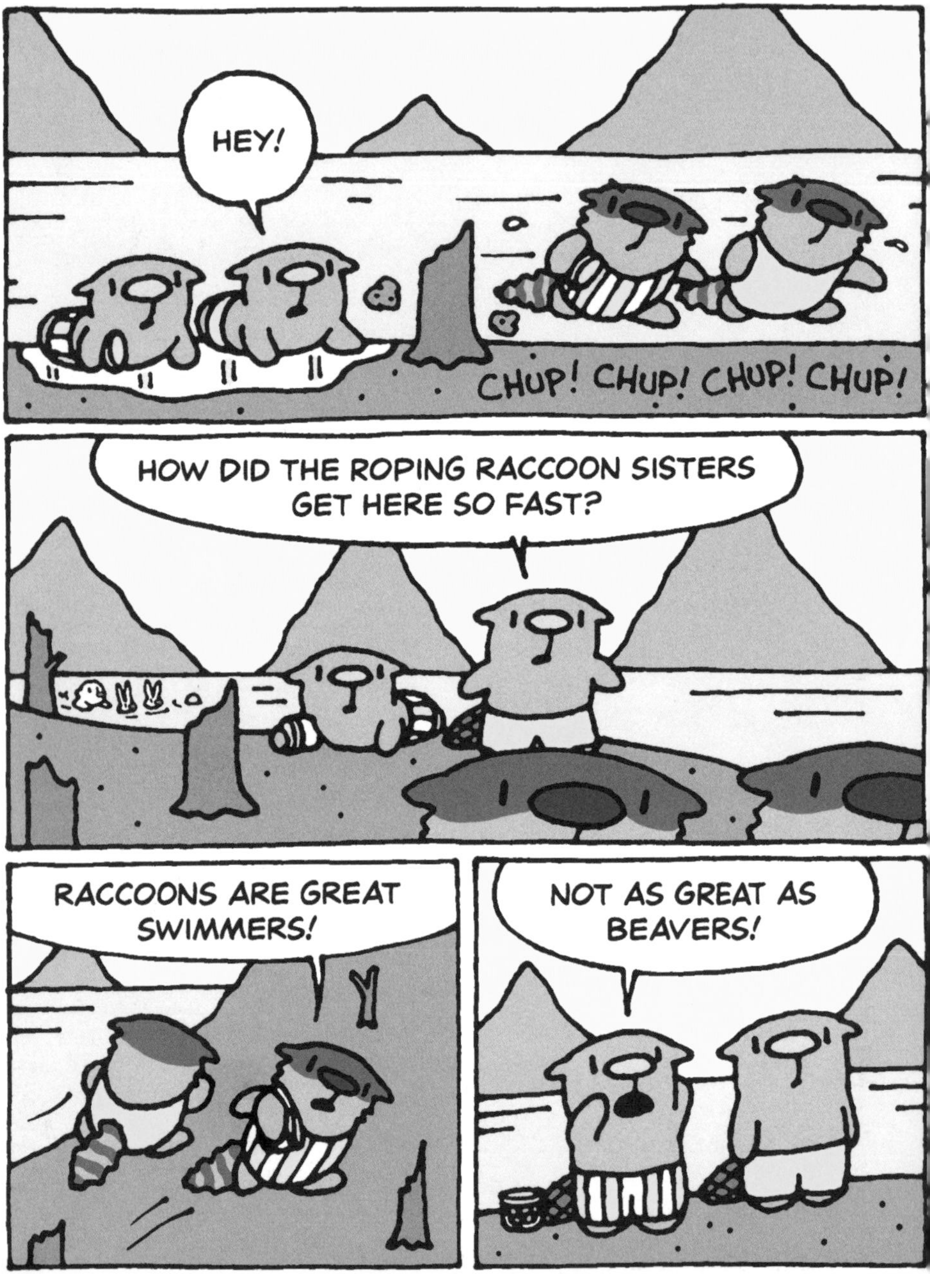
HEY!
CHUP! CHUP! CHUP! CHUP!
HOW DID THE ROPING RACCOON SISTERS GET HERE SO FAST?
RACCOONS ARE GREAT SWIMMERS!
NOT AS GREAT AS BEAVERS!

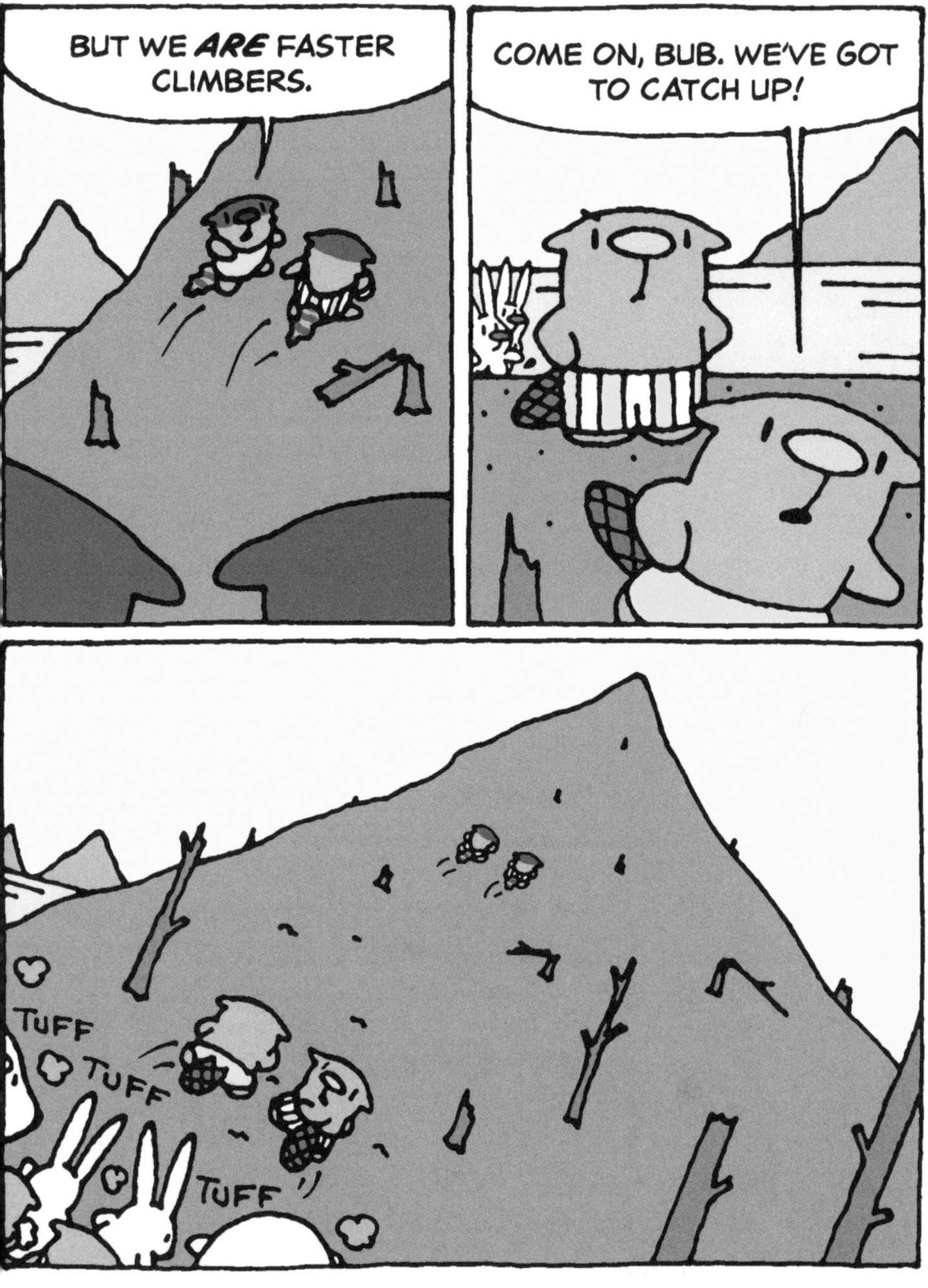
BUT WE ARE FASTER CLIMBERS.
COME ON, BUB. WE'VE GOT TO CATCH UP!
TUFF
TUFF
TUFF

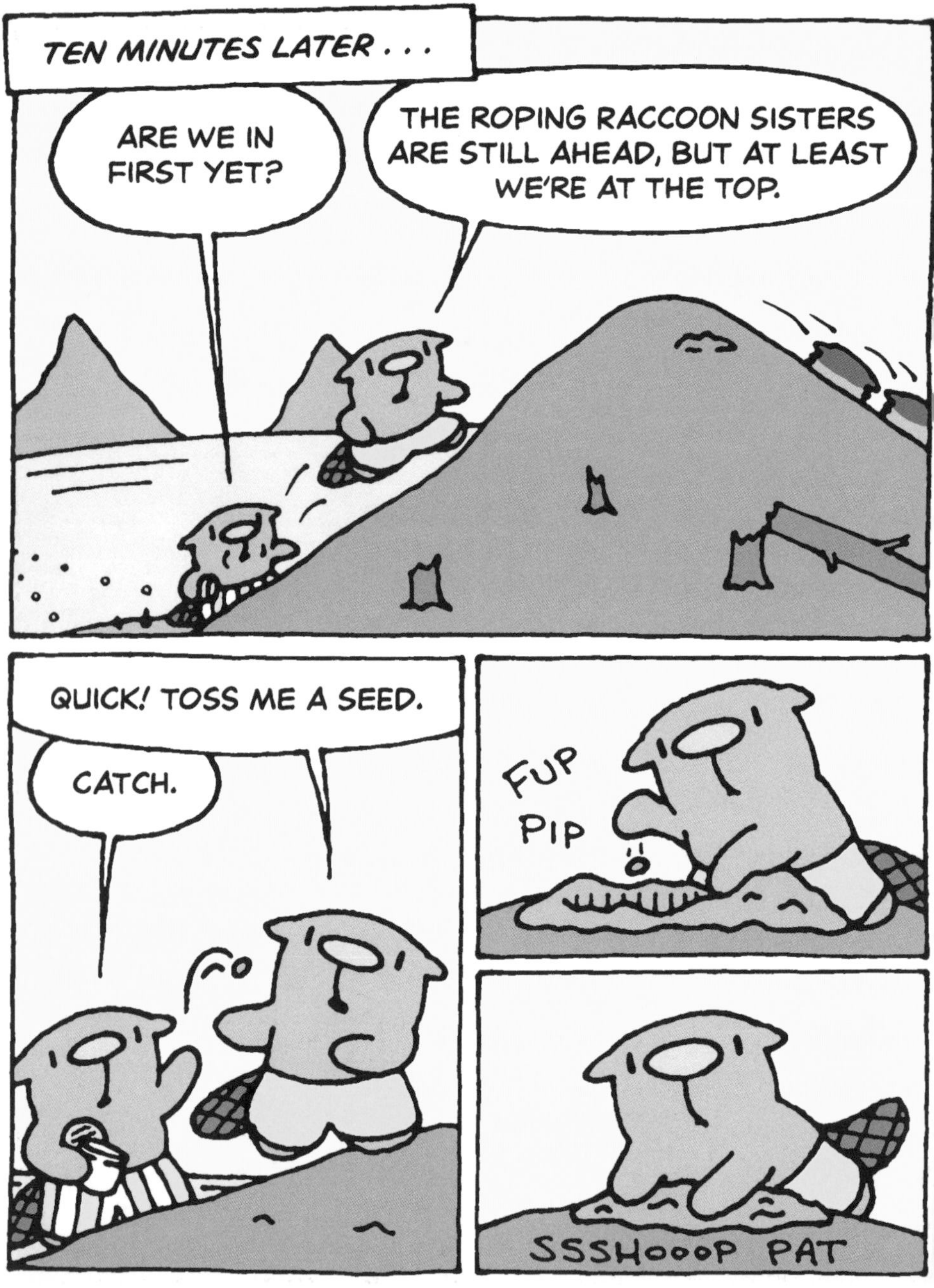
TEN MINUTES LATER . . .
ARE WE IN FIRST YET?
THE ROPING RACCOON SISTERS ARE STILL AHEAD, BUT AT LEAST WE'RE AT THE TOP.
QUICK! TOSS ME A SEED.
CATCH.
FUP
PIP
SSSHOOOP PAT

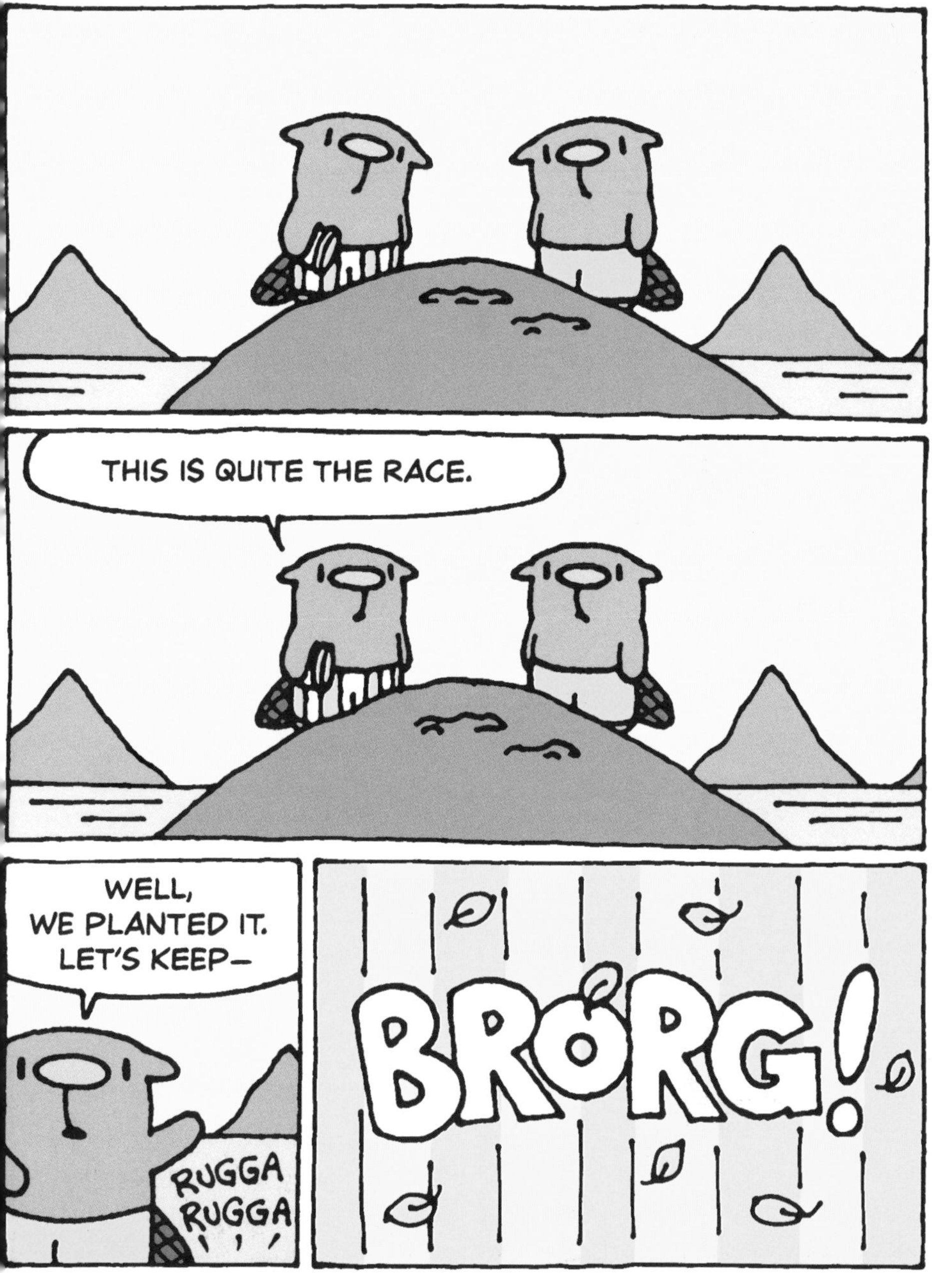

THIS IS QUITE THE RACE.
WELL, WE PLANTED IT. LET'S KEEP—
RUGGA RUGGA
BRORG!

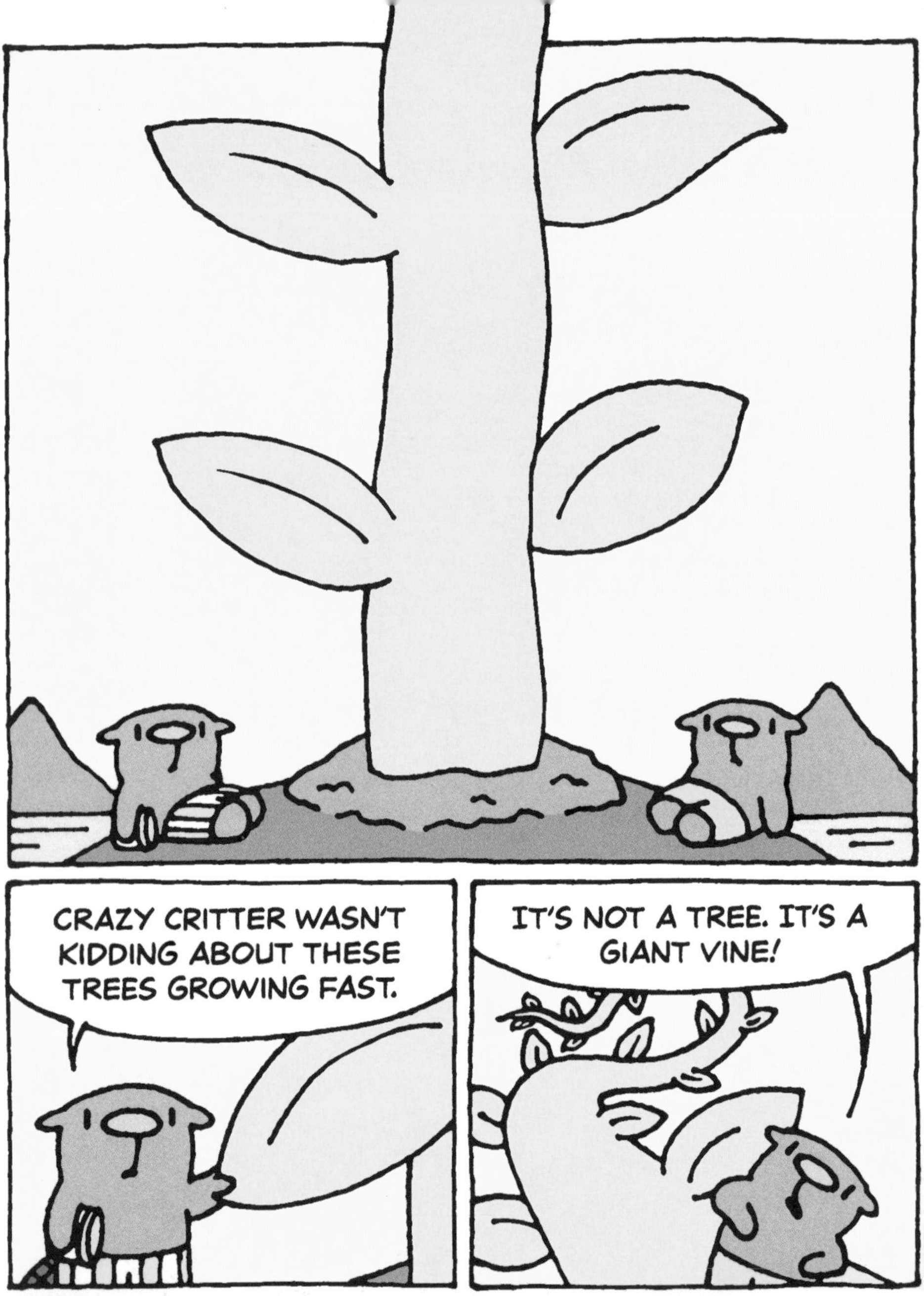
CRAZY CRITTER WASN'T KIDDING ABOUT THESE TREES GROWING FAST.
IT'S NOT A TREE. IT'S A GIANT VINE!

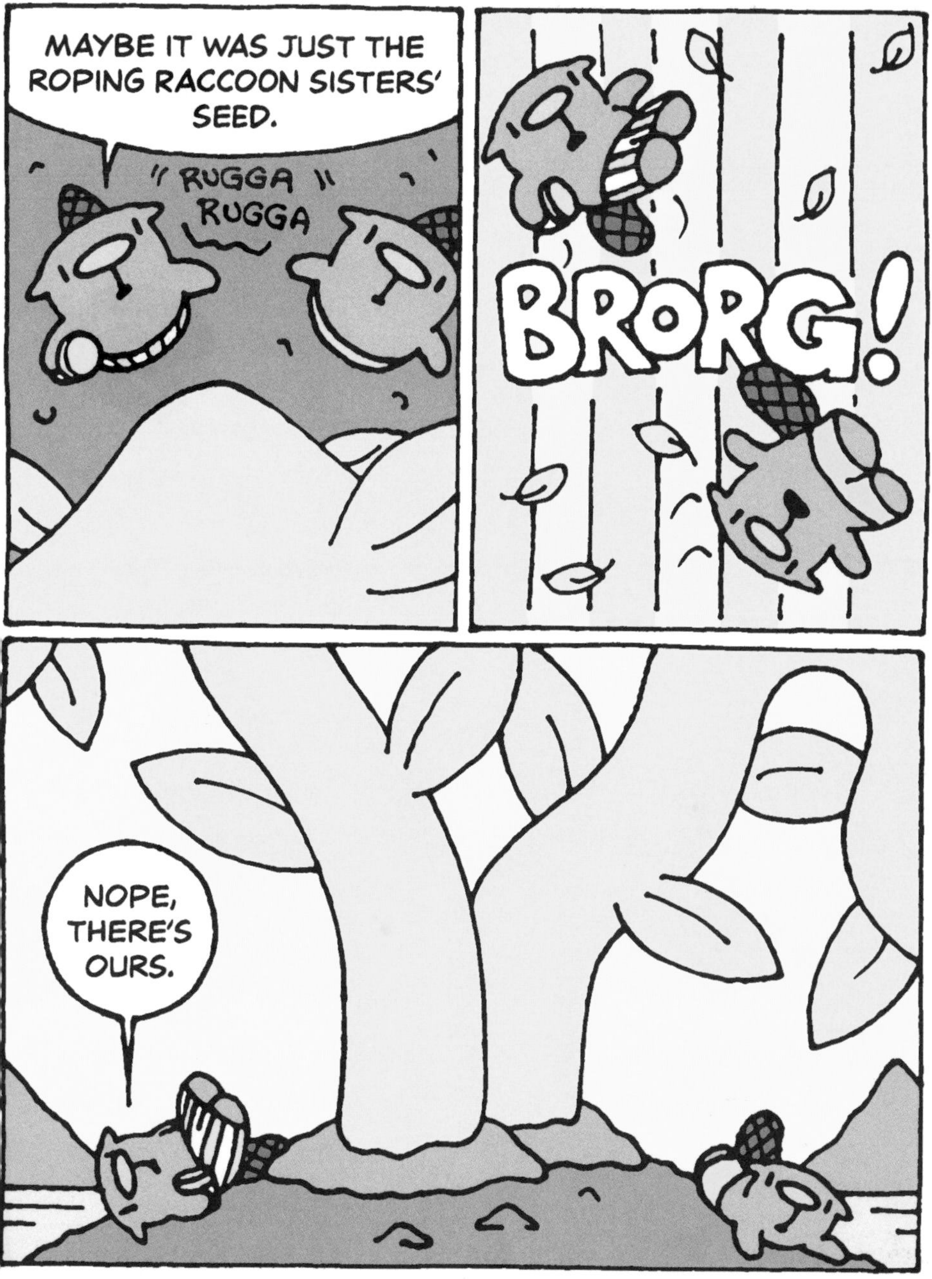
MAYBE IT WAS JUST THE ROPING RACCOON SISTERS' SEED.
"RUGGA RUGGA"
BRORG!
NOPE, THERE'S OURS.

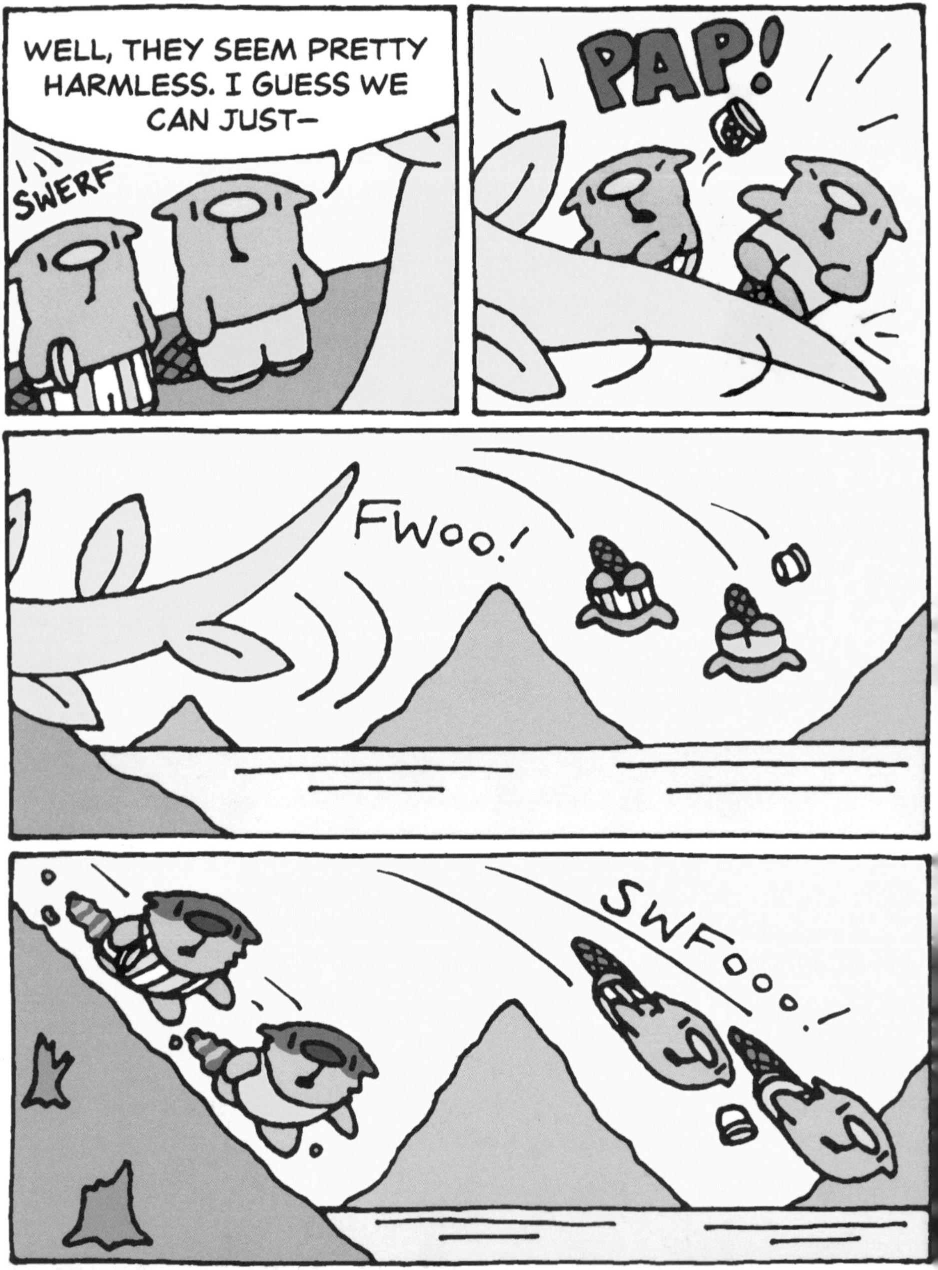
WELL, THEY SEEM PRETTY HARMLESS. I GUESS WE CAN JUST–
SWERF
PAP!
FWOO!
SWFOOO!

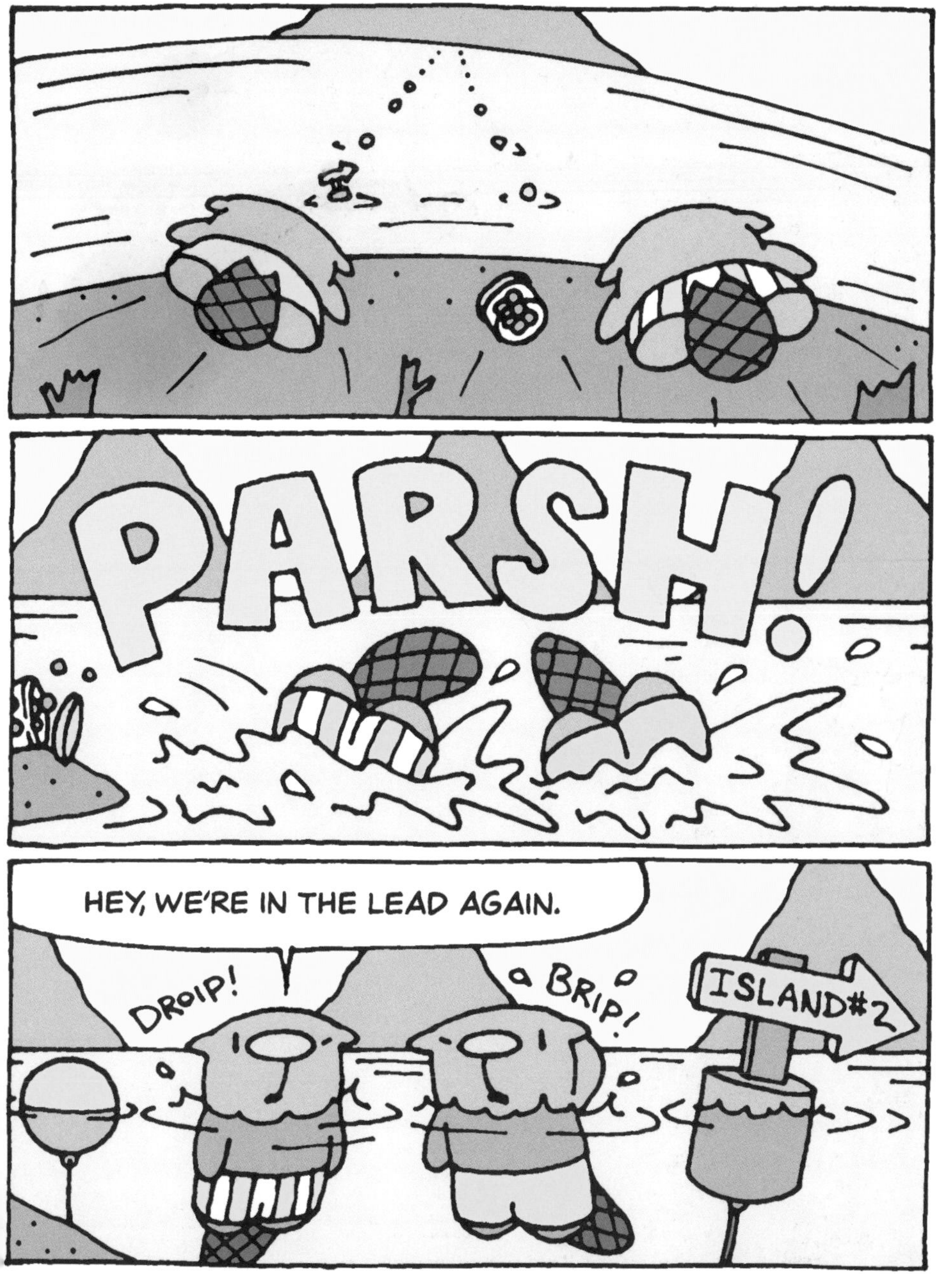
PARSH!
HEY, WE'RE IN THE LEAD AGAIN.
DROIP!
BRIP!
ISLAND#2

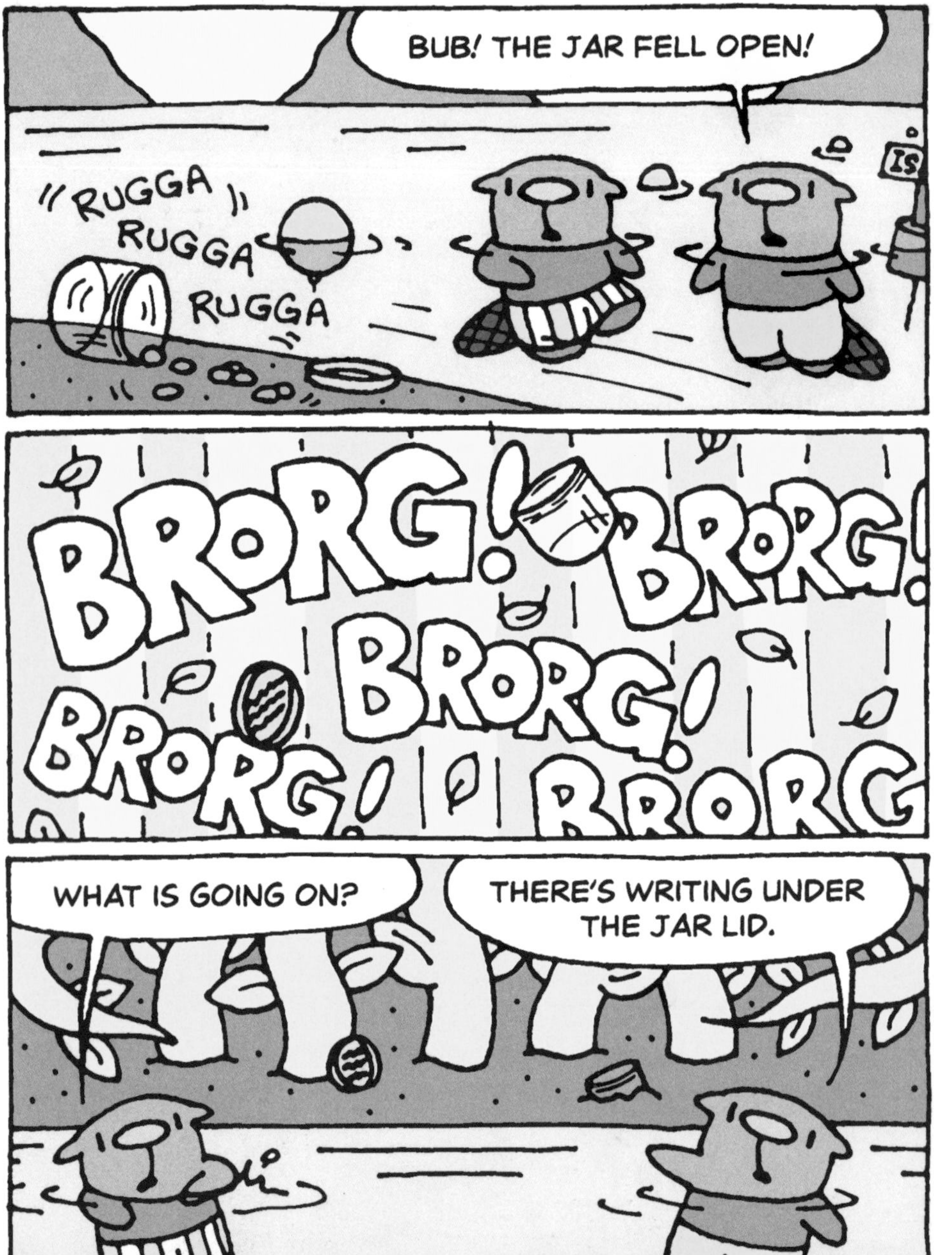
BUB! THE JAR FELL OPEN!
"RUGGA RUGGA RUGGA"
IS
BRORG! BRORG! BRORG! BRORG! BRORG
WHAT IS GOING ON?
THERE'S WRITING UNDER THE JAR LID.

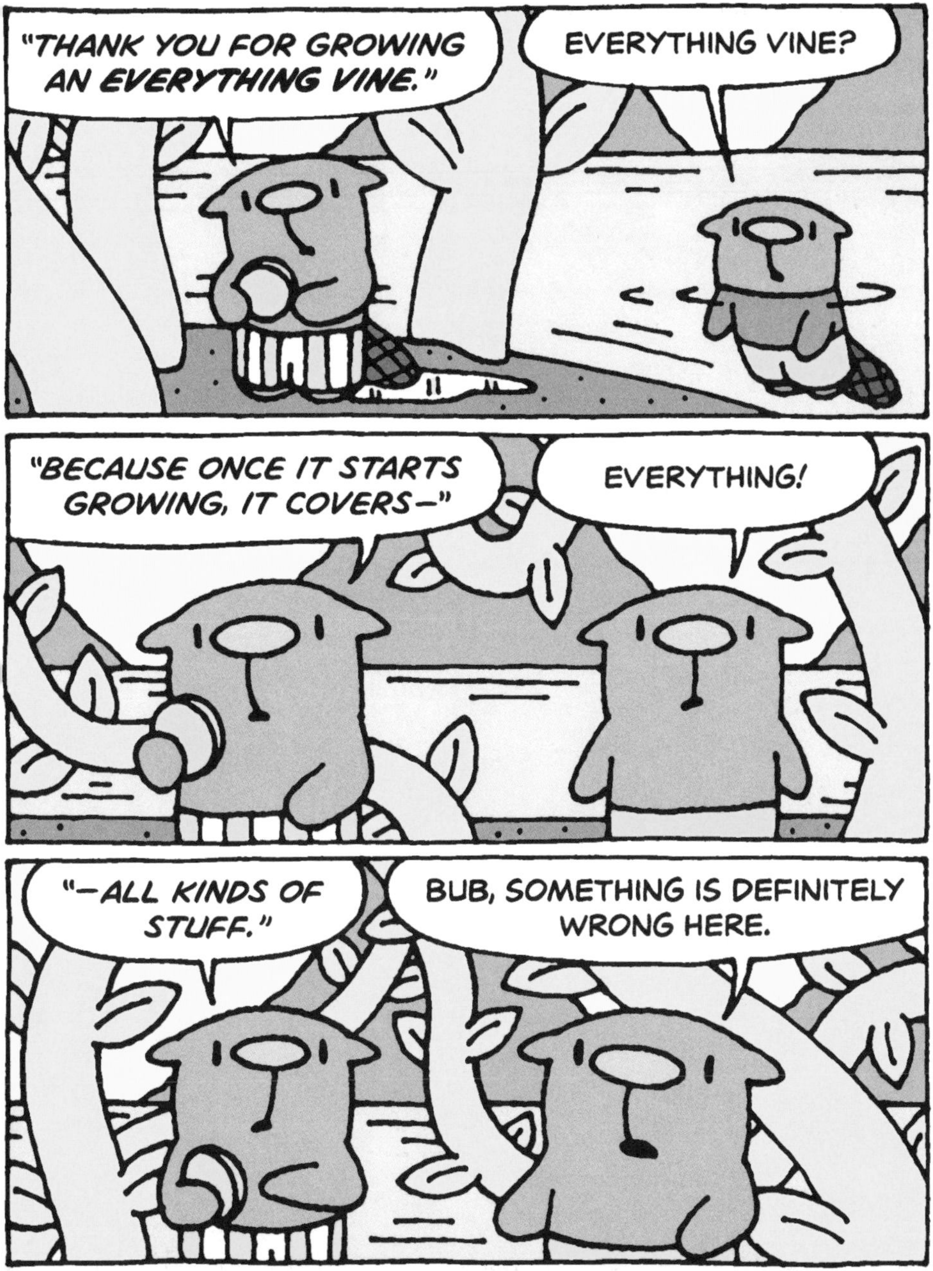
"THANK YOU FOR GROWING AN EVERYTHING VINE."
EVERYTHING VINE?
"BECAUSE ONCE IT STARTS GROWING, IT COVERS—"
EVERYTHING!
"—ALL KINDS OF STUFF."
BUB, SOMETHING IS DEFINITELY WRONG HERE.

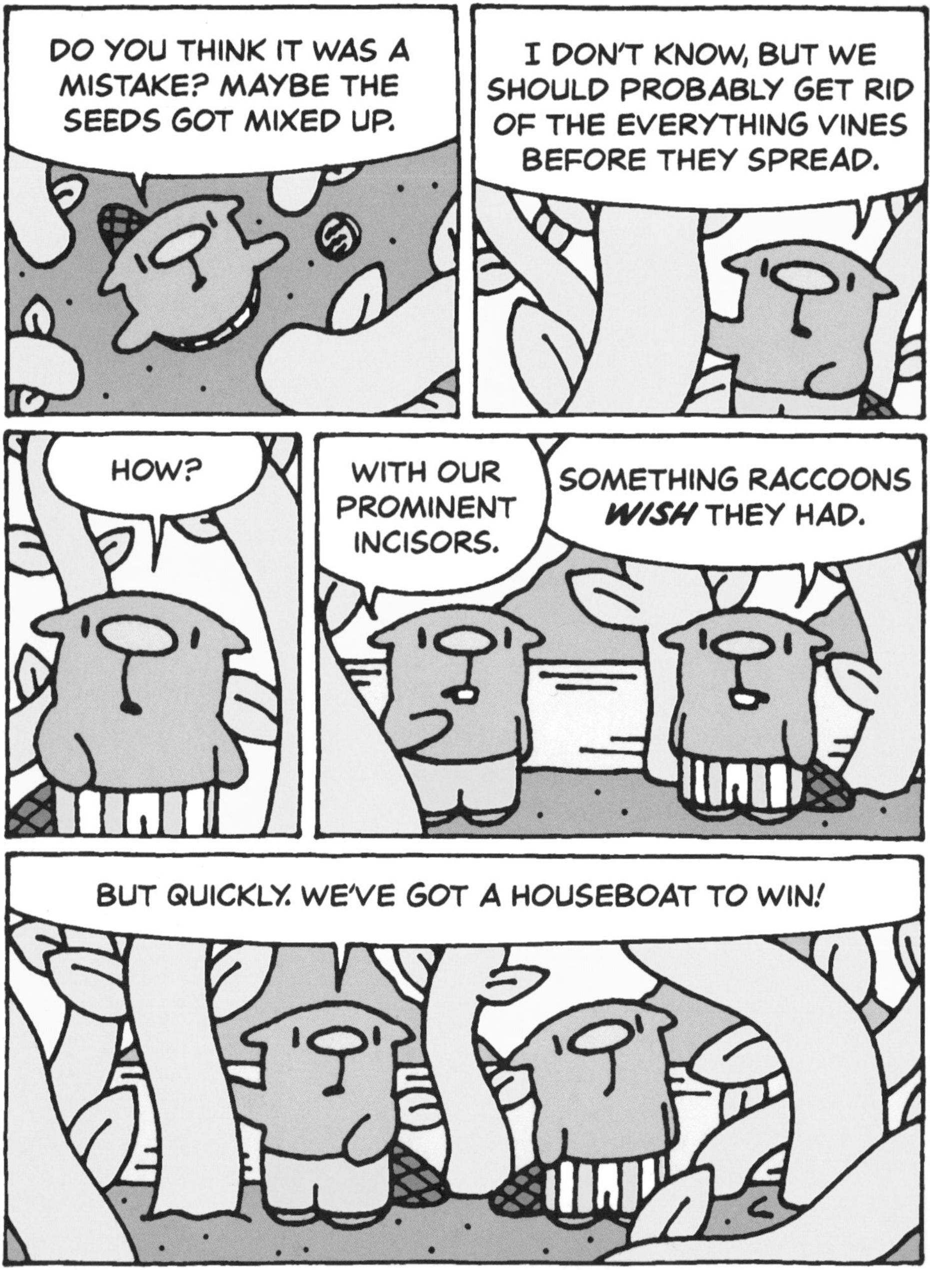
DO YOU THINK IT WAS A MISTAKE? MAYBE THE SEEDS GOT MIXED UP.
I DON'T KNOW, BUT WE SHOULD PROBABLY GET RID OF THE EVERYTHING VINES BEFORE THEY SPREAD.
HOW?
WITH OUR PROMINENT INCISORS.
SOMETHING RACCOONS *WISH* THEY HAD.
BUT QUICKLY. WE'VE GOT A HOUSEBOAT TO WIN!

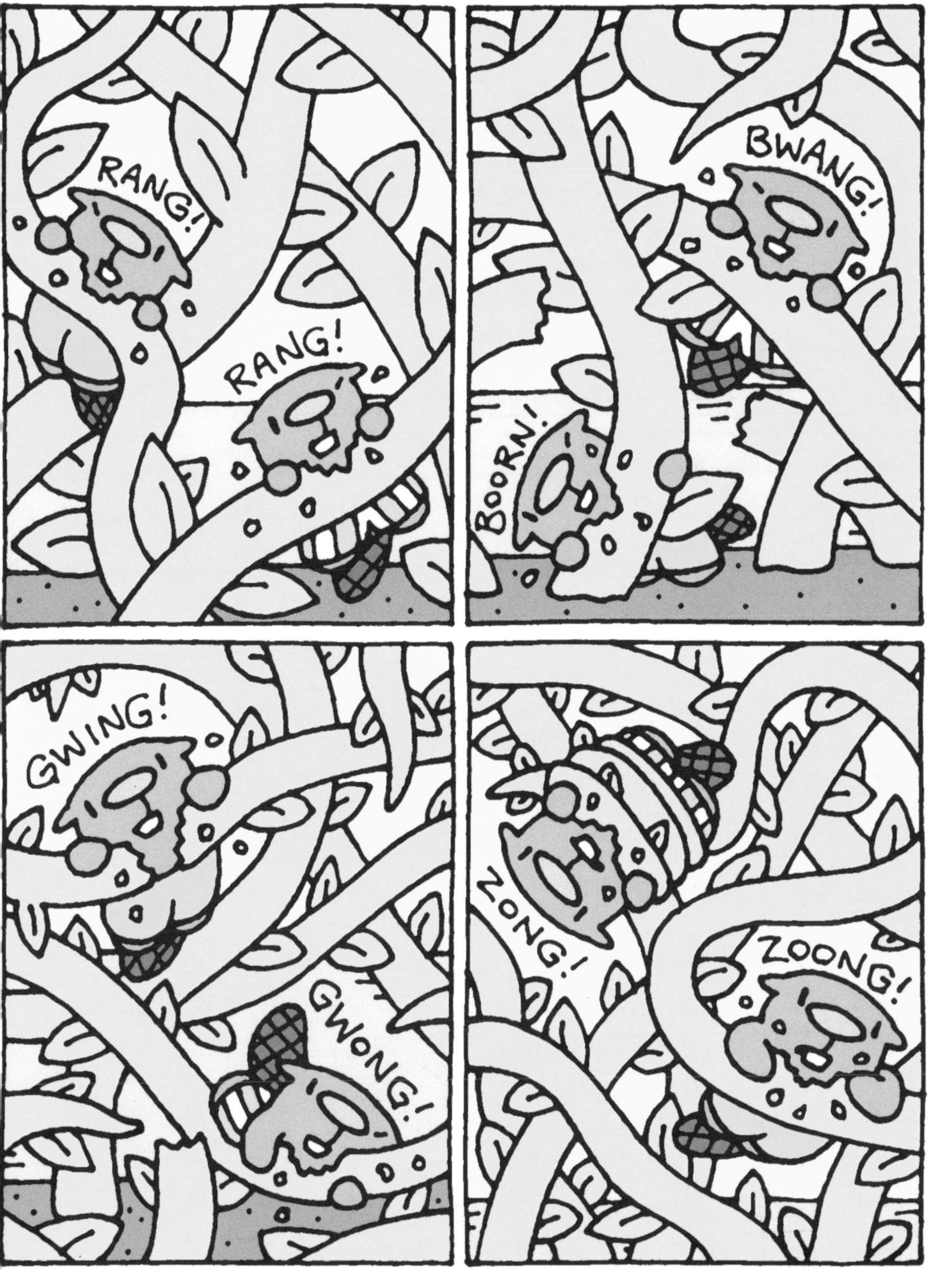
RANG!
RANG!
BWANG!
BOORN!
GWING!
GWONG!
ZONG!
ZOONG!

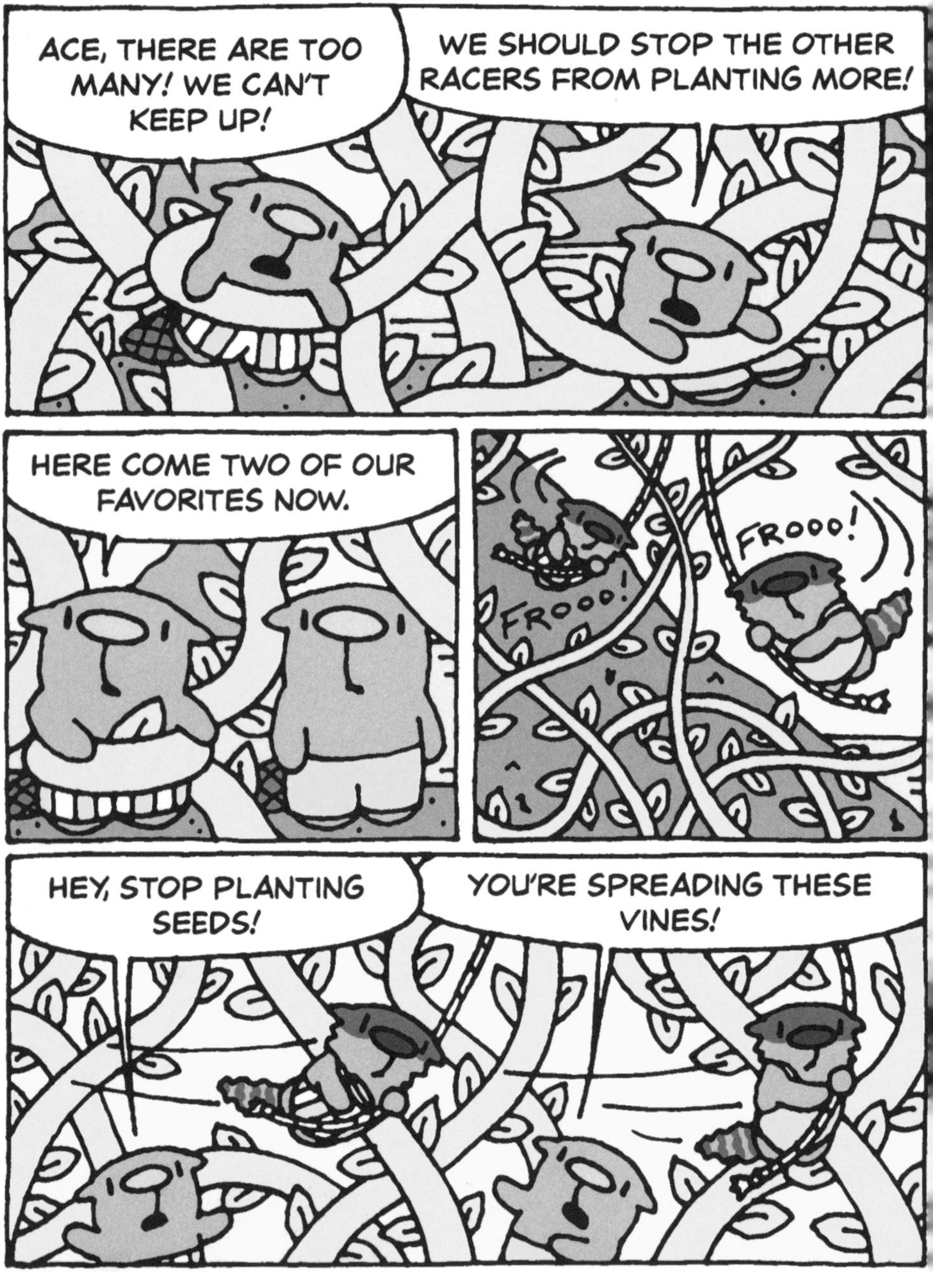
ACE, THERE ARE TOO MANY! WE CAN'T KEEP UP!
WE SHOULD STOP THE OTHER RACERS FROM PLANTING MORE!
HERE COME TWO OF OUR FAVORITES NOW.
FROOO!
FROOO!
HEY, STOP PLANTING SEEDS!
YOU'RE SPREADING THESE VINES!

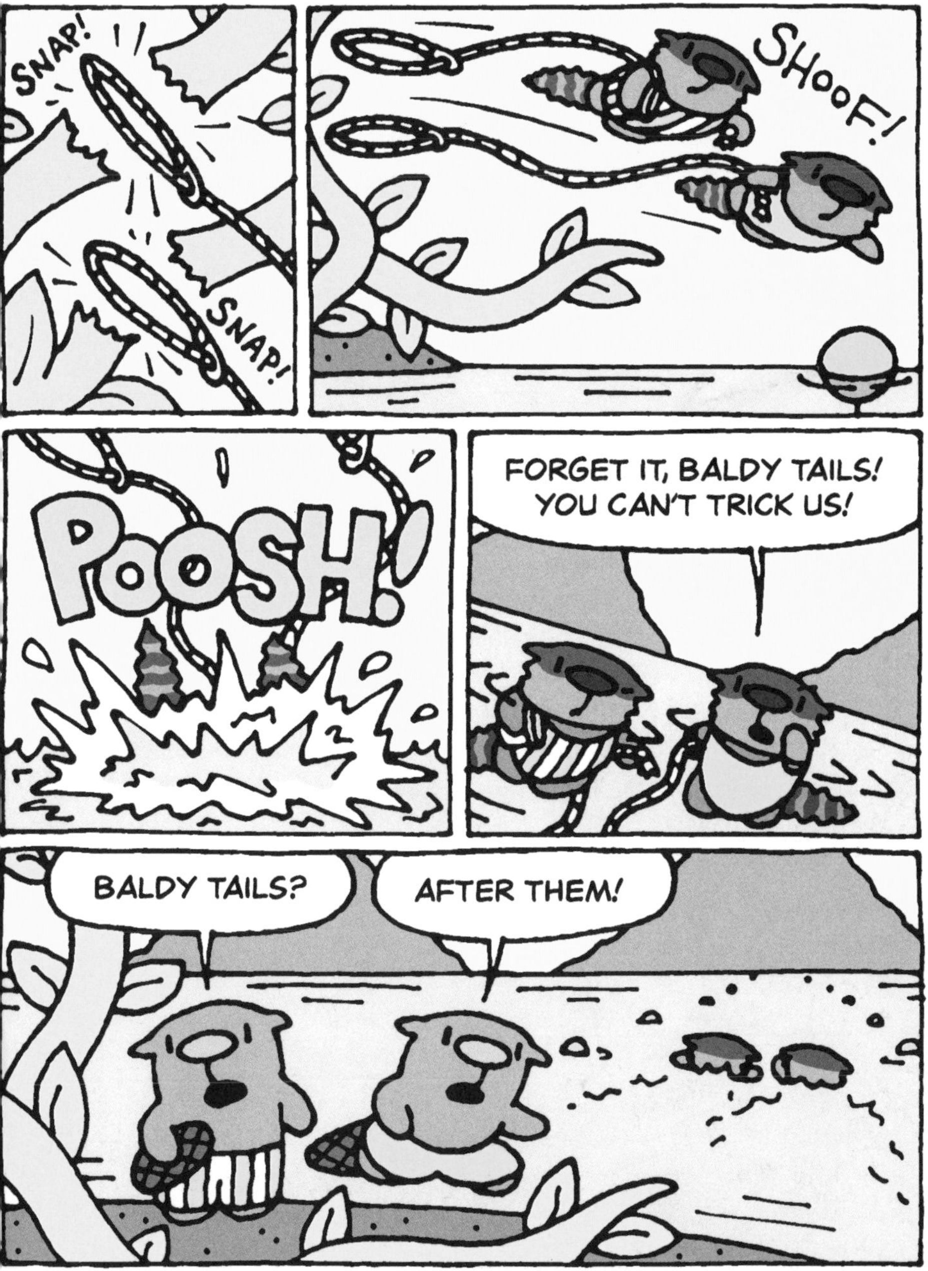
SNAP!
SNAP!
SHOOF!
POOSH!
FORGET IT, BALDY TAILS! YOU CAN'T TRICK US!
BALDY TAILS?
AFTER THEM!

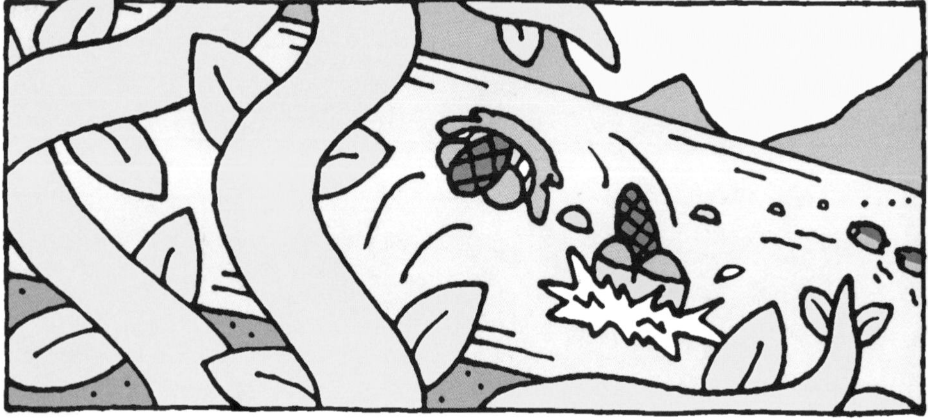

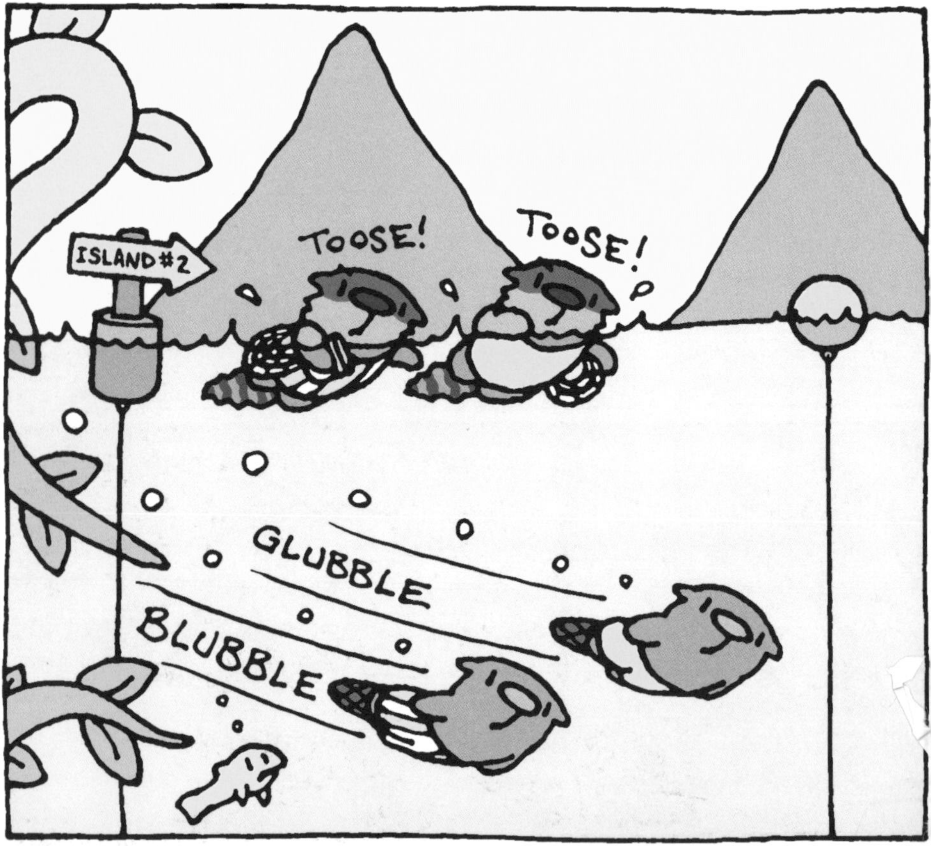
ISLAND #2
TOOSE!
TOOSE!
GLUBBLE
BLUBBLE

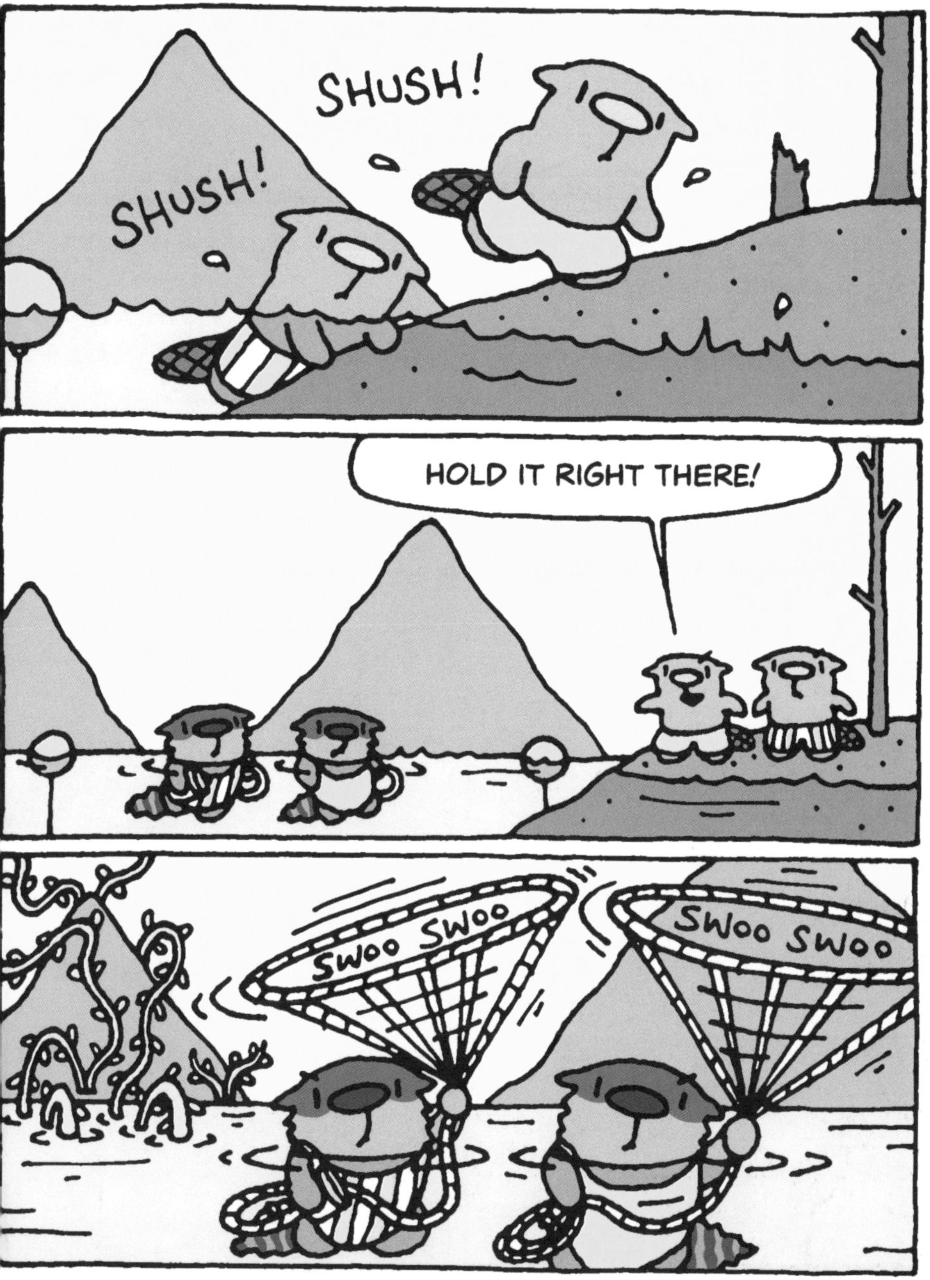
SHUSH!
SHUSH!
HOLD IT RIGHT THERE!
SWOO SWOO
SWOO SWOO

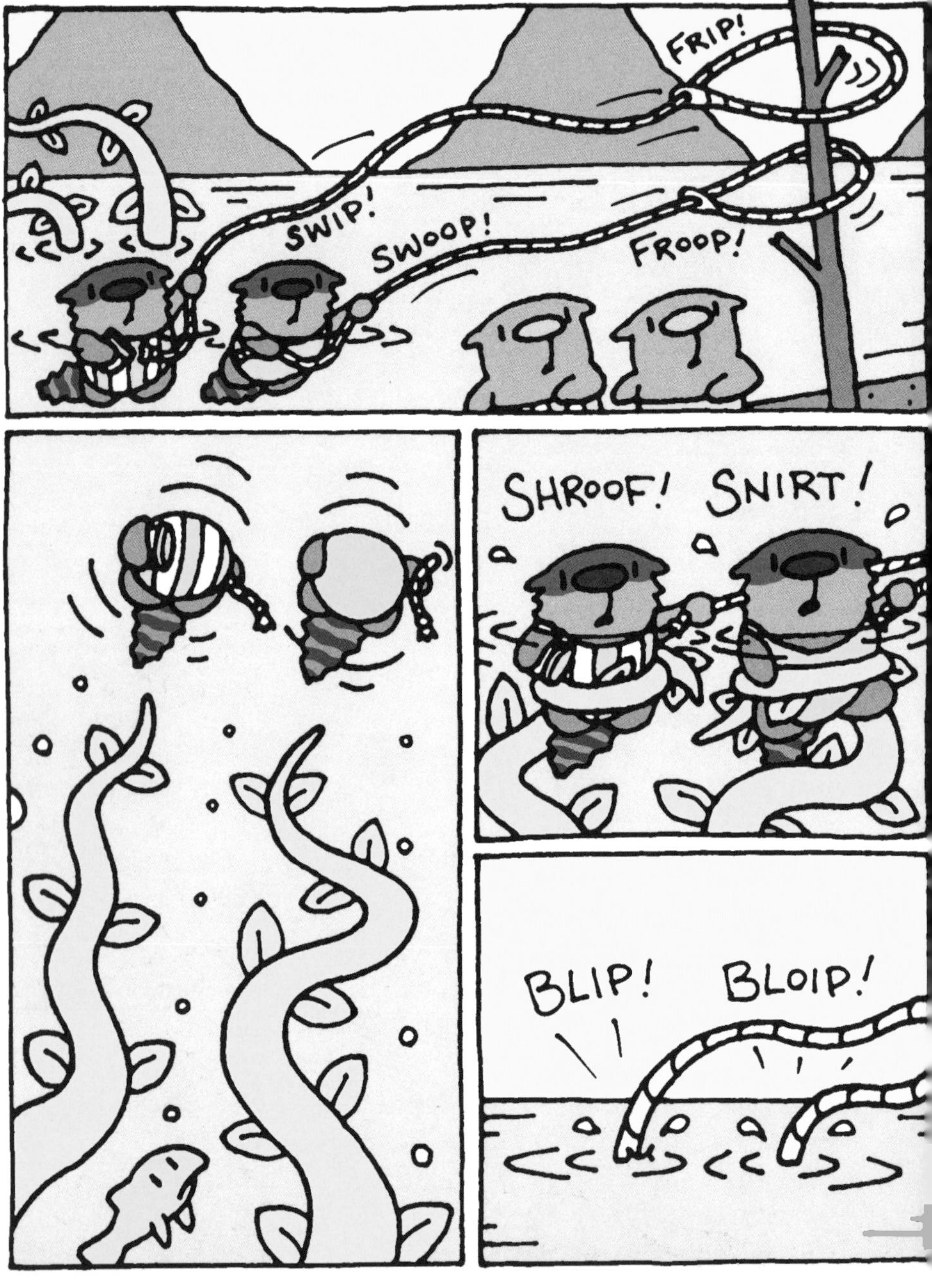
FRIP!
SWIP!
SWOOP!
FROOP!
SHROOF!
SNIRT!
BLIP!
BLOIP!

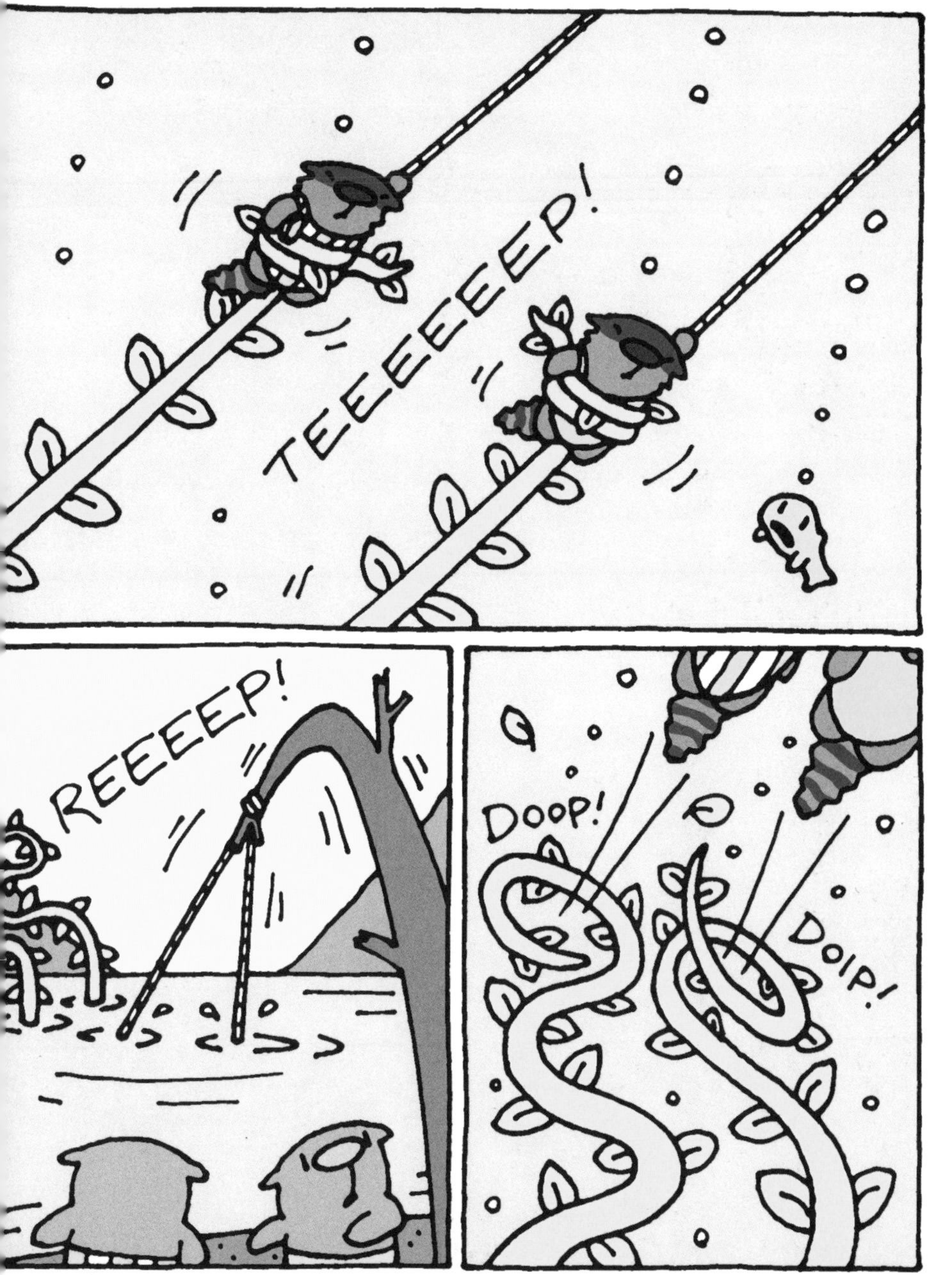
TEEEEEEEP!
REEEEEP!
DOOP!
DOIP!

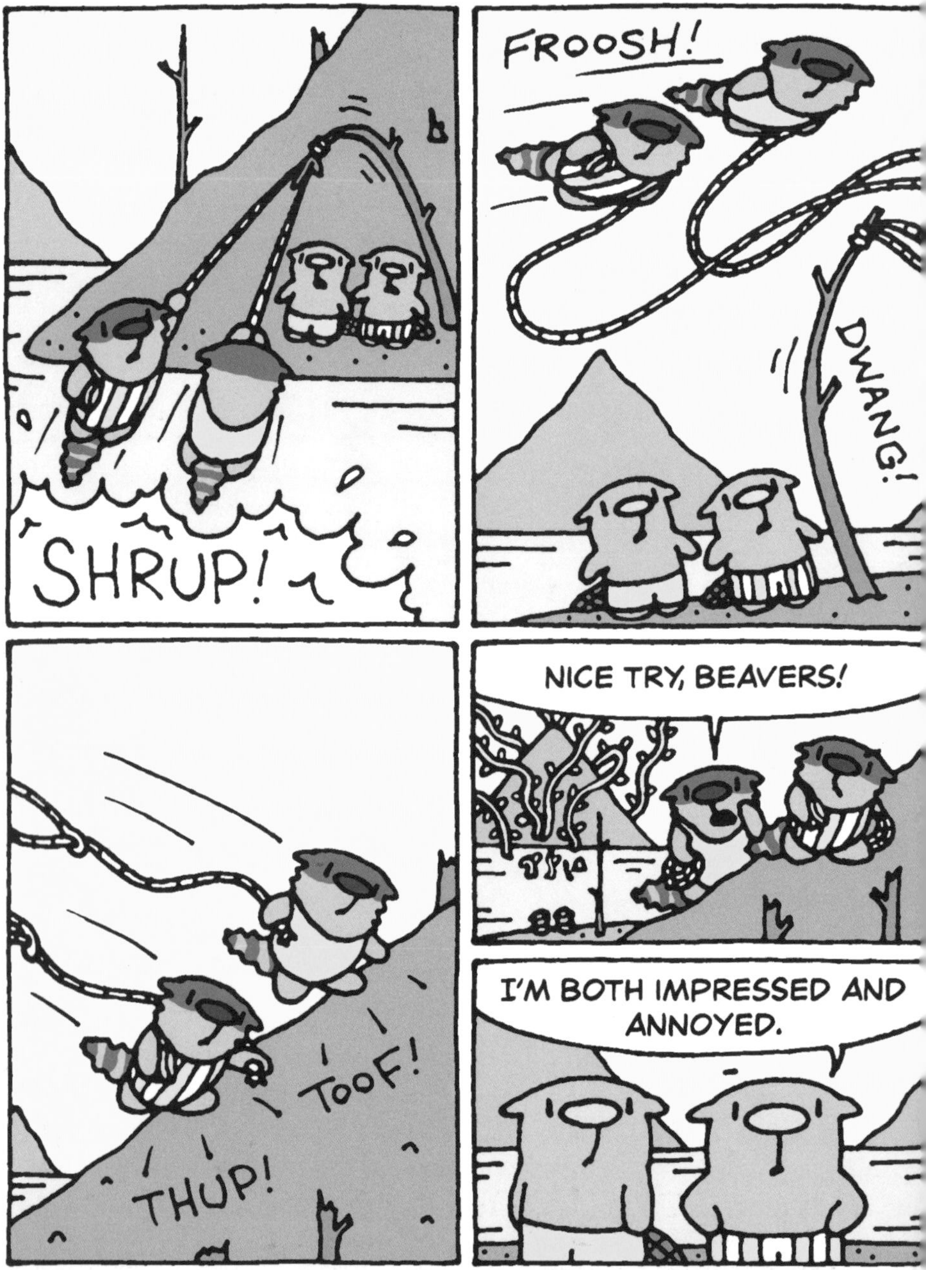
SHRUP!
FROOSH!
DWANG!
TOOF!
THUP!
NICE TRY, BEAVERS!
I'M BOTH IMPRESSED AND ANNOYED.

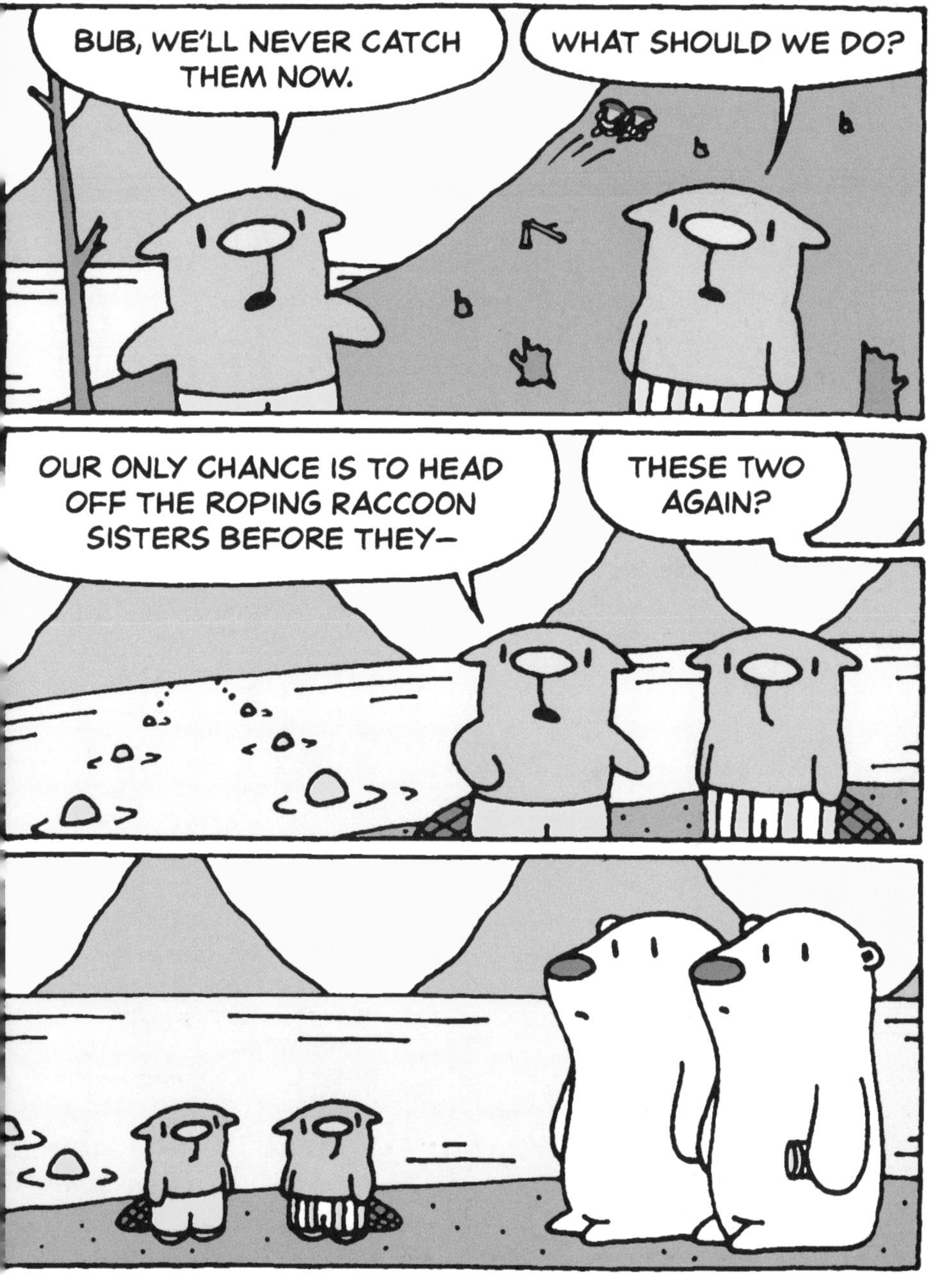
BUB, WE'LL NEVER CATCH THEM NOW.
WHAT SHOULD WE DO?
OUR ONLY CHANCE IS TO HEAD OFF THE ROPING RACCOON SISTERS BEFORE THEY—
THESE TWO AGAIN?

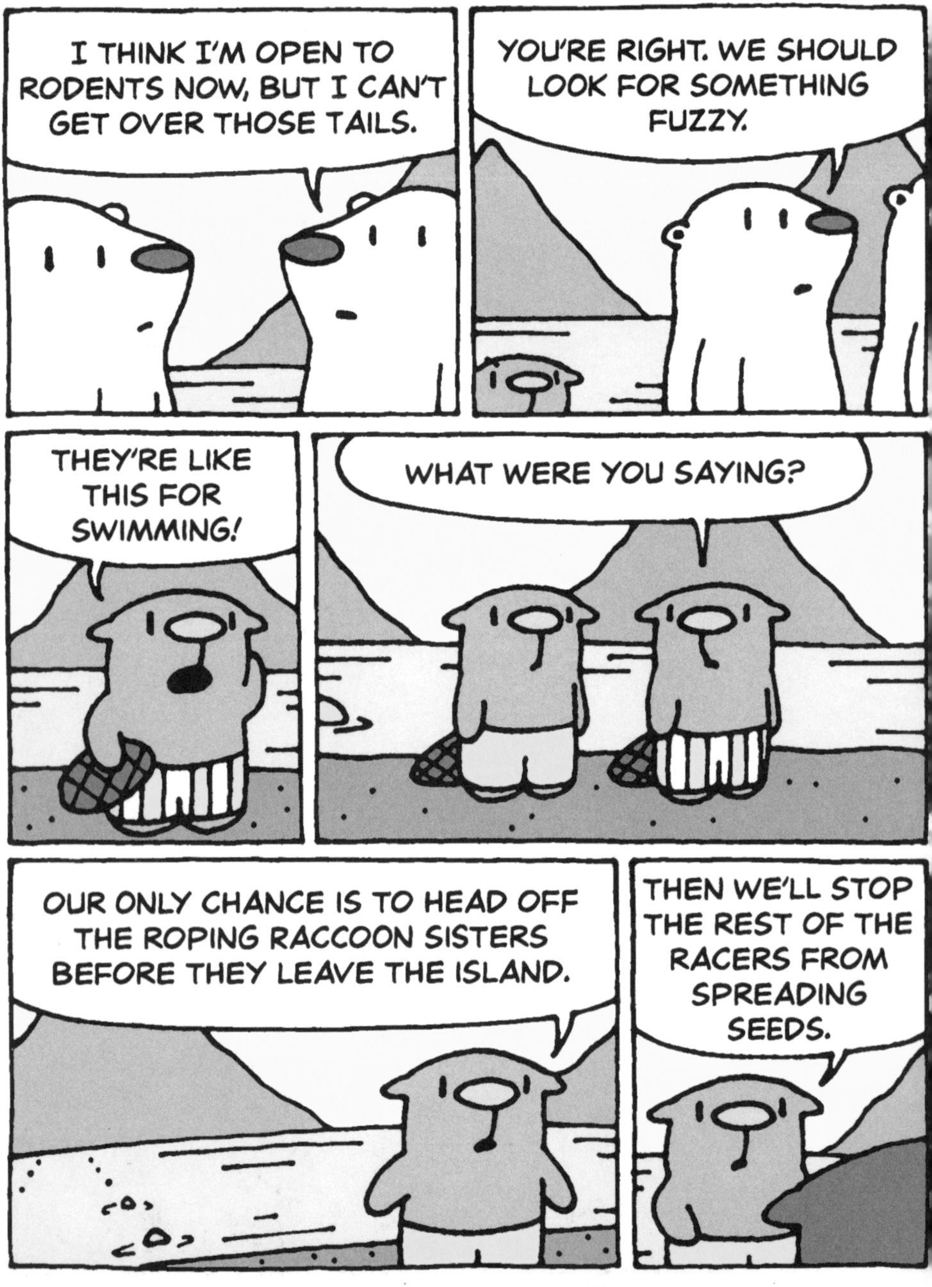
I THINK I'M OPEN TO RODENTS NOW, BUT I CAN'T GET OVER THOSE TAILS.
YOU'RE RIGHT. WE SHOULD LOOK FOR SOMETHING FUZZY.
THEY'RE LIKE THIS FOR SWIMMING!
WHAT WERE YOU SAYING?
OUR ONLY CHANCE IS TO HEAD OFF THE ROPING RACCOON SISTERS BEFORE THEY LEAVE THE ISLAND.
THEN WE'LL STOP THE REST OF THE RACERS FROM SPREADING SEEDS.

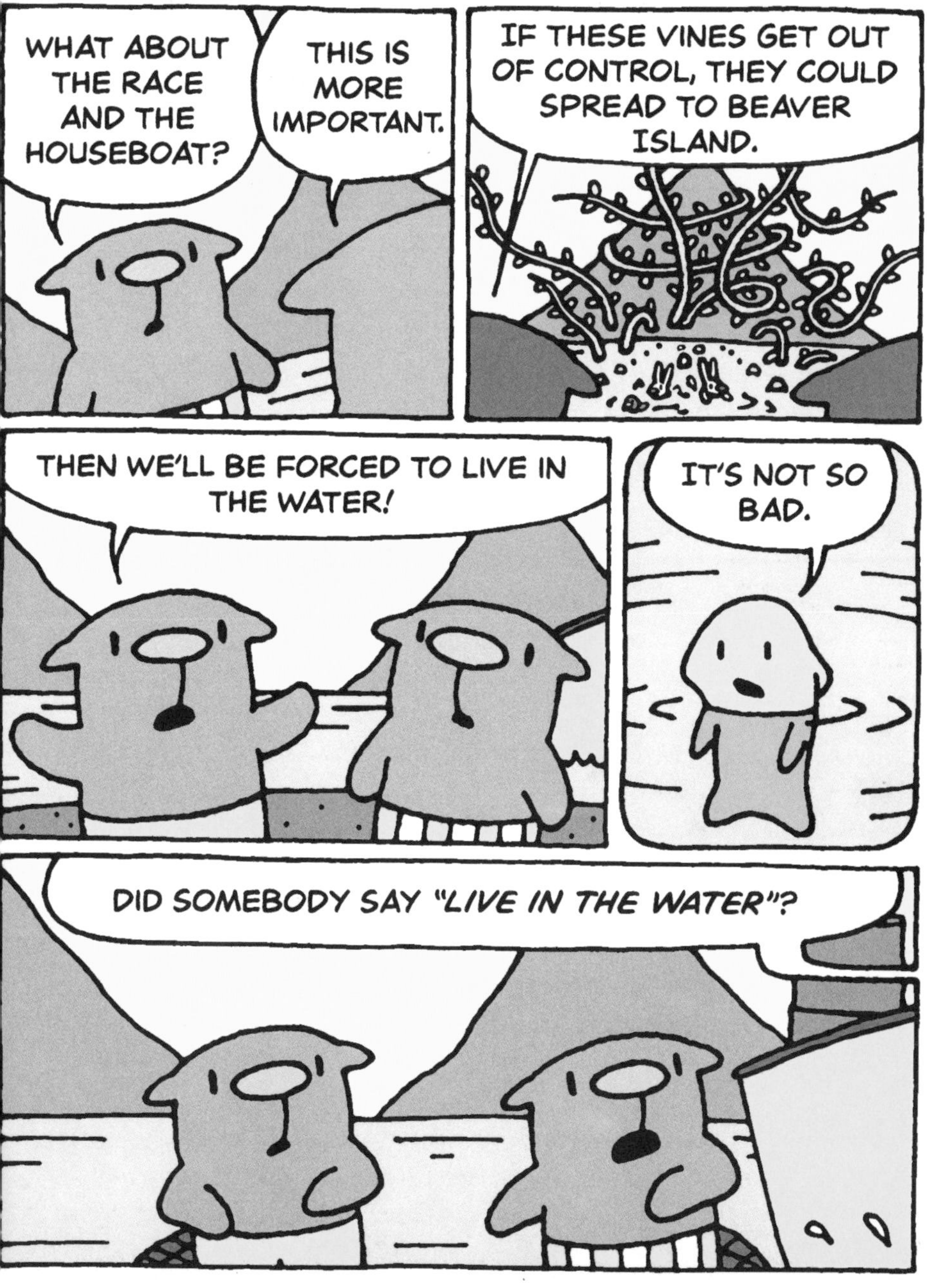
WHAT ABOUT THE RACE AND THE HOUSEBOAT?
THIS IS MORE IMPORTANT.
IF THESE VINES GET OUT OF CONTROL, THEY COULD SPREAD TO BEAVER ISLAND.
THEN WE'LL BE FORCED TO LIVE IN THE WATER!
IT'S NOT SO BAD.
DID SOMEBODY SAY "*LIVE IN THE WATER*"?

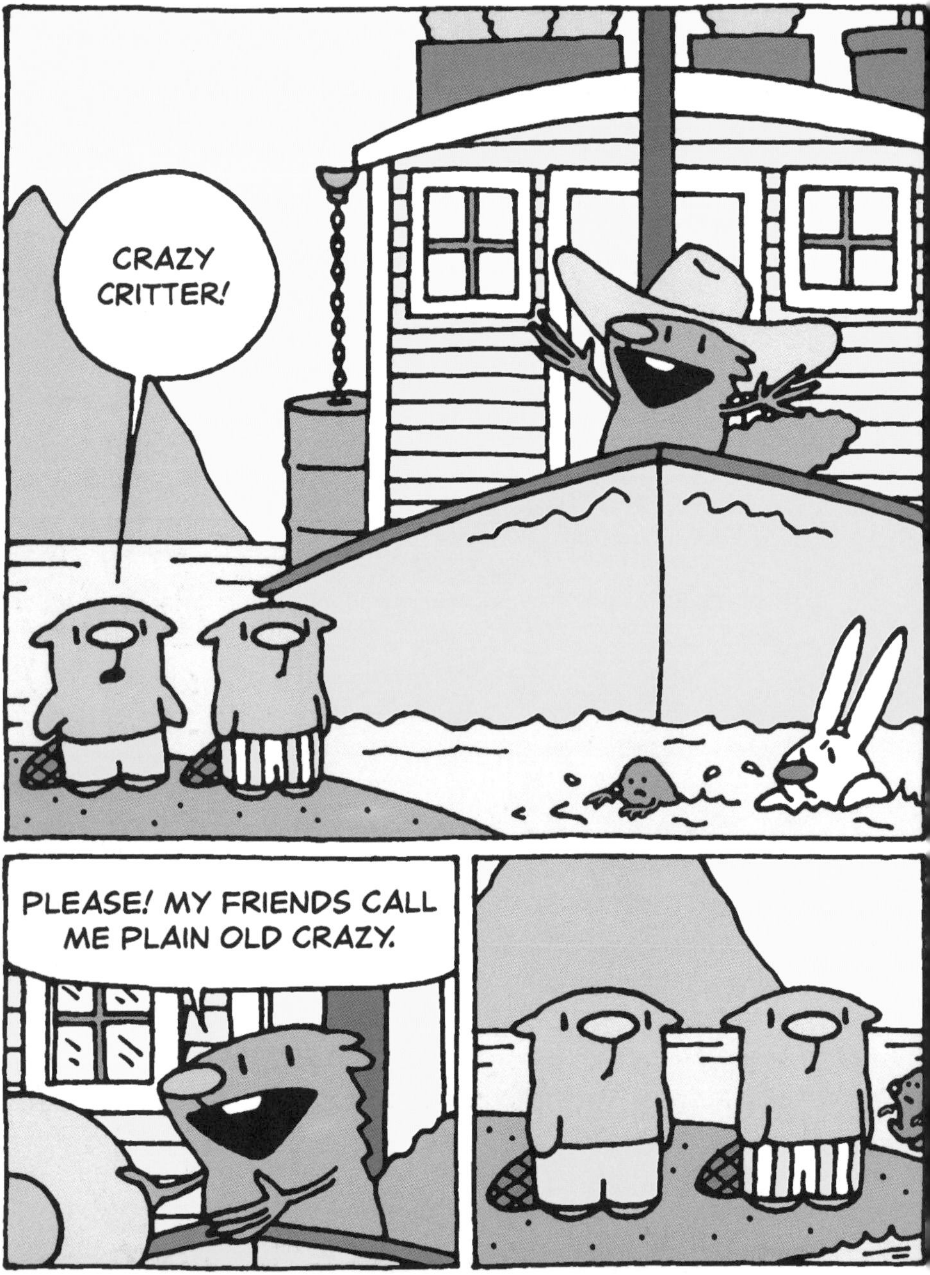
CRAZY CRITTER!
PLEASE! MY FRIENDS CALL ME PLAIN OLD CRAZY.

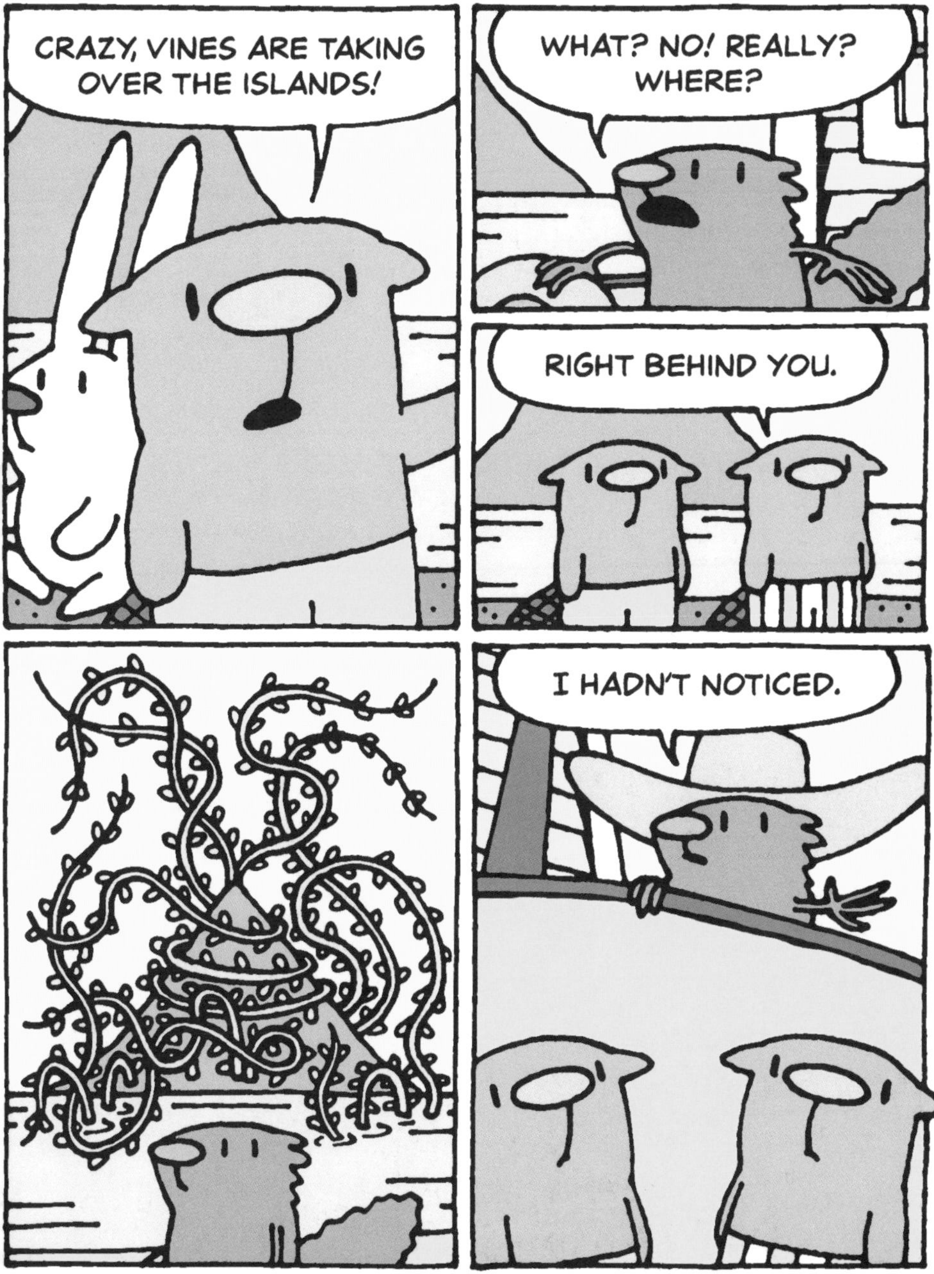
CRAZY, VINES ARE TAKING OVER THE ISLANDS!
WHAT? NO! REALLY? WHERE?
RIGHT BEHIND YOU.
I HADN'T NOTICED.

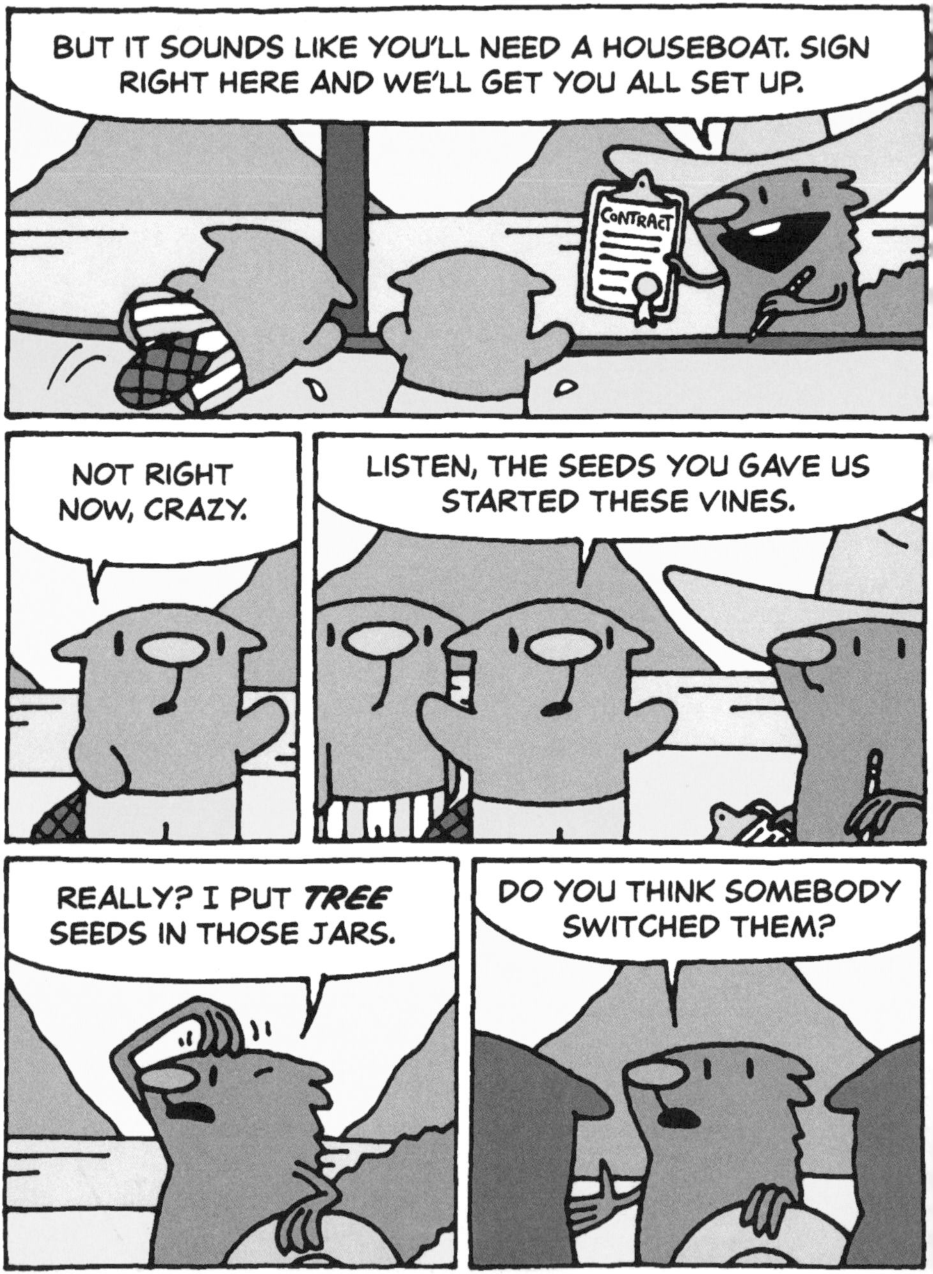
BUT IT SOUNDS LIKE YOU'LL NEED A HOUSEBOAT. SIGN RIGHT HERE AND WE'LL GET YOU ALL SET UP.
CONTRACT
NOT RIGHT NOW, CRAZY.
LISTEN, THE SEEDS YOU GAVE US STARTED THESE VINES.
REALLY? I PUT *TREE* SEEDS IN THOSE JARS.
DO YOU THINK SOMEBODY SWITCHED THEM?

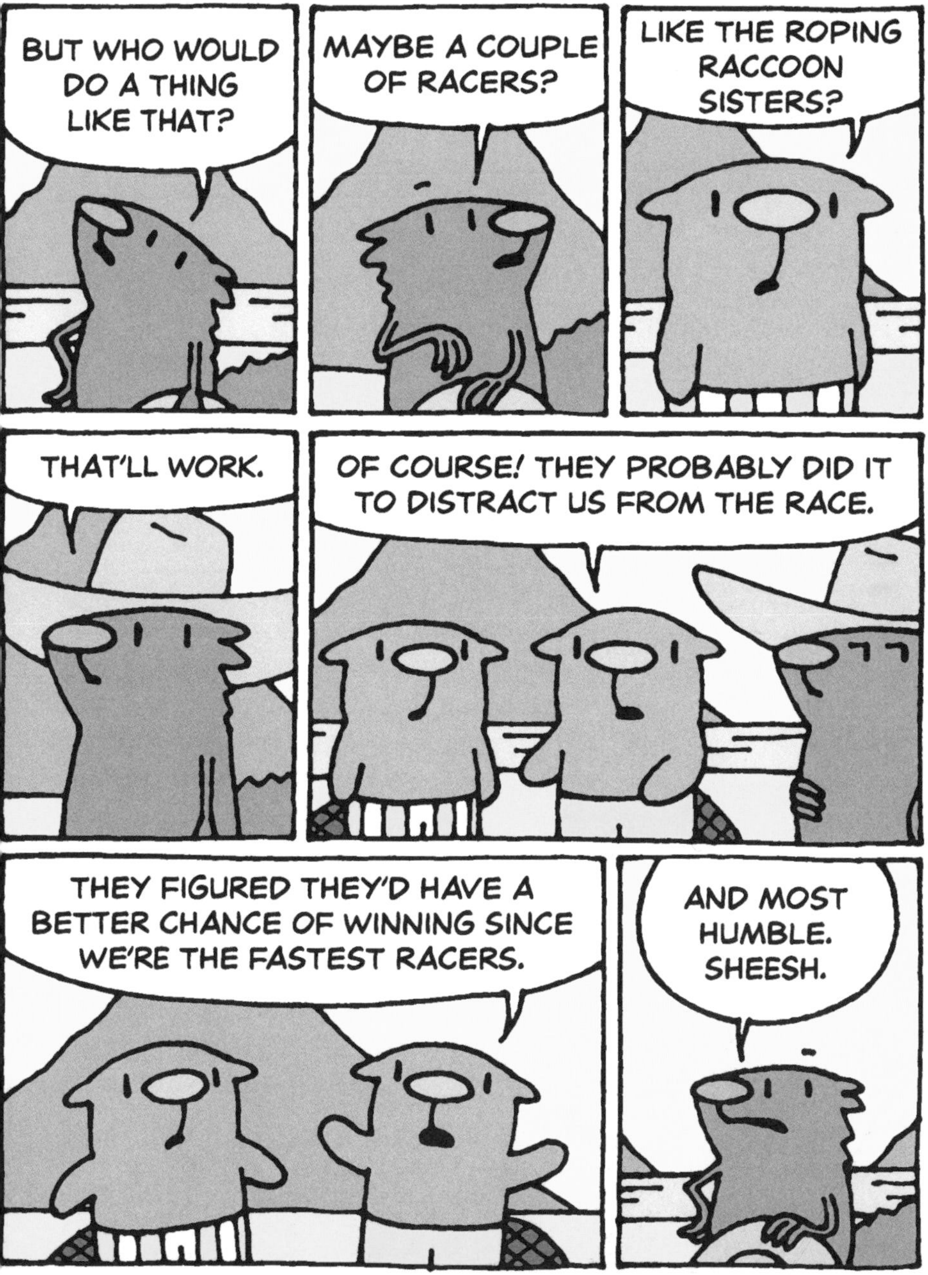
BUT WHO WOULD DO A THING LIKE THAT?
MAYBE A COUPLE OF RACERS?
LIKE THE ROPING RACCOON SISTERS?
THAT'LL WORK.
OF COURSE! THEY PROBABLY DID IT TO DISTRACT US FROM THE RACE.
THEY FIGURED THEY'D HAVE A BETTER CHANCE OF WINNING SINCE WE'RE THE FASTEST RACERS.
AND MOST HUMBLE. SHEESH.

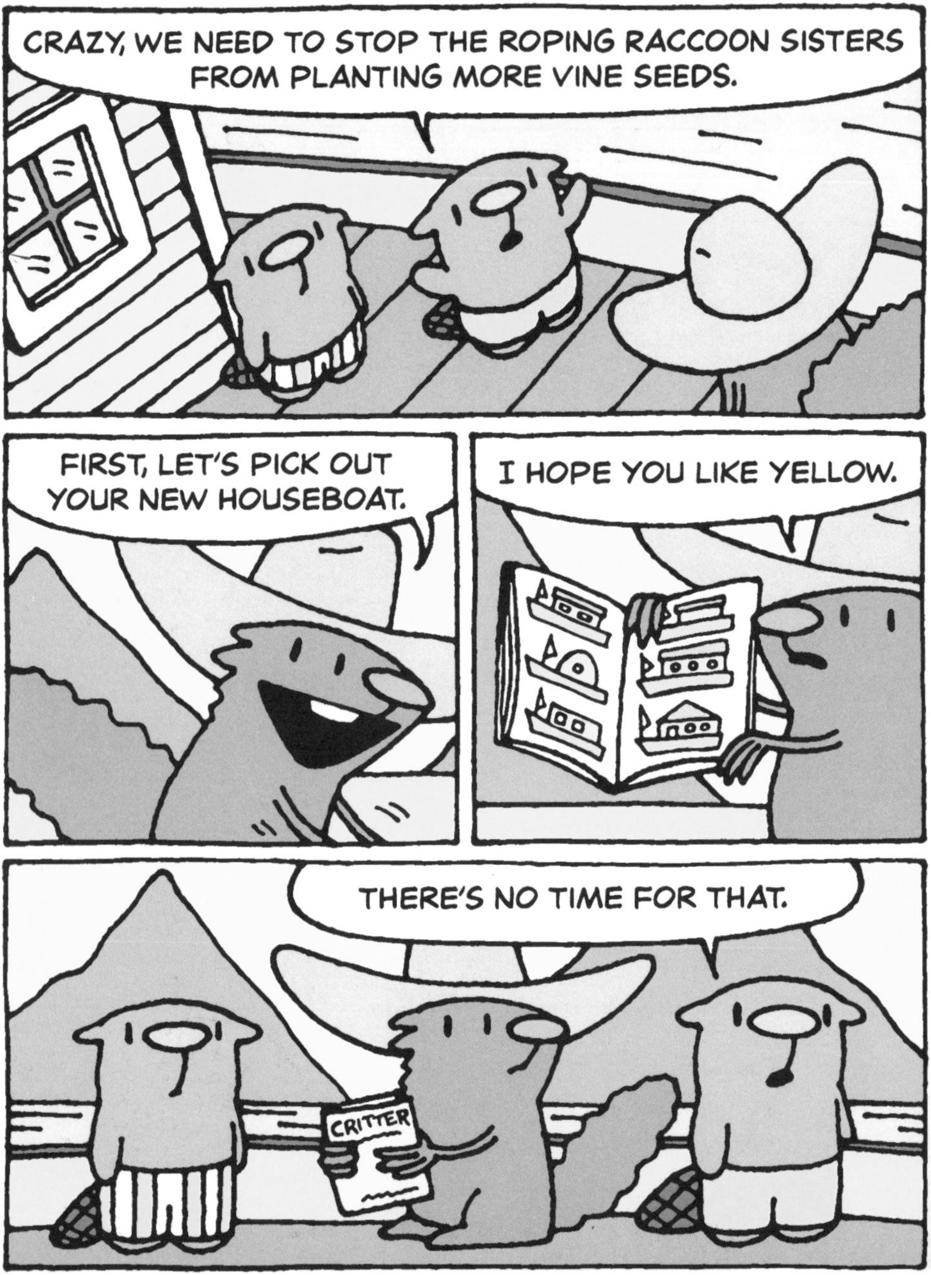
CRAZY, WE NEED TO STOP THE ROPING RACCOON SISTERS FROM PLANTING MORE VINE SEEDS.
FIRST, LET'S PICK OUT YOUR NEW HOUSEBOAT.
I HOPE YOU LIKE YELLOW.
THERE'S NO TIME FOR THAT.
CRITTER

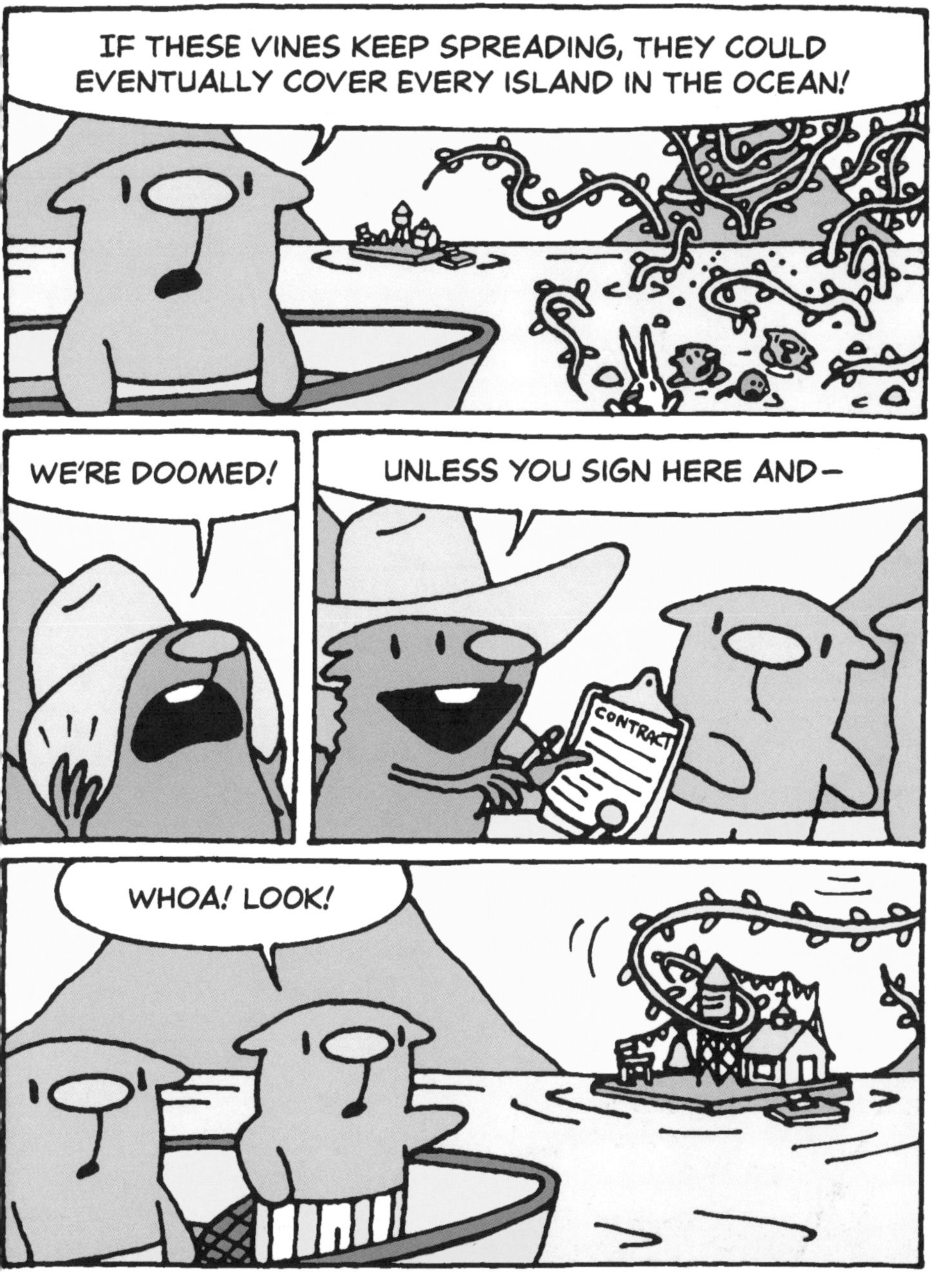
IF THESE VINES KEEP SPREADING, THEY COULD EVENTUALLY COVER EVERY ISLAND IN THE OCEAN!
WE'RE DOOMED!
UNLESS YOU SIGN HERE AND—
CONTRACT
WHOA! LOOK!

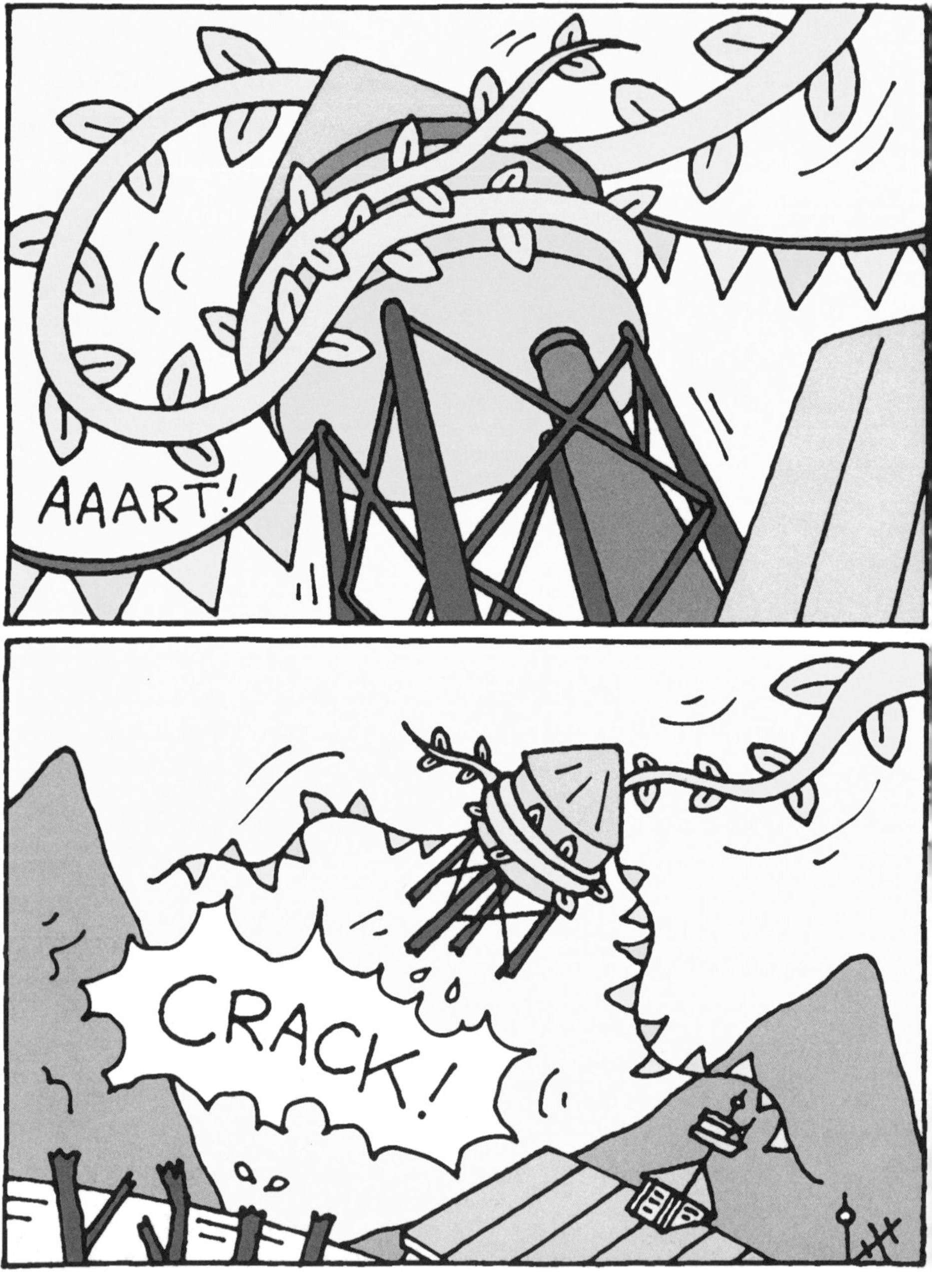
AAART!
CRACK!

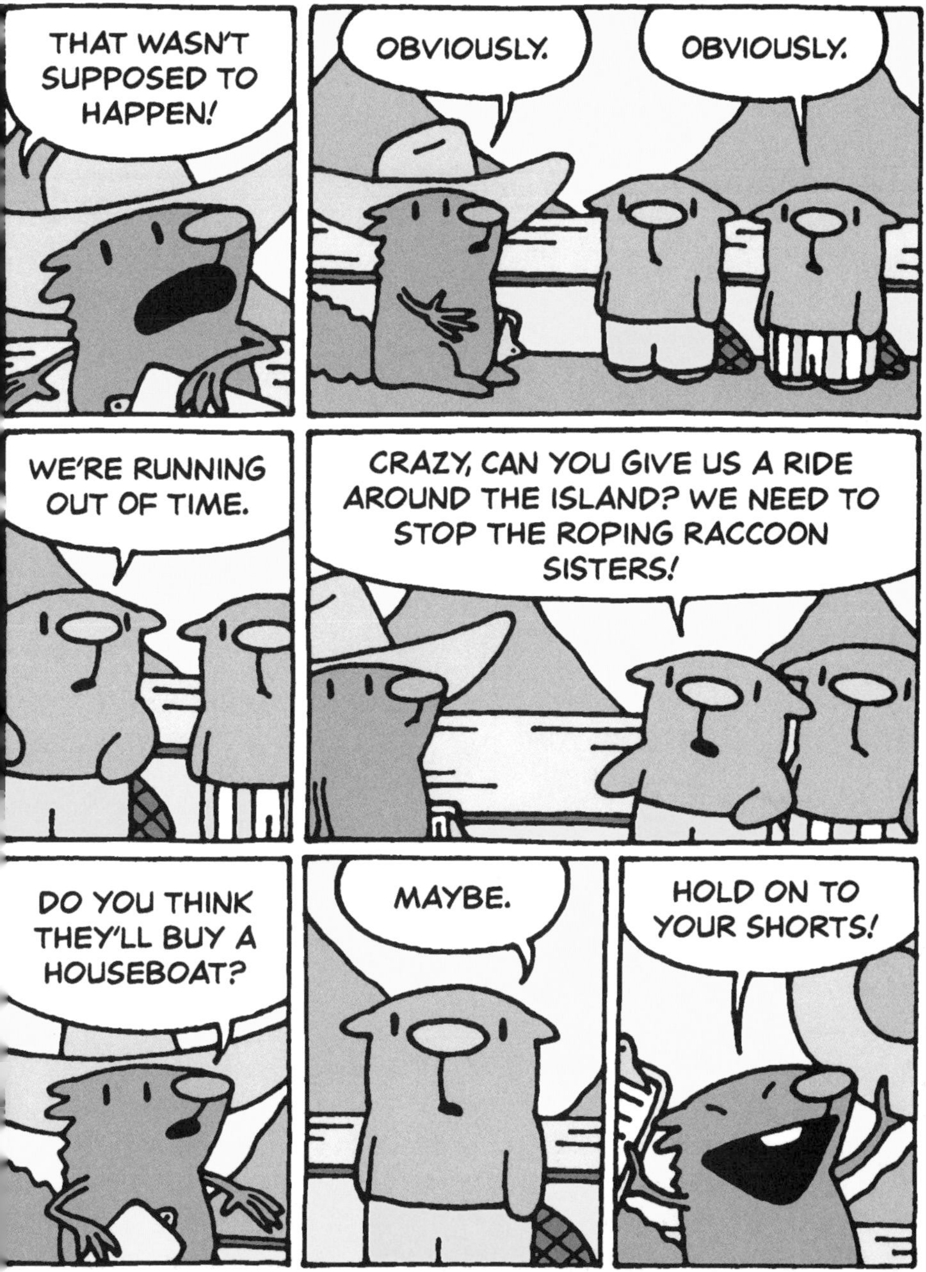
THAT WASN'T SUPPOSED TO HAPPEN!
OBVIOUSLY.
OBVIOUSLY.
WE'RE RUNNING OUT OF TIME.
CRAZY, CAN YOU GIVE US A RIDE AROUND THE ISLAND? WE NEED TO STOP THE ROPING RACCOON SISTERS!
DO YOU THINK THEY'LL BUY A HOUSEBOAT?
MAYBE.
HOLD ON TO YOUR SHORTS!

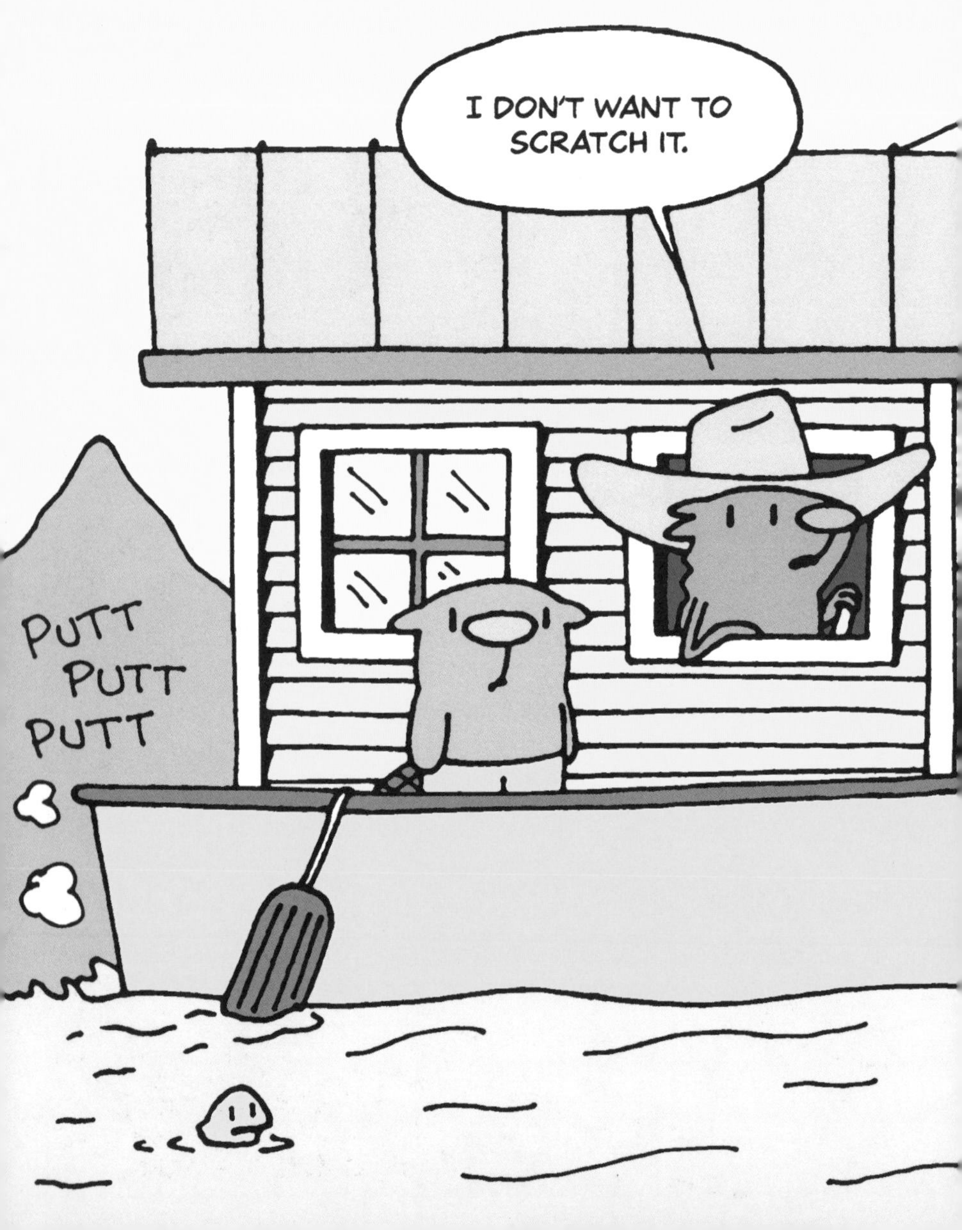
I DON'T WANT TO SCRATCH IT.
PUTT PUTT PUTT

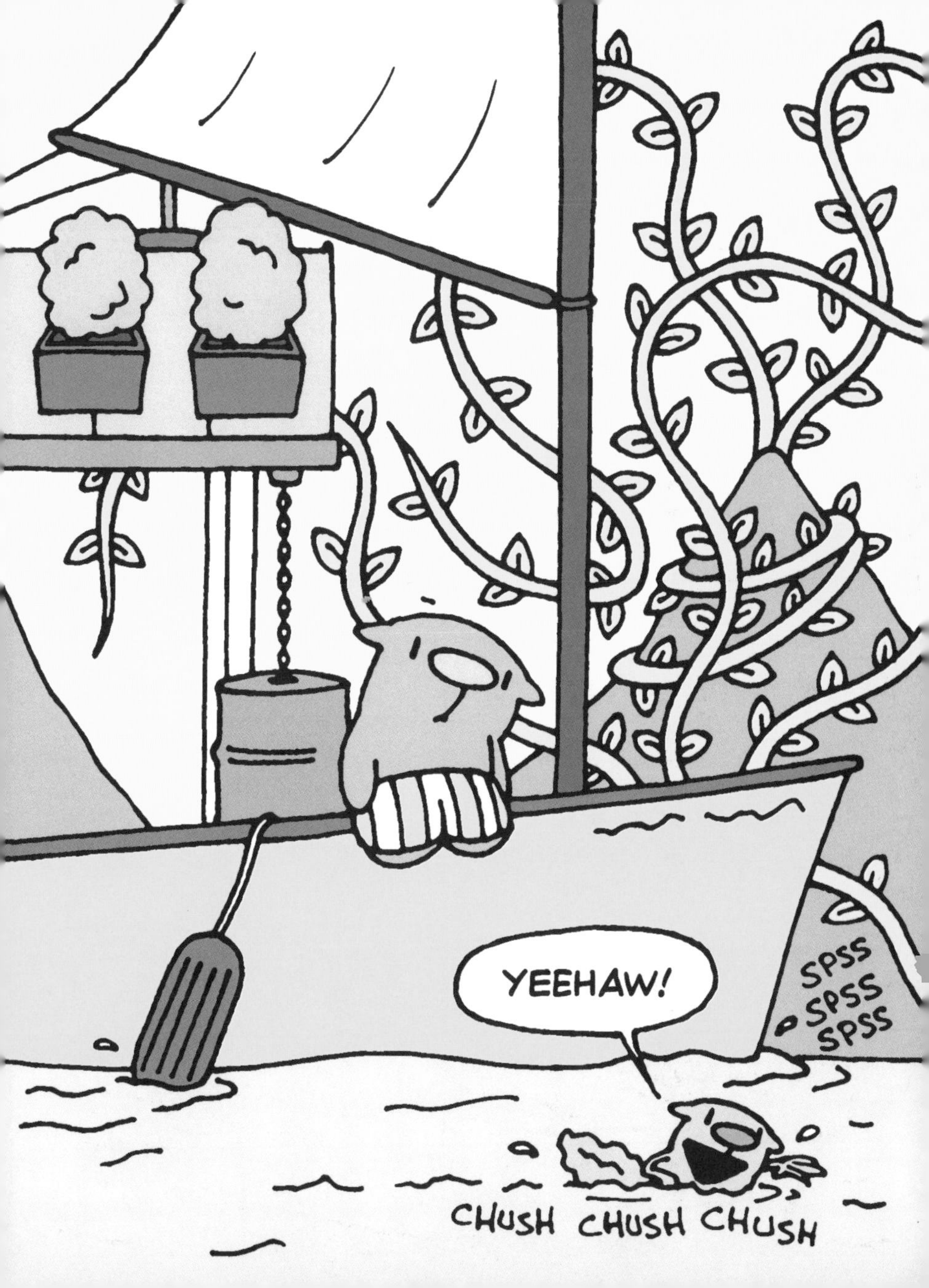
YEEHAW!
SPSS
SPSS
SPSS
CHUSH CHUSH CHUSH

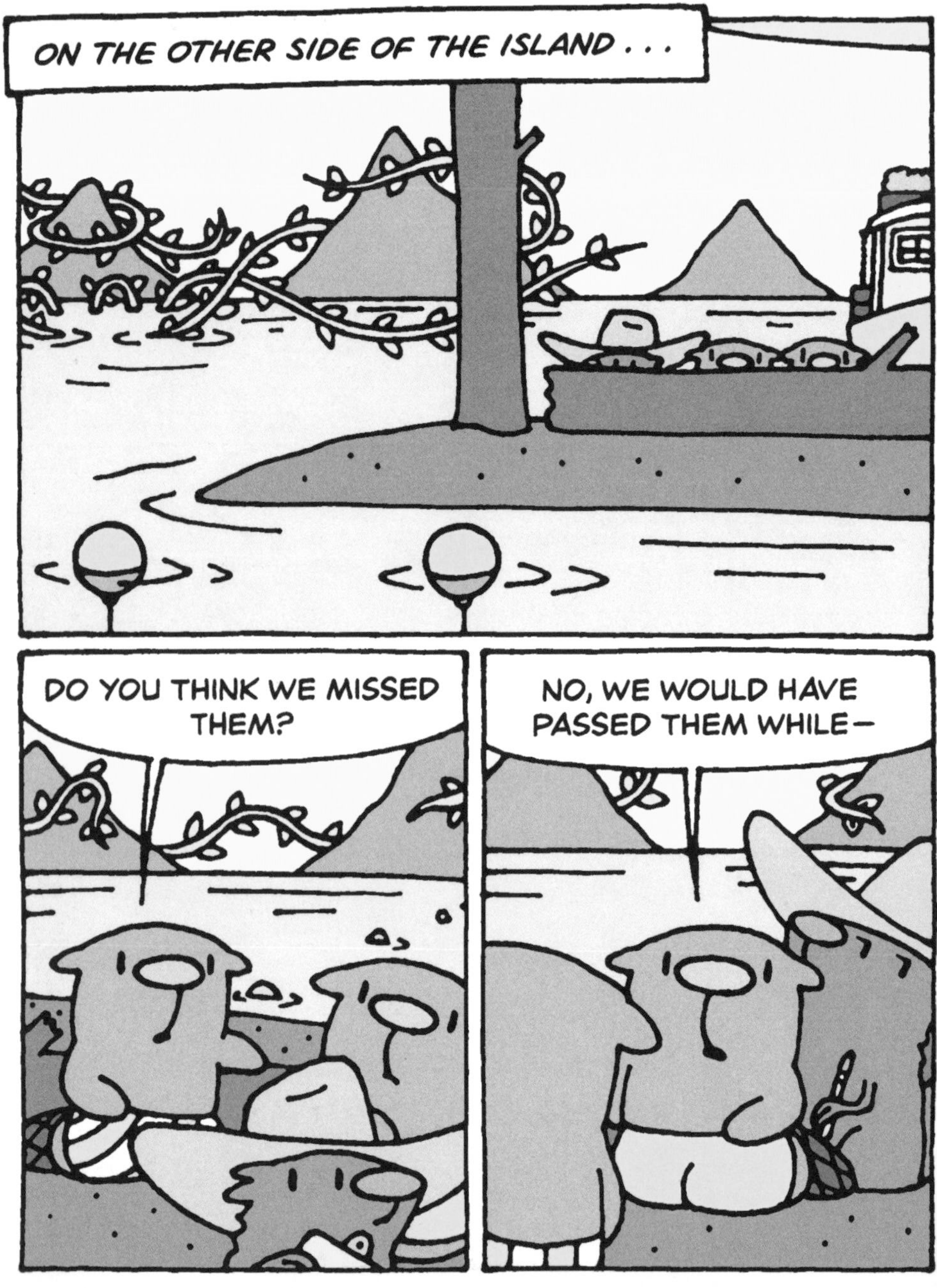
ON THE OTHER SIDE OF THE ISLAND . . .
DO YOU THINK WE MISSED THEM?
NO, WE WOULD HAVE PASSED THEM WHILE—

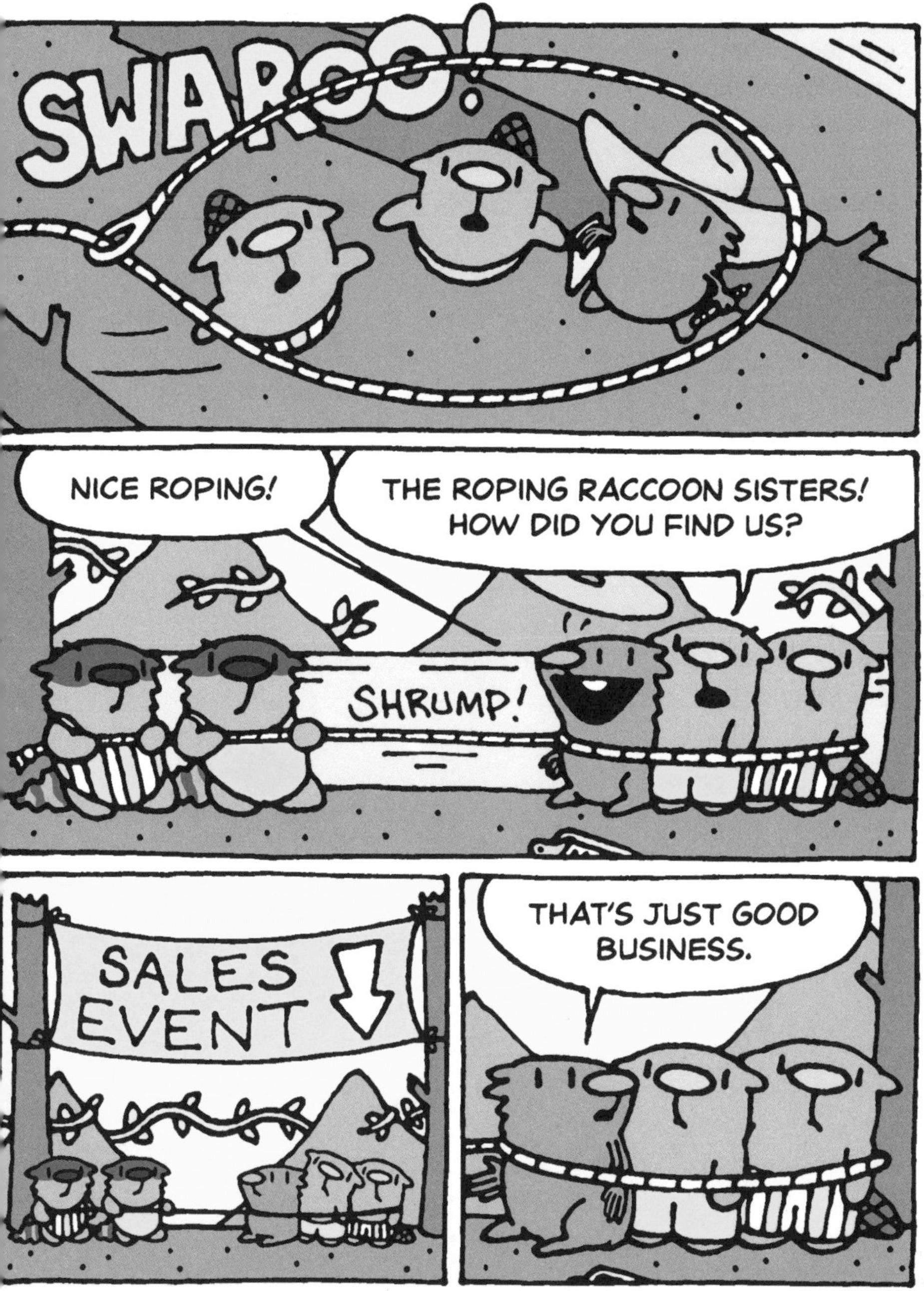
SWAROO!
NICE ROPING!
THE ROPING RACCOON SISTERS! HOW DID YOU FIND US?
SHRUMP!
SALES EVENT
THAT'S JUST GOOD BUSINESS.

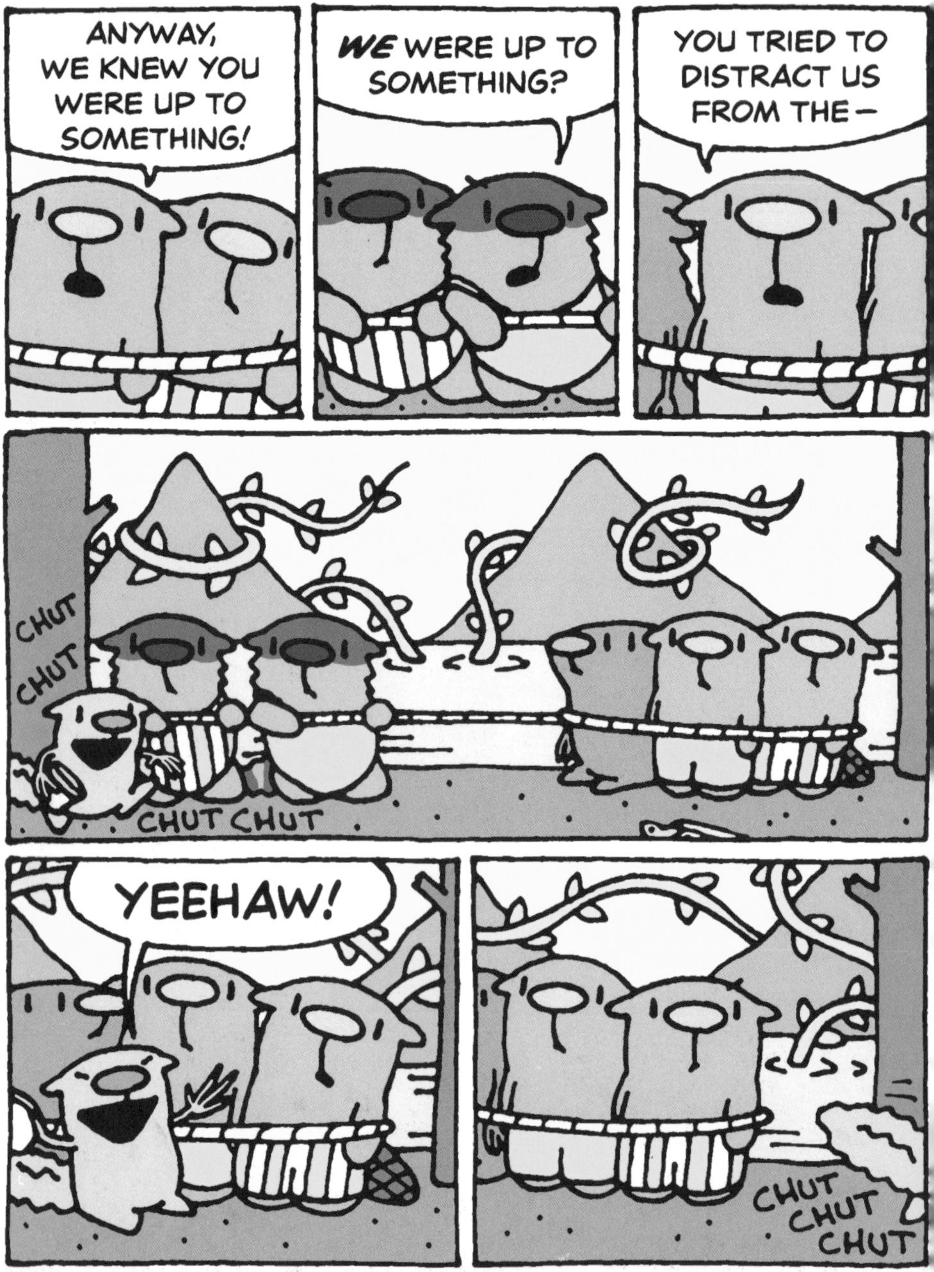
ANYWAY, WE KNEW YOU WERE UP TO SOMETHING!
WE WERE UP TO SOMETHING?
YOU TRIED TO DISTRACT US FROM THE—
CHUT CHUT
CHUT CHUT
YEEHAW!
CHUT CHUT CHUT

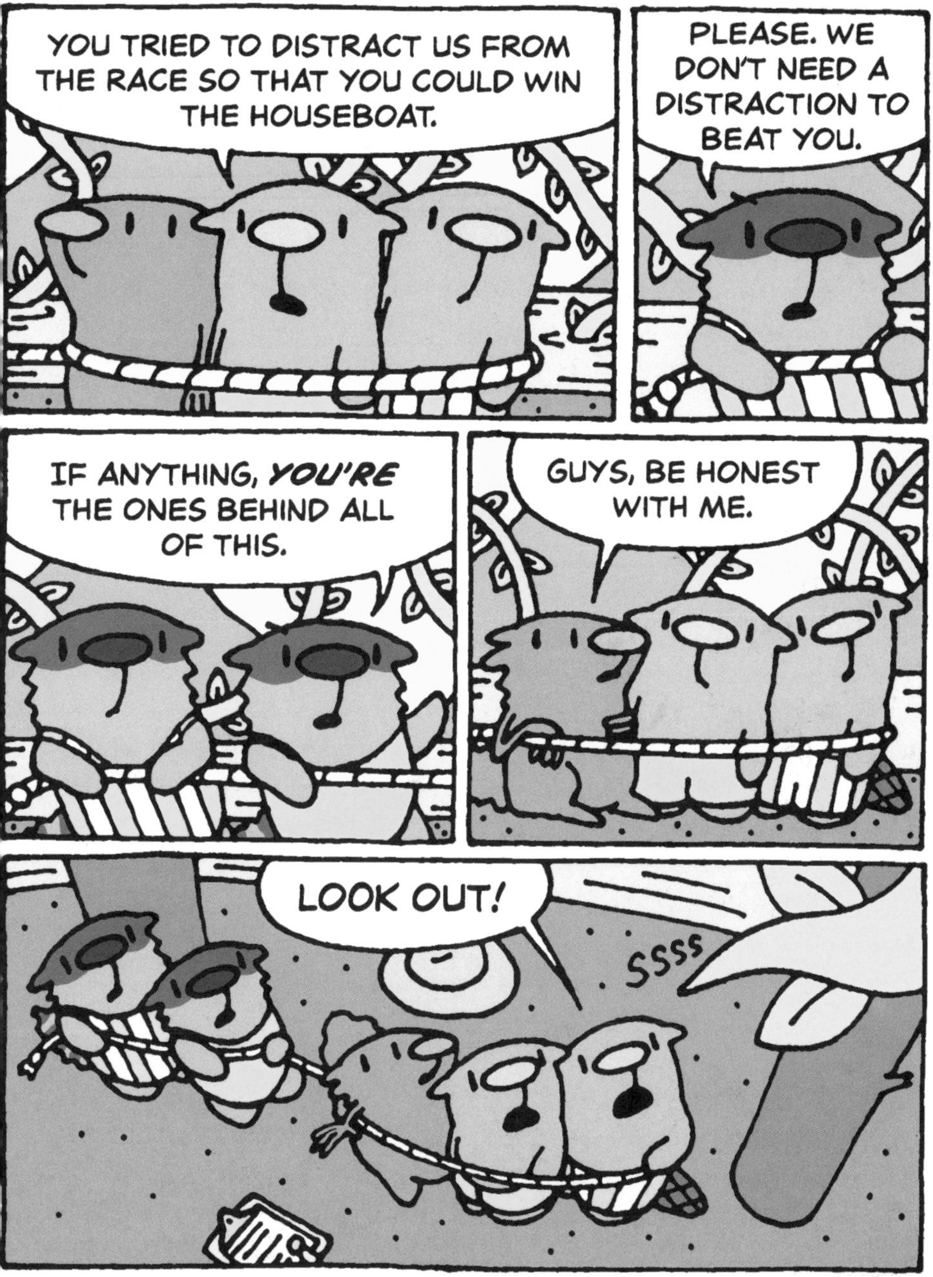
YOU TRIED TO DISTRACT US FROM THE RACE SO THAT YOU COULD WIN THE HOUSEBOAT.
PLEASE. WE DON'T NEED A DISTRACTION TO BEAT YOU.
IF ANYTHING, *YOU'RE* THE ONES BEHIND ALL OF THIS.
GUYS, BE HONEST WITH ME.
LOOK OUT!
SSSS

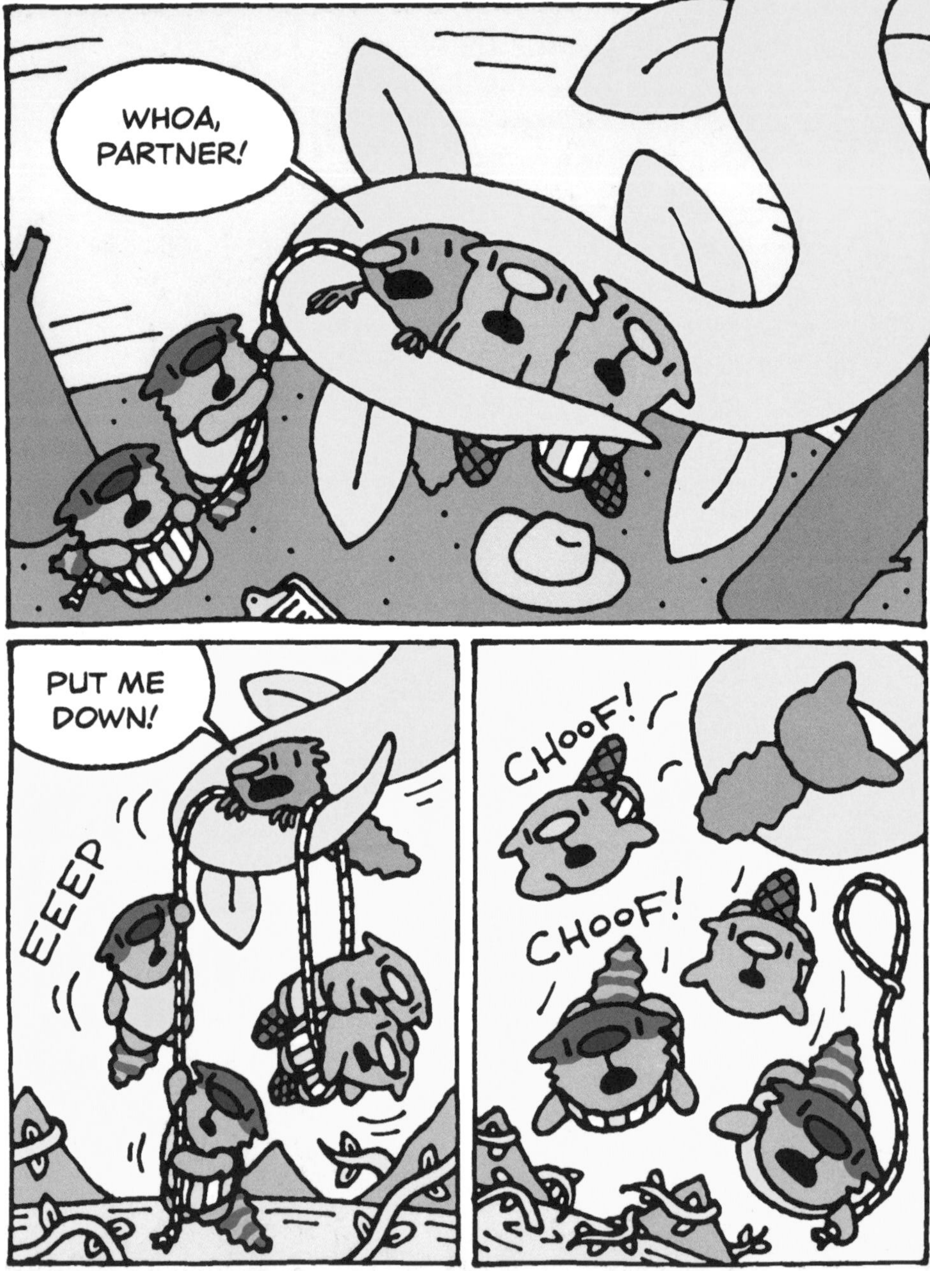
WHOA, PARTNER!
PUT ME DOWN!
EEEEP
CHOOF!
CHOOF!

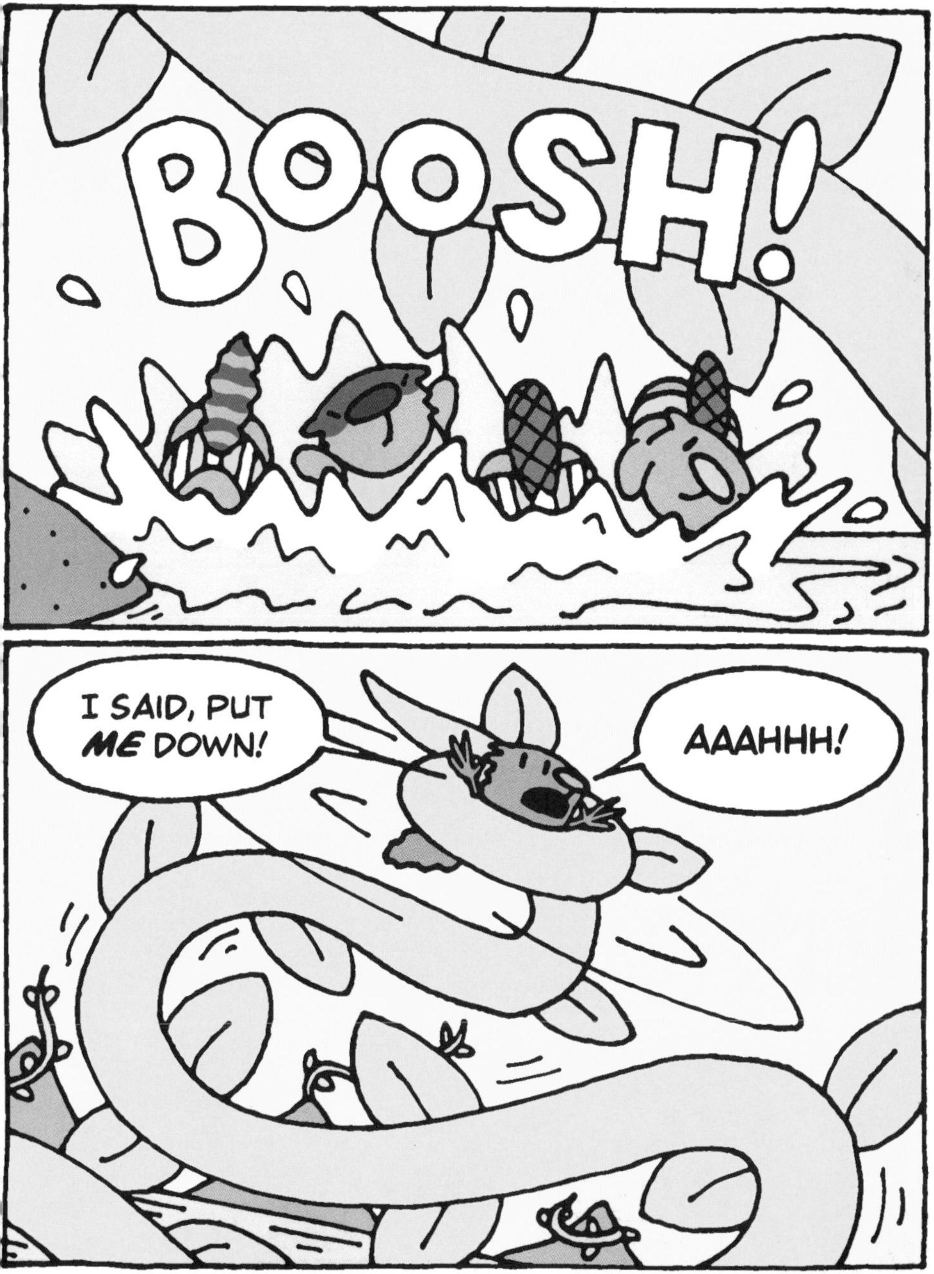
BOOSH!
I SAID, PUT ME DOWN!
AAAHHH!

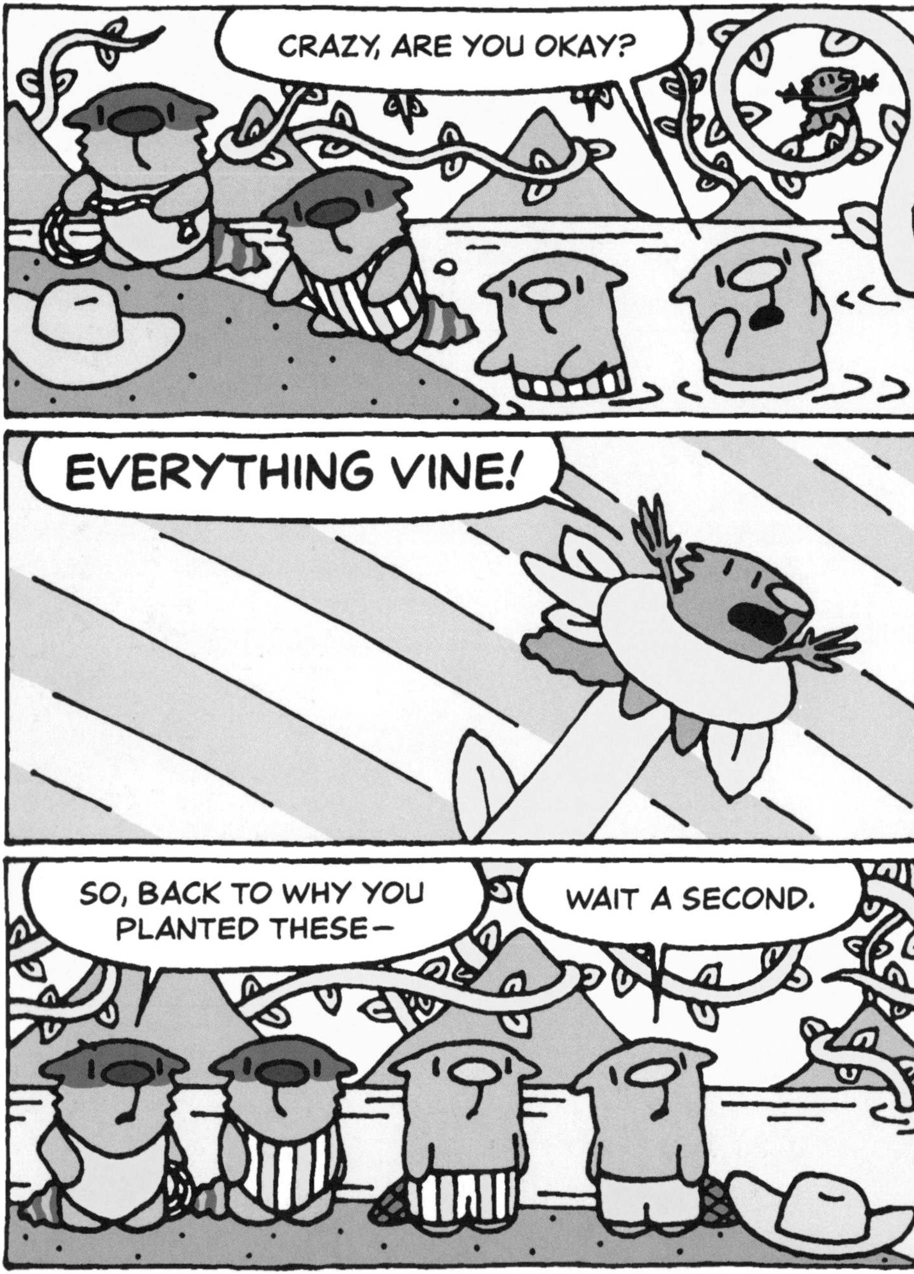
CRAZY, ARE YOU OKAY?
EVERYTHING VINE!
SO, BACK TO WHY YOU PLANTED THESE—
WAIT A SECOND.

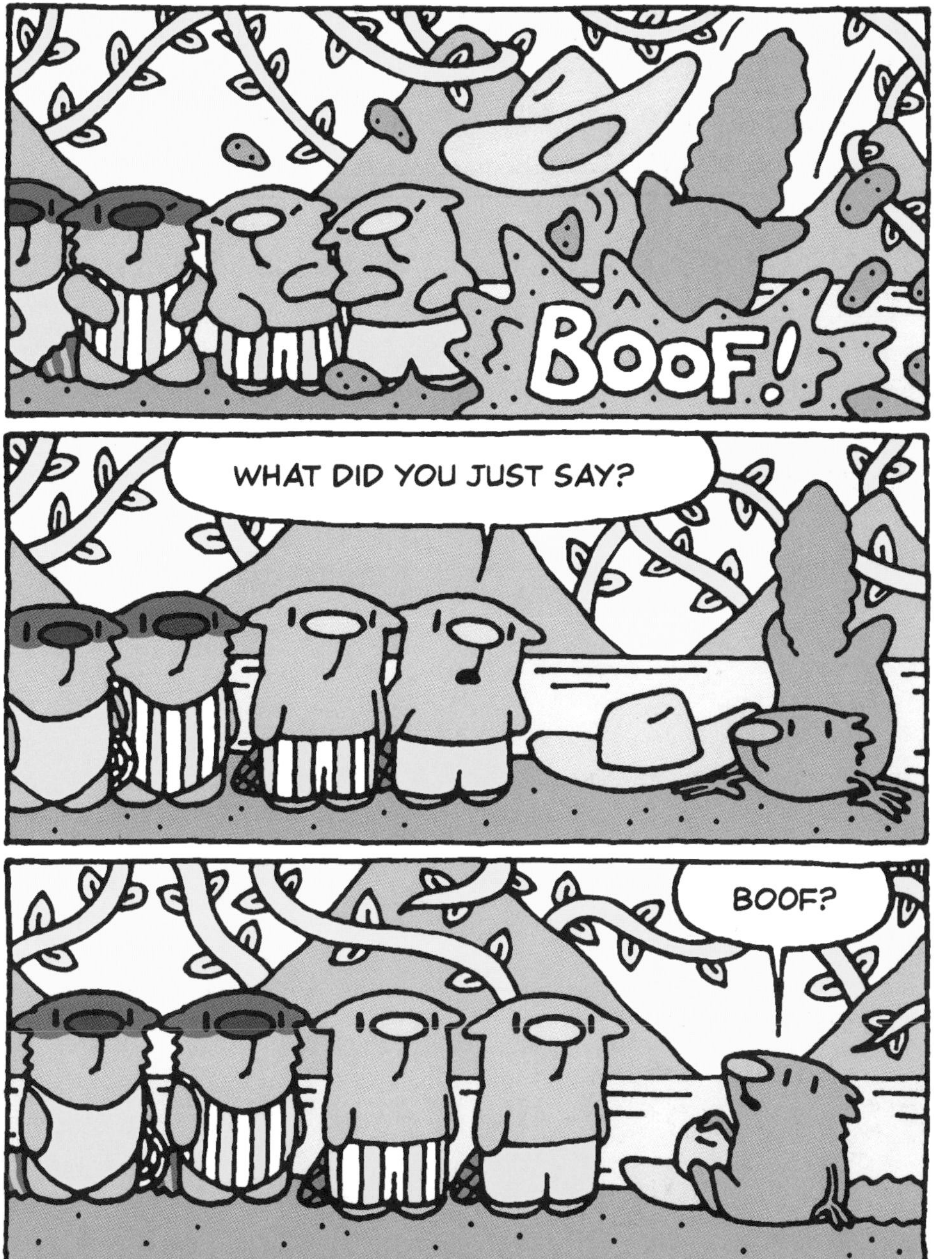
BOOF!
WHAT DID YOU JUST SAY?
BOOF?

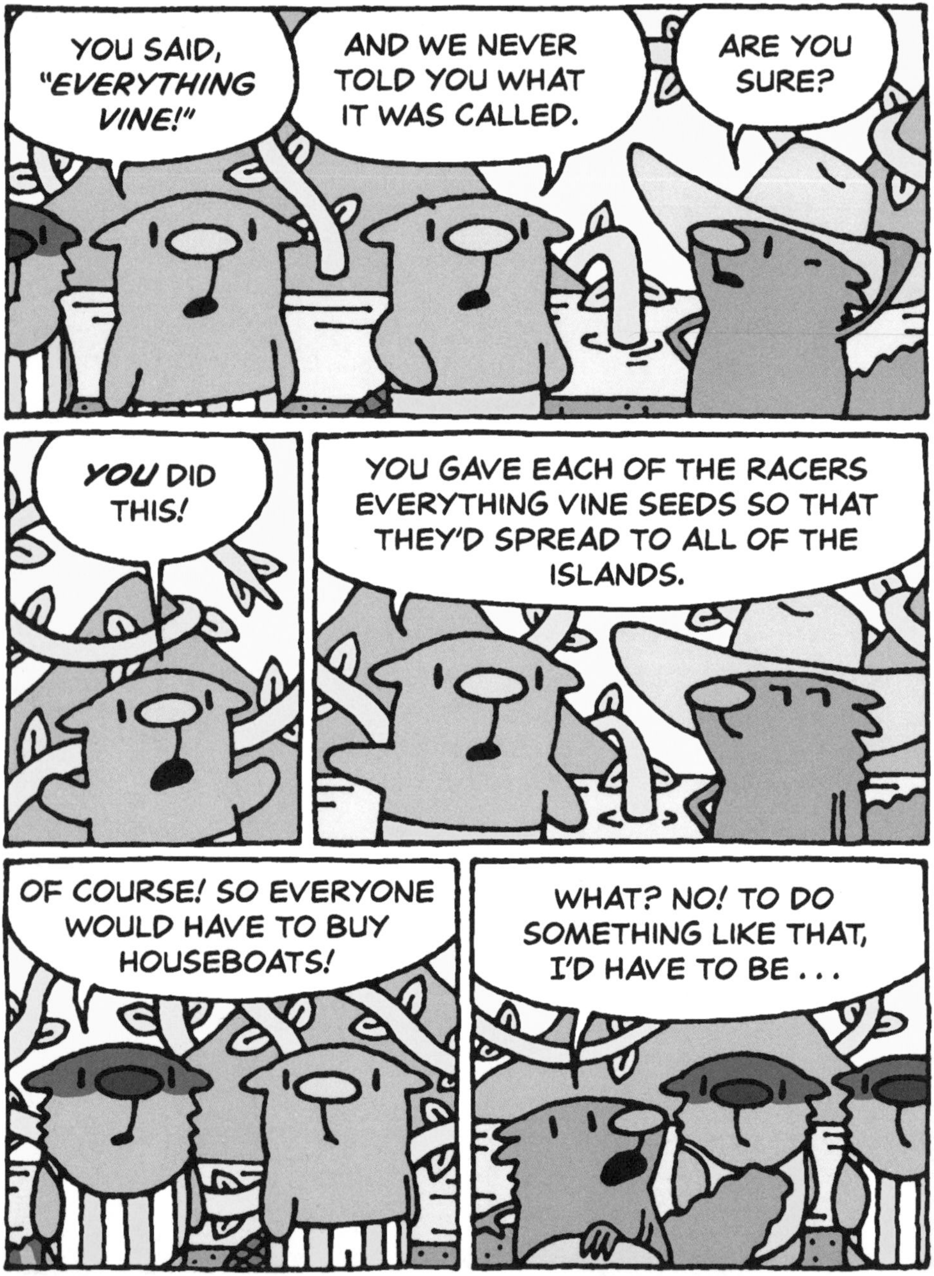
YOU SAID, "*EVERYTHING VINE!*"
AND WE NEVER TOLD YOU WHAT IT WAS CALLED.
ARE YOU SURE?
YOU DID THIS!
YOU GAVE EACH OF THE RACERS EVERYTHING VINE SEEDS SO THAT THEY'D SPREAD TO ALL OF THE ISLANDS.
OF COURSE! SO EVERYONE WOULD HAVE TO BUY HOUSEBOATS!
WHAT? NO! TO DO SOMETHING LIKE THAT, I'D HAVE TO BE . . .

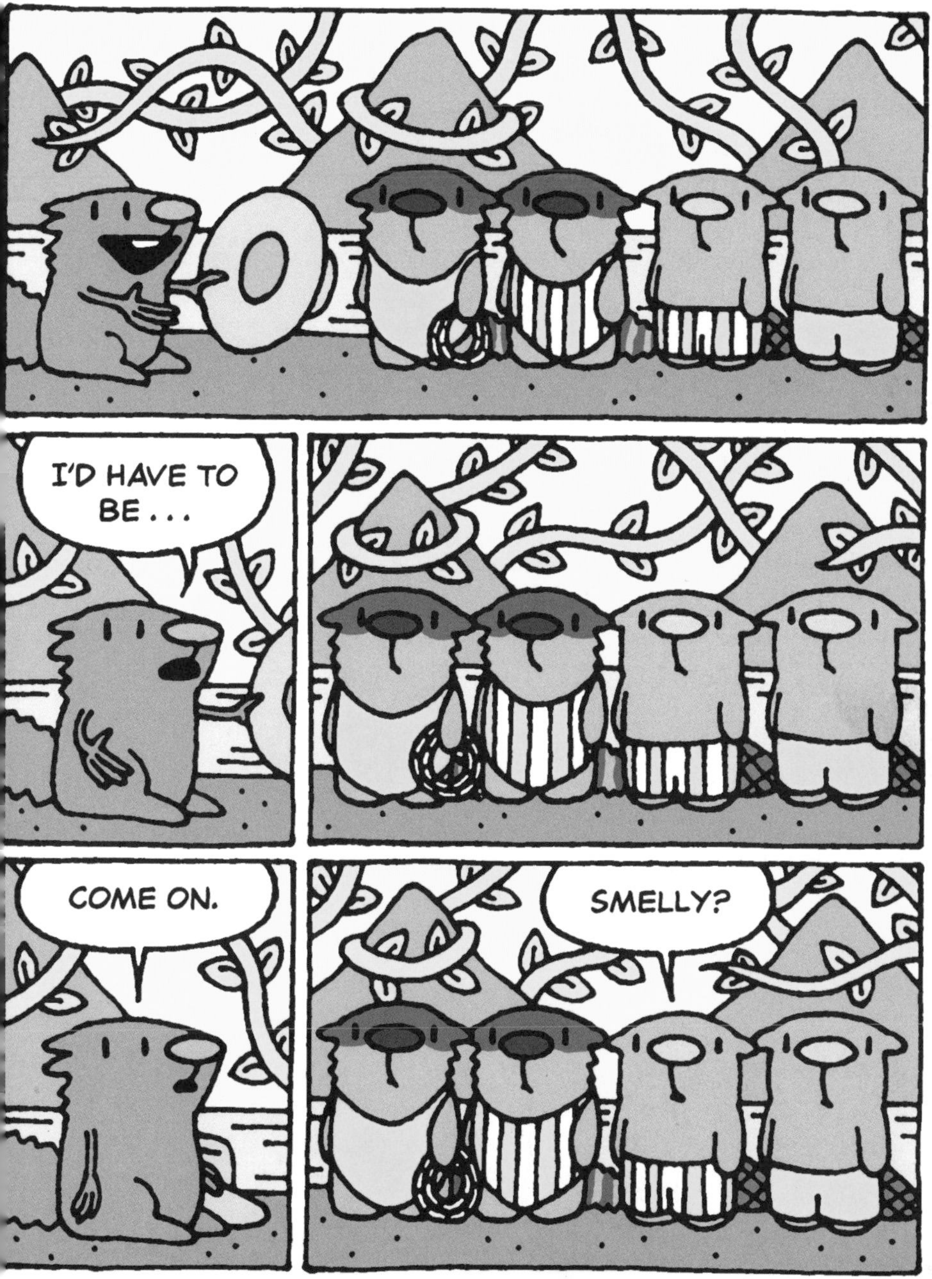
I'D HAVE TO BE . . .
COME ON.
SMELLY?

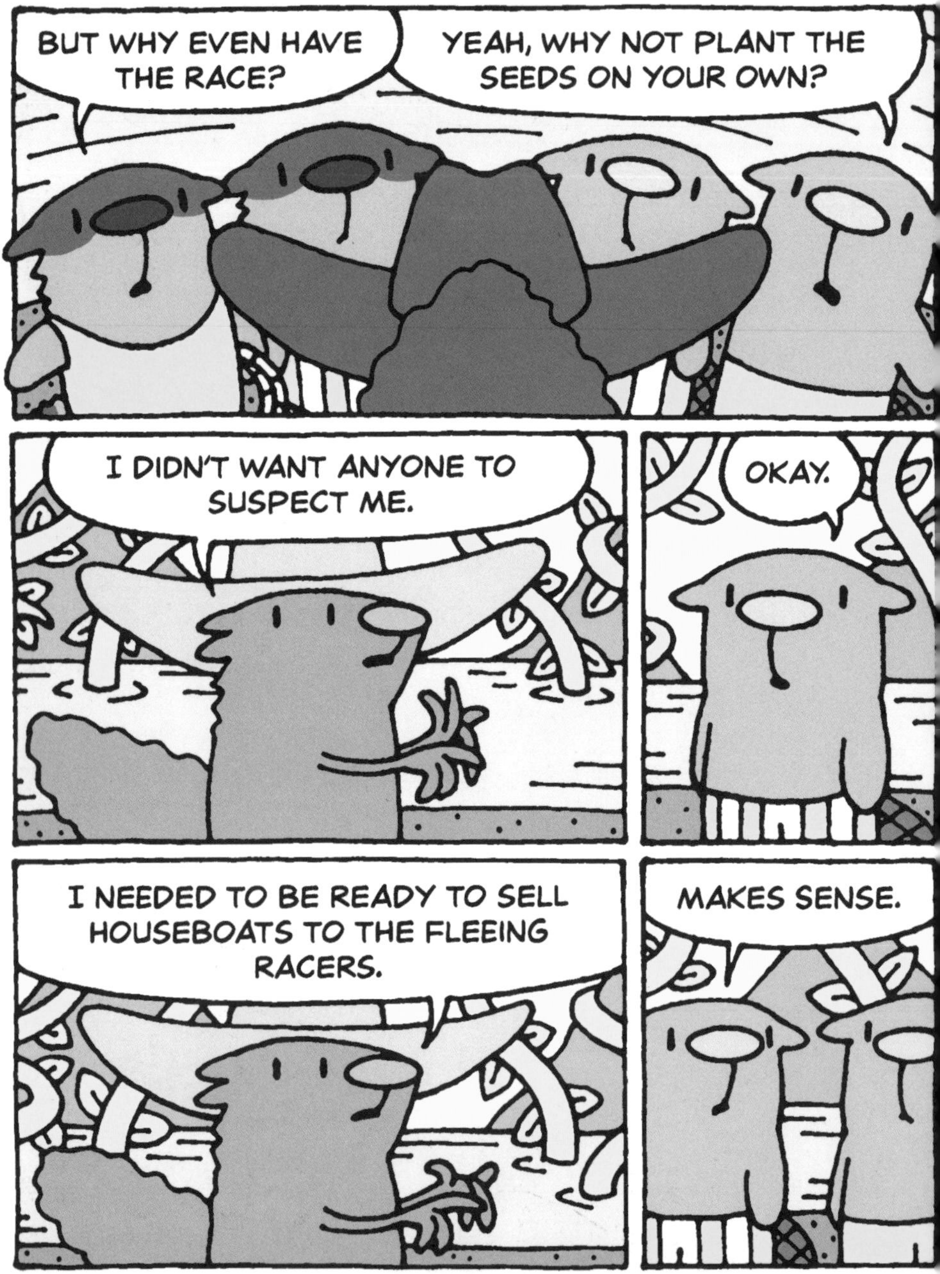
BUT WHY EVEN HAVE THE RACE?
YEAH, WHY NOT PLANT THE SEEDS ON YOUR OWN?
I DIDN'T WANT ANYONE TO SUSPECT ME.
OKAY.
I NEEDED TO BE READY TO SELL HOUSEBOATS TO THE FLEEING RACERS.
MAKES SENSE.

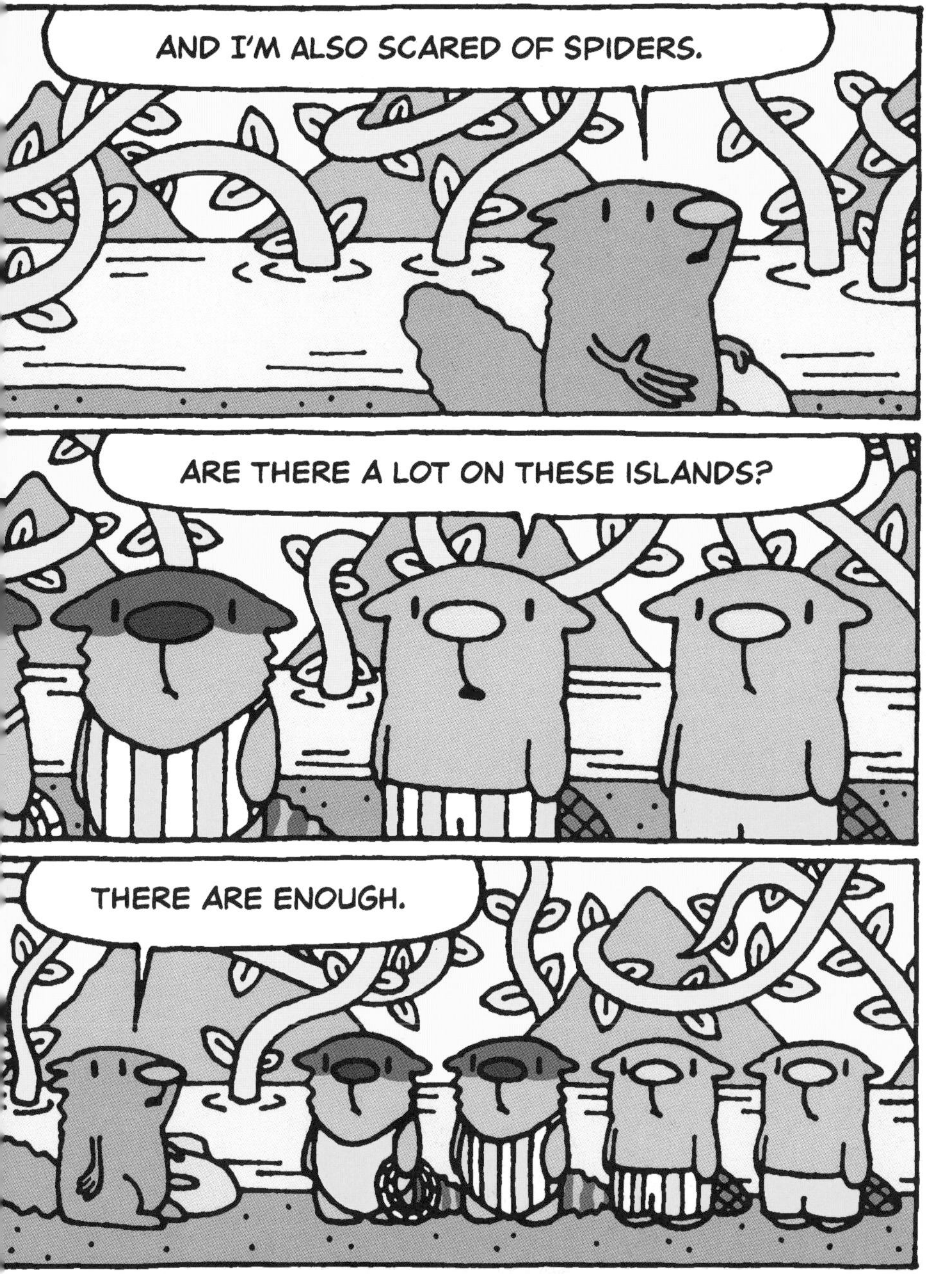
AND I'M ALSO SCARED OF SPIDERS.
ARE THERE A LOT ON THESE ISLANDS?
THERE ARE ENOUGH.

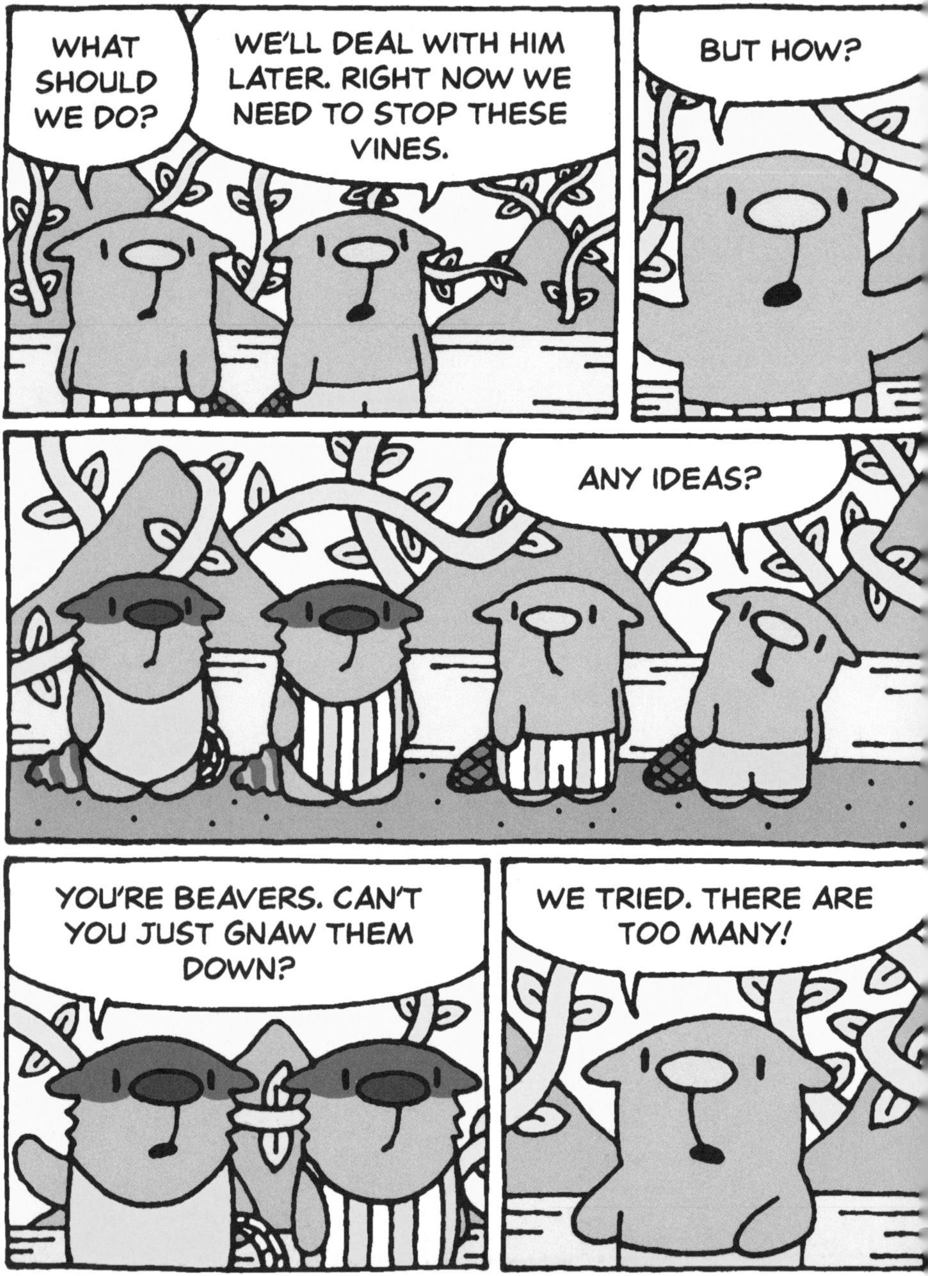
WHAT SHOULD WE DO?
WE'LL DEAL WITH HIM LATER. RIGHT NOW WE NEED TO STOP THESE VINES.
BUT HOW?
ANY IDEAS?
YOU'RE BEAVERS. CAN'T YOU JUST GNAW THEM DOWN?
WE TRIED. THERE ARE TOO MANY!

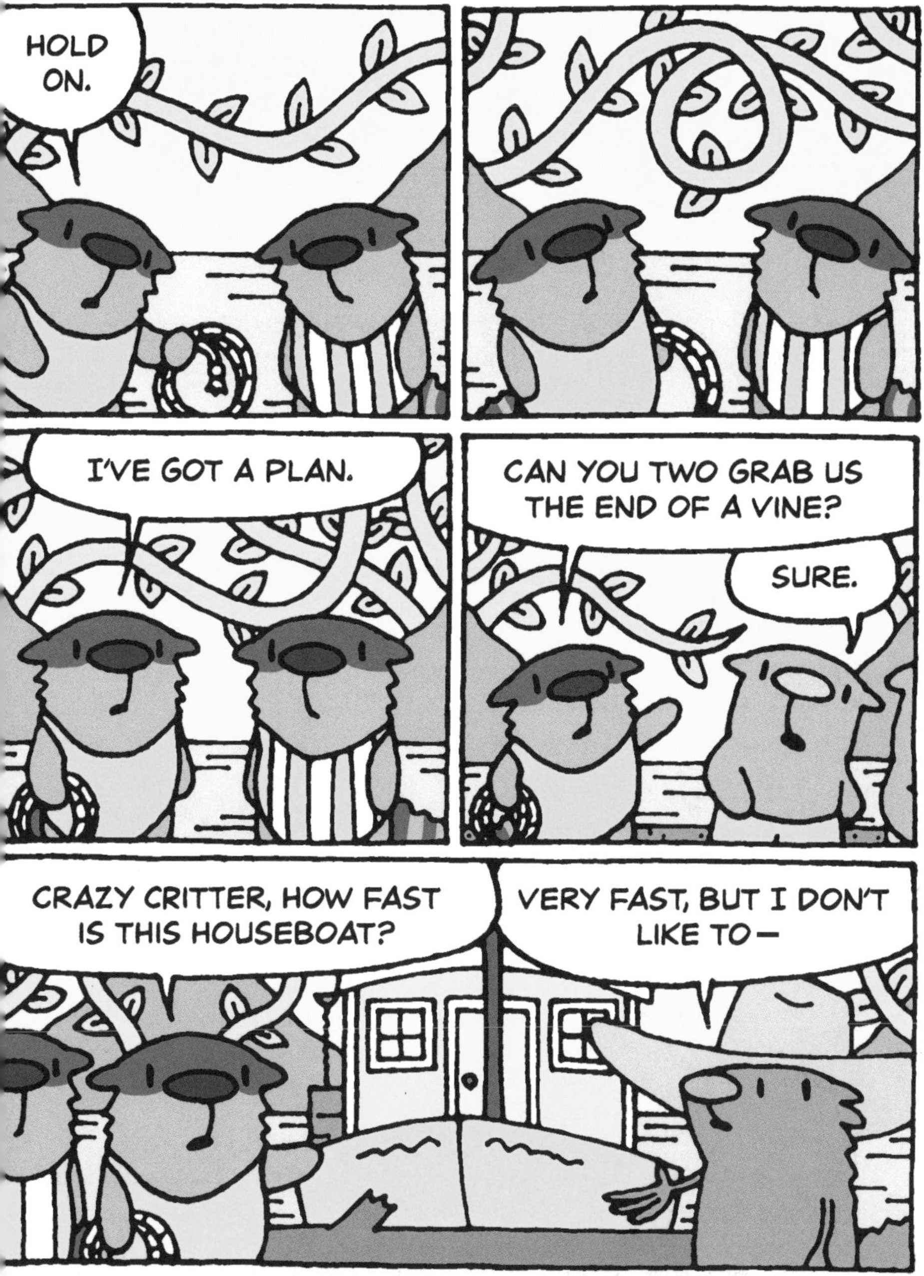
HOLD ON.
I'VE GOT A PLAN.
CAN YOU TWO GRAB US THE END OF A VINE?
SURE.
CRAZY CRITTER, HOW FAST IS THIS HOUSEBOAT?
VERY FAST, BUT I DON'T LIKE TO—

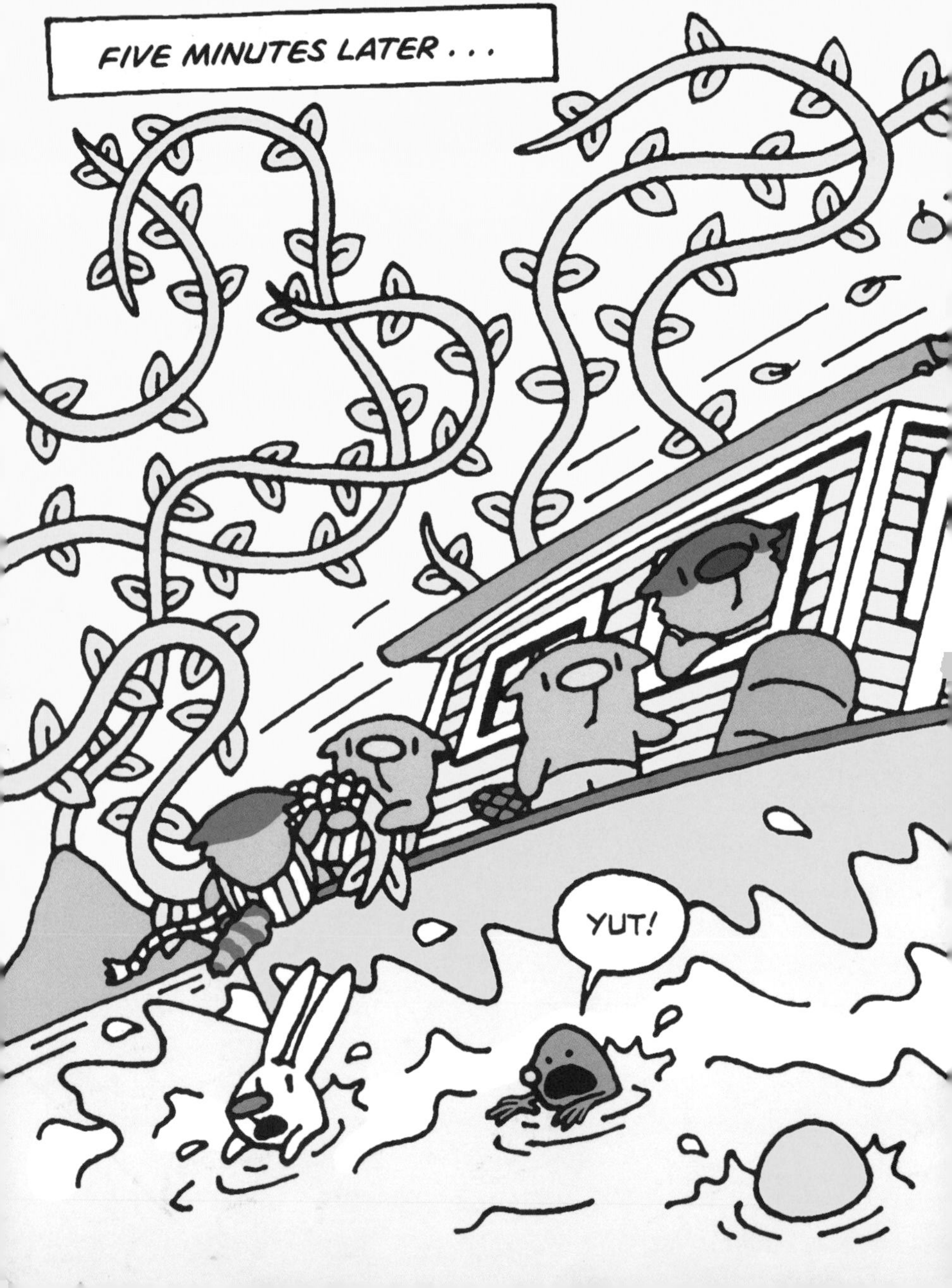
FIVE MINUTES LATER . . .
YUT!

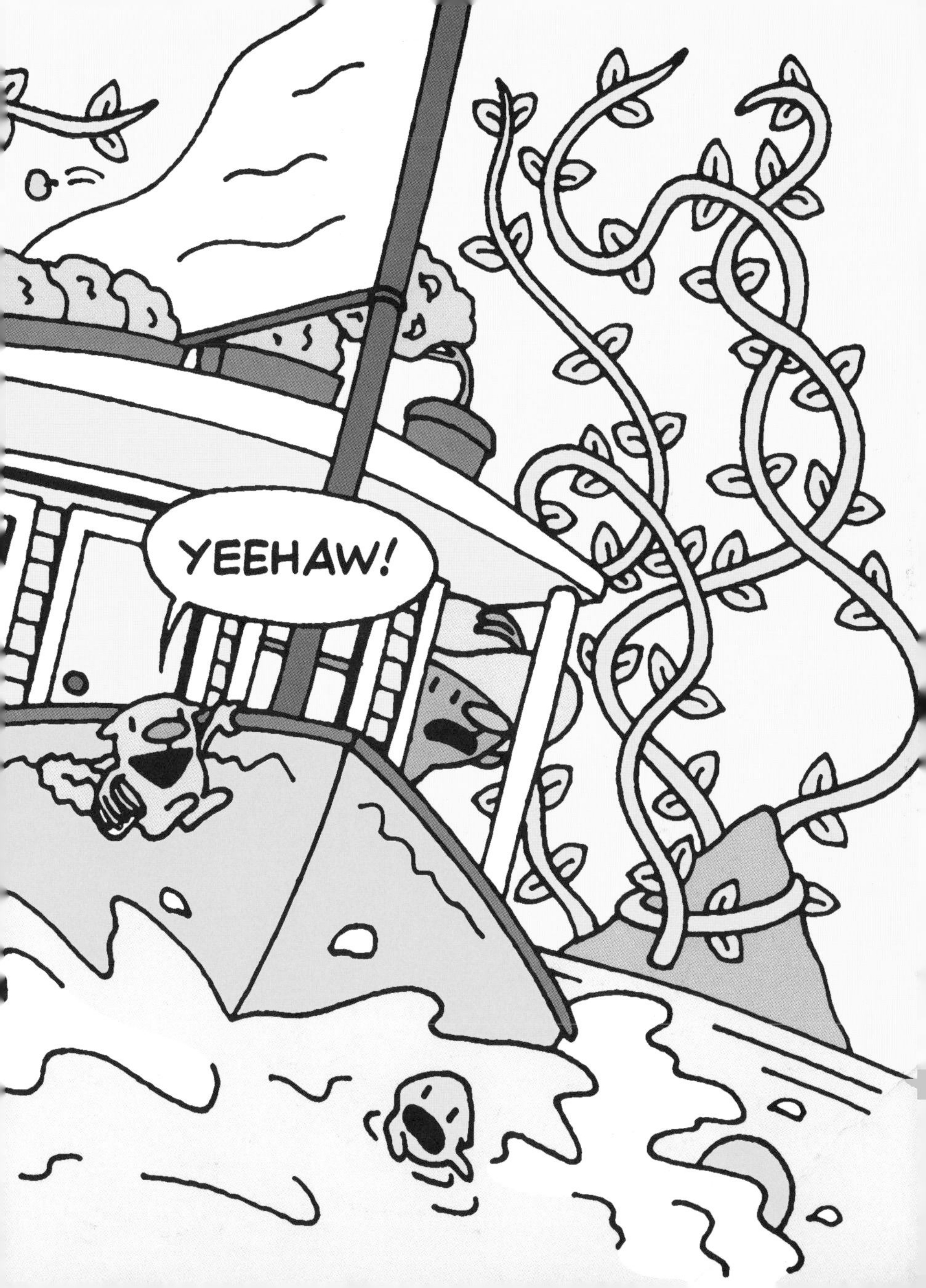
YEEHAW!

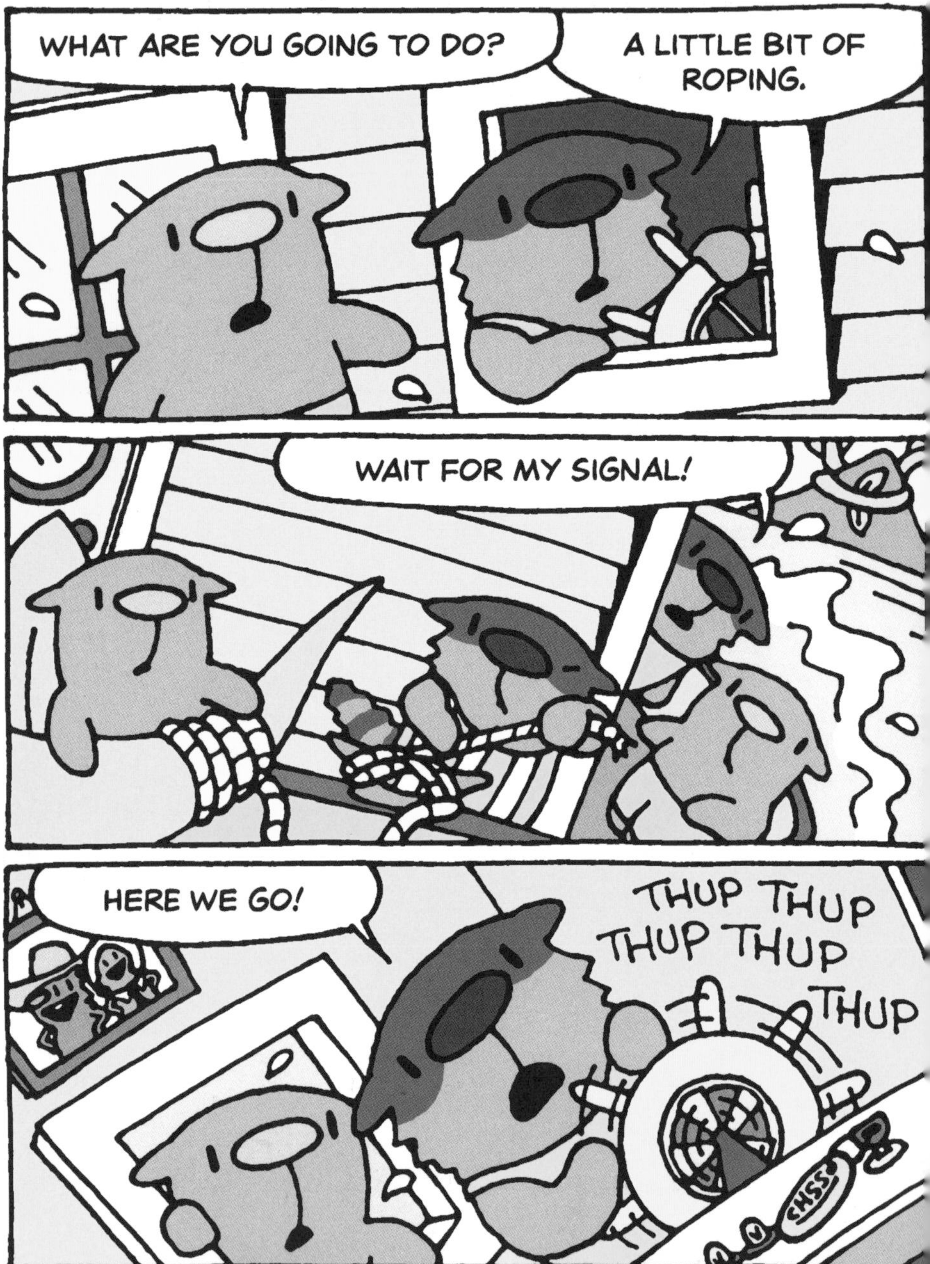
WHAT ARE YOU GOING TO DO?
A LITTLE BIT OF ROPING.
WAIT FOR MY SIGNAL!
HERE WE GO!
THUP THUP THUP THUP THUP

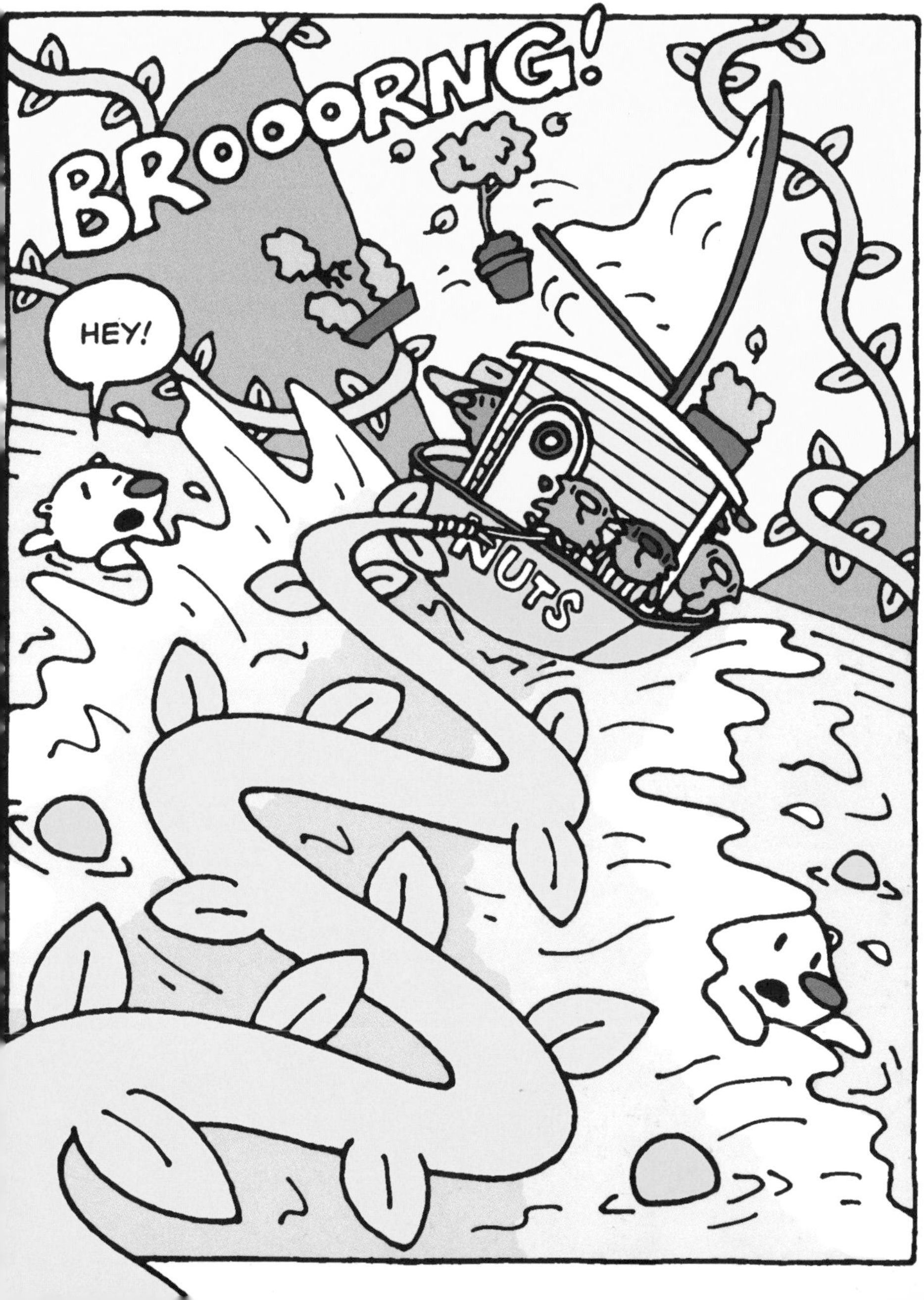
BROOORNG!
HEY!
NUTS

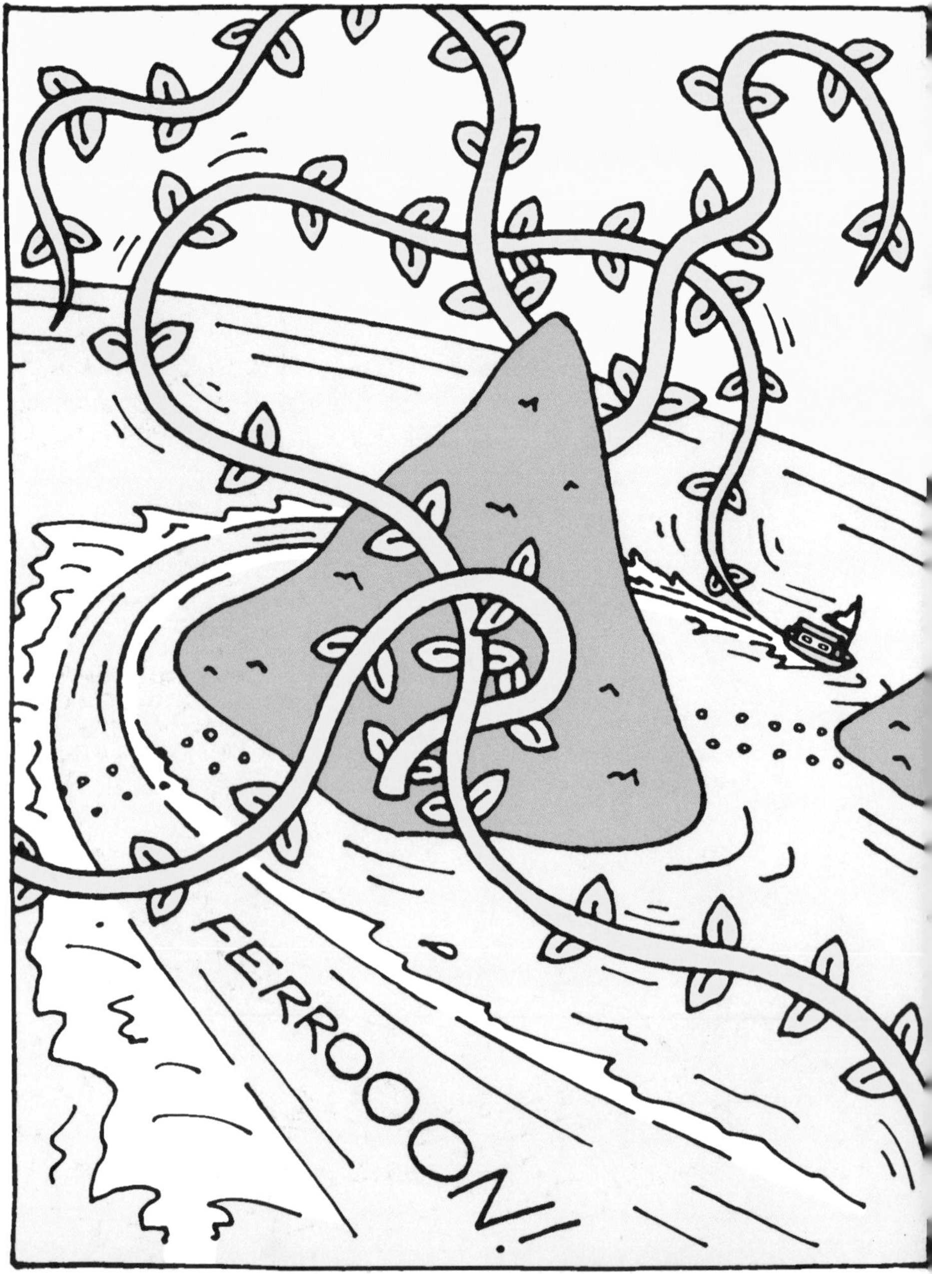
FERROOOON!

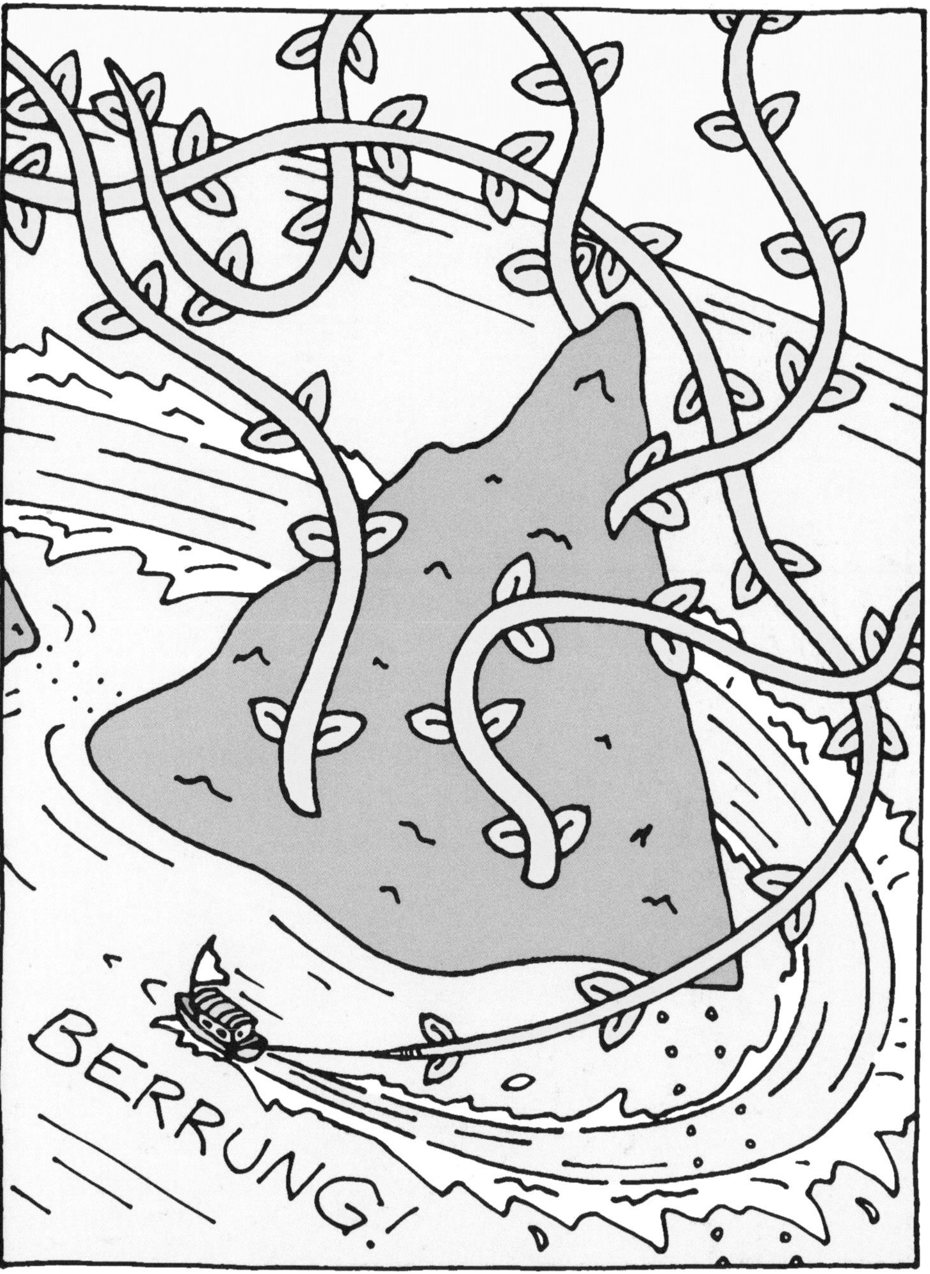
BERRUNG!

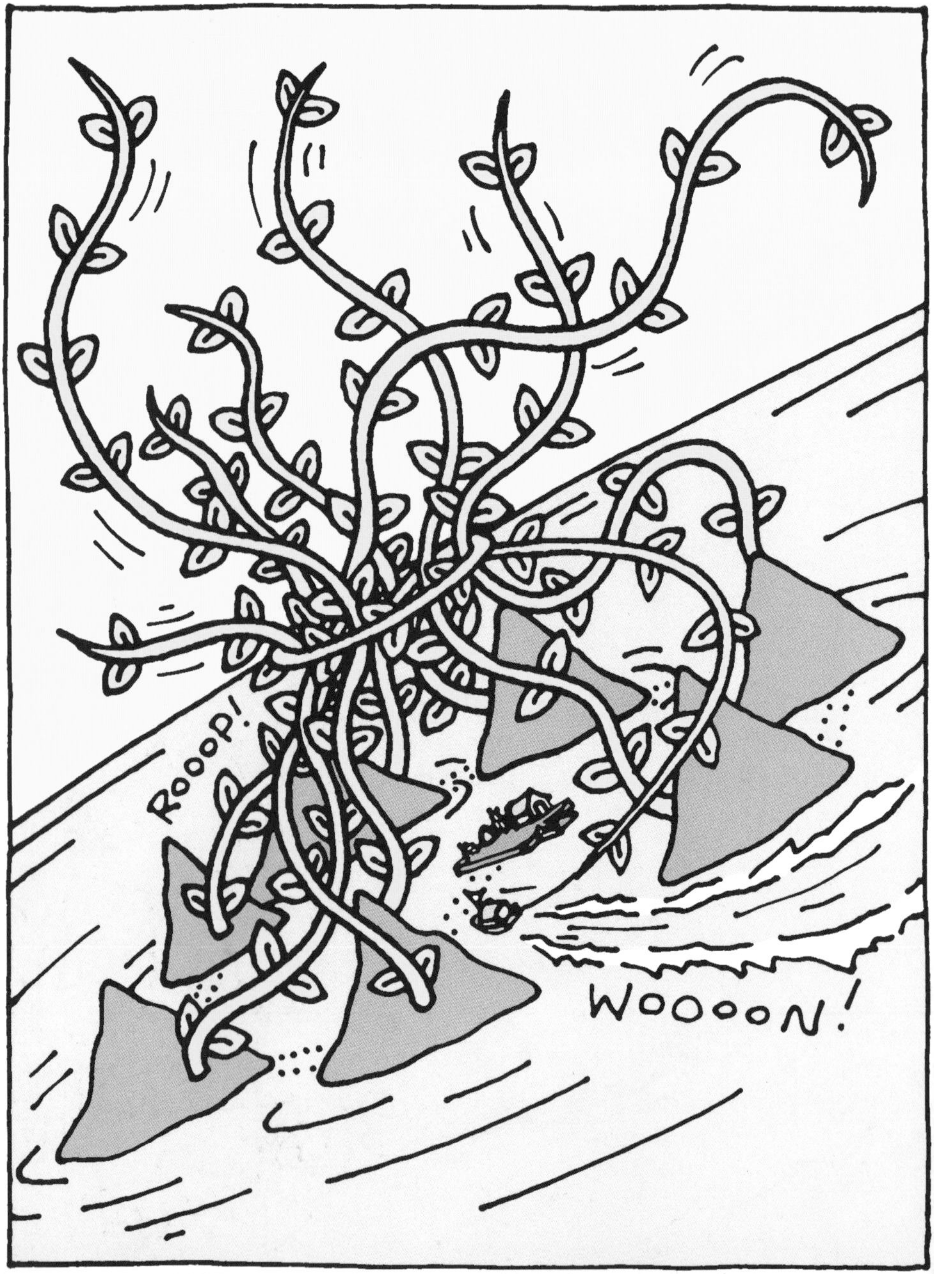

ROOOP!
WOOOOON!

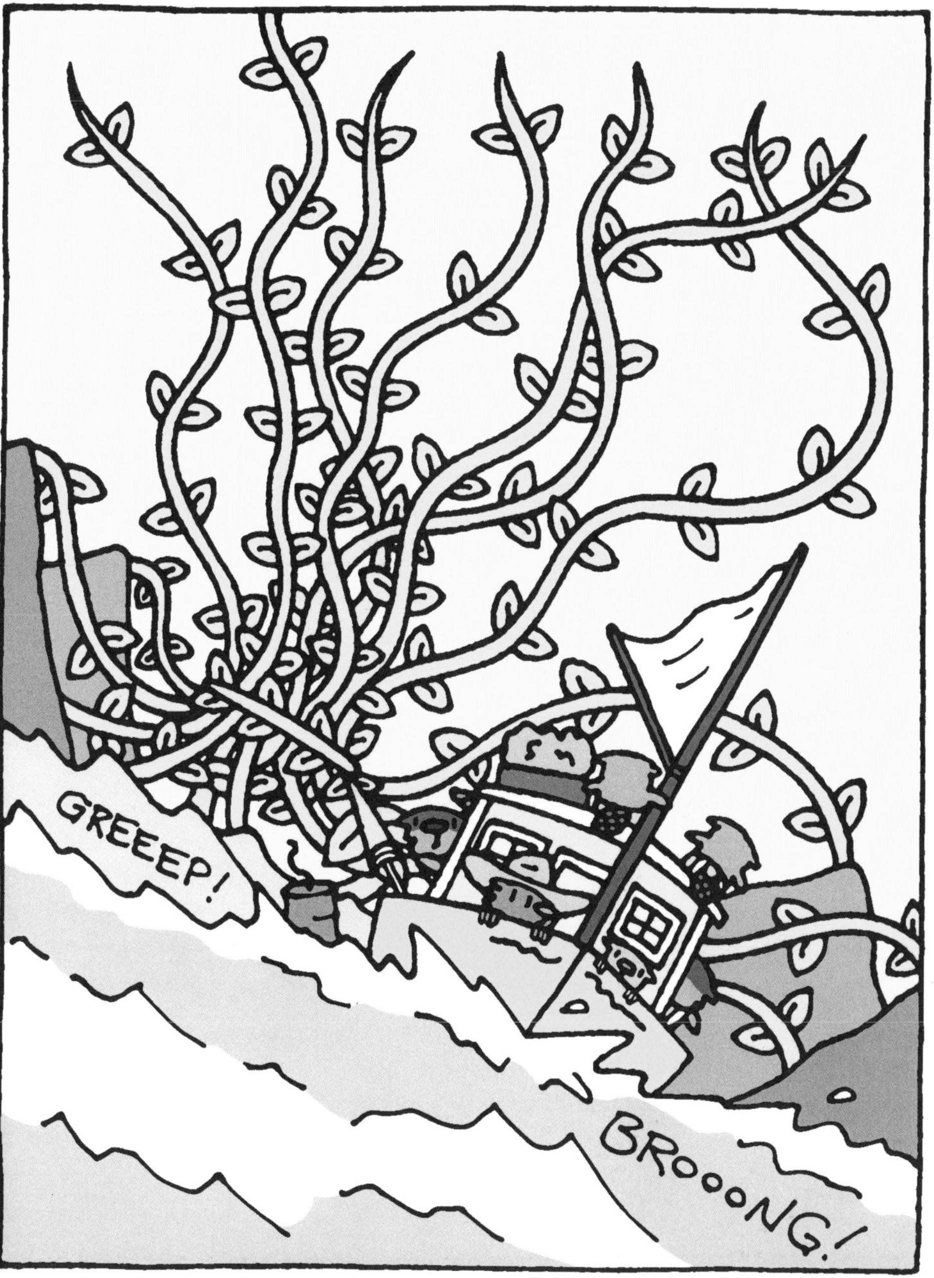
GREEEEP!
BROOONG!

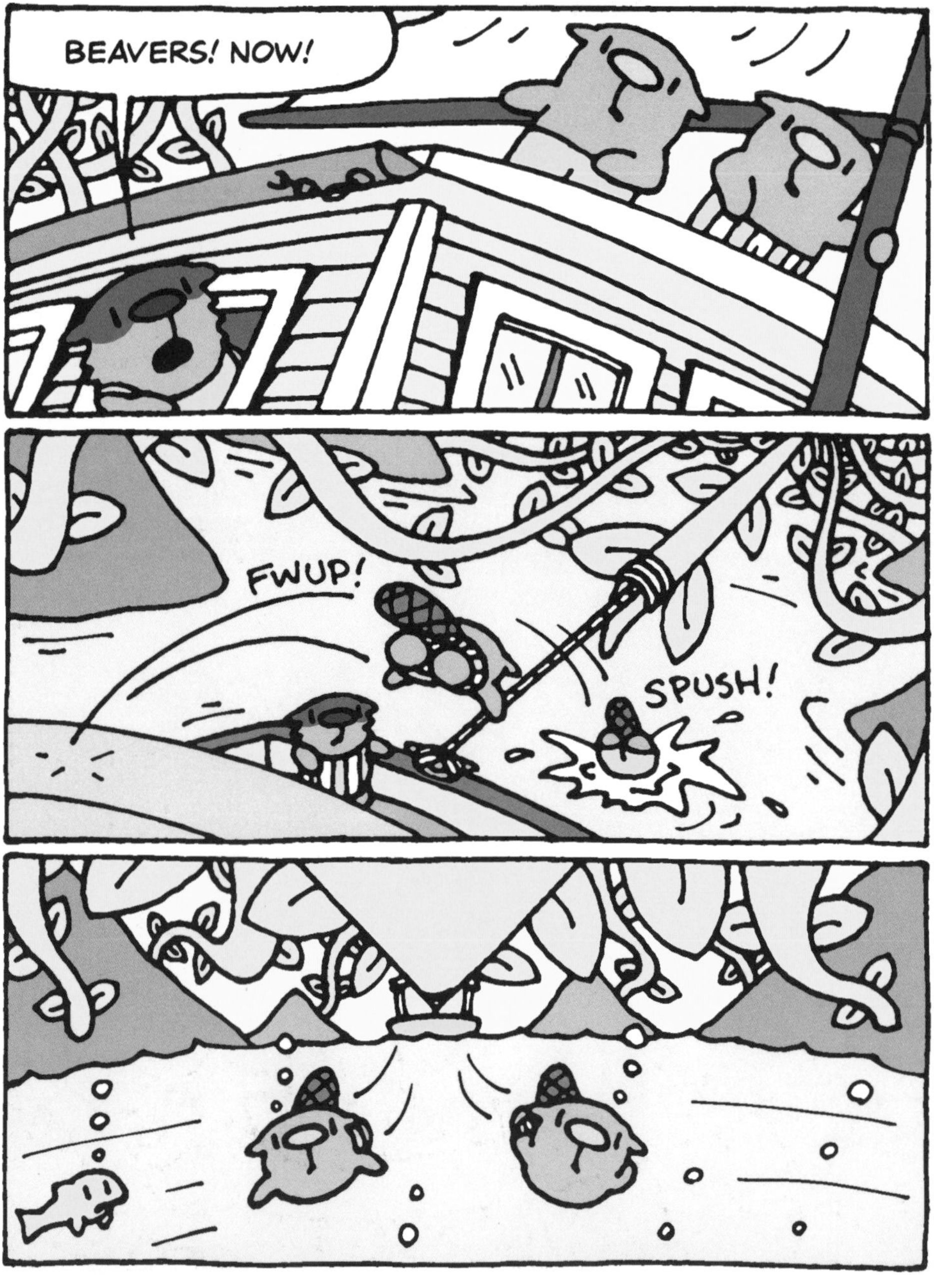
BEAVERS! NOW!
FWUP!
SPUSH!

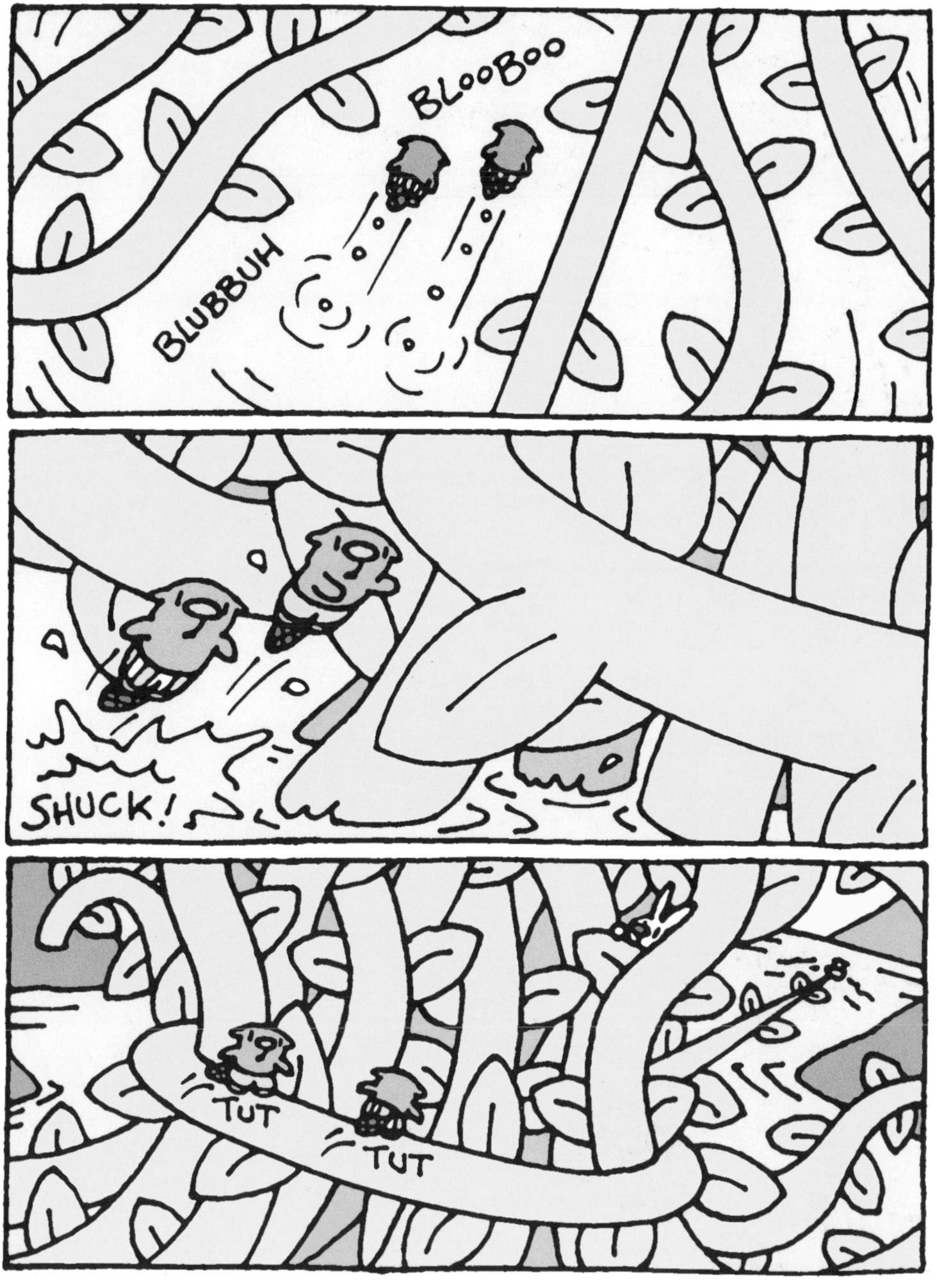
BLUBBUH
BLOOBOO
SHUCK!
TUT
TUT

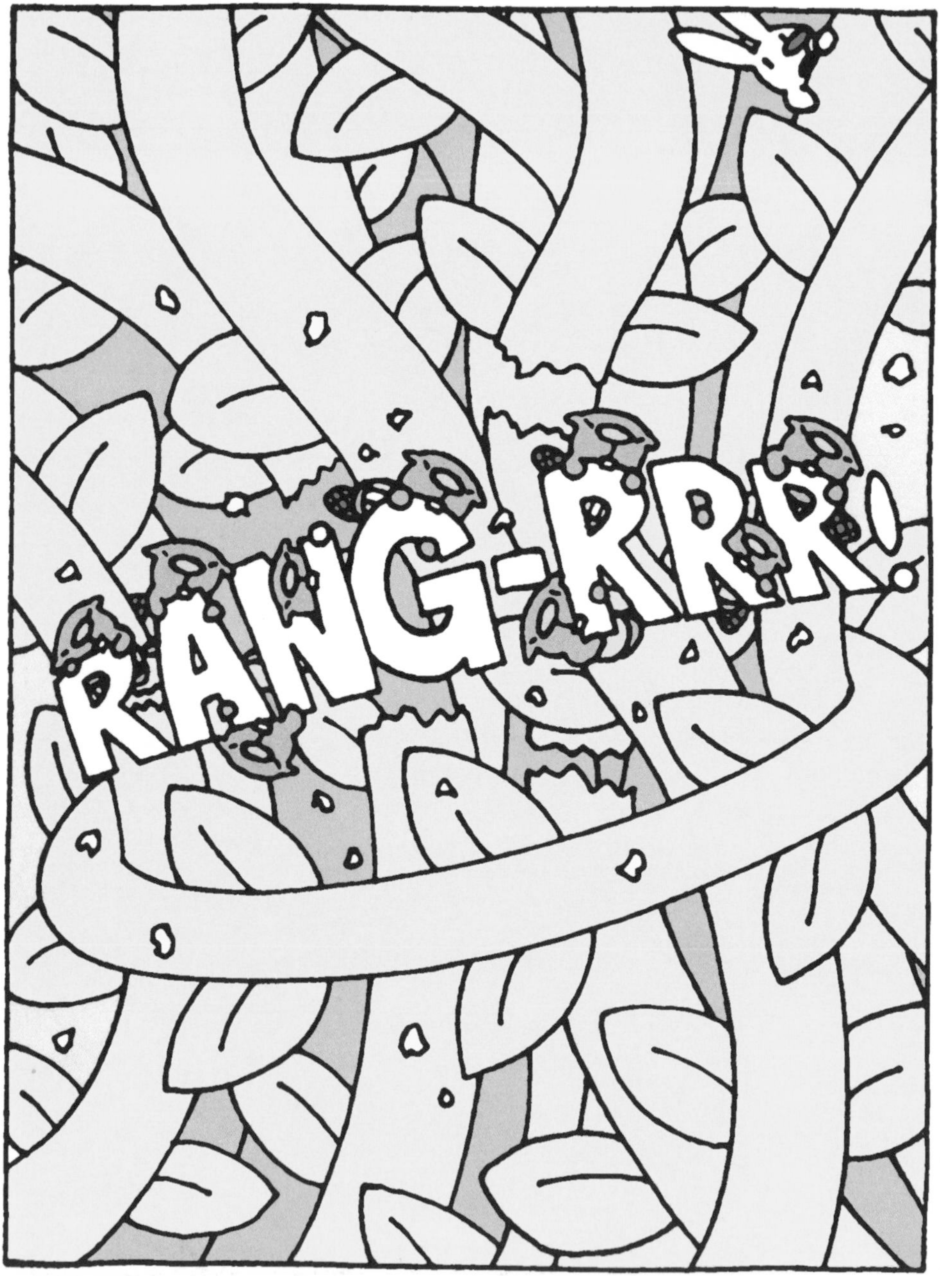
RANG-RRR!

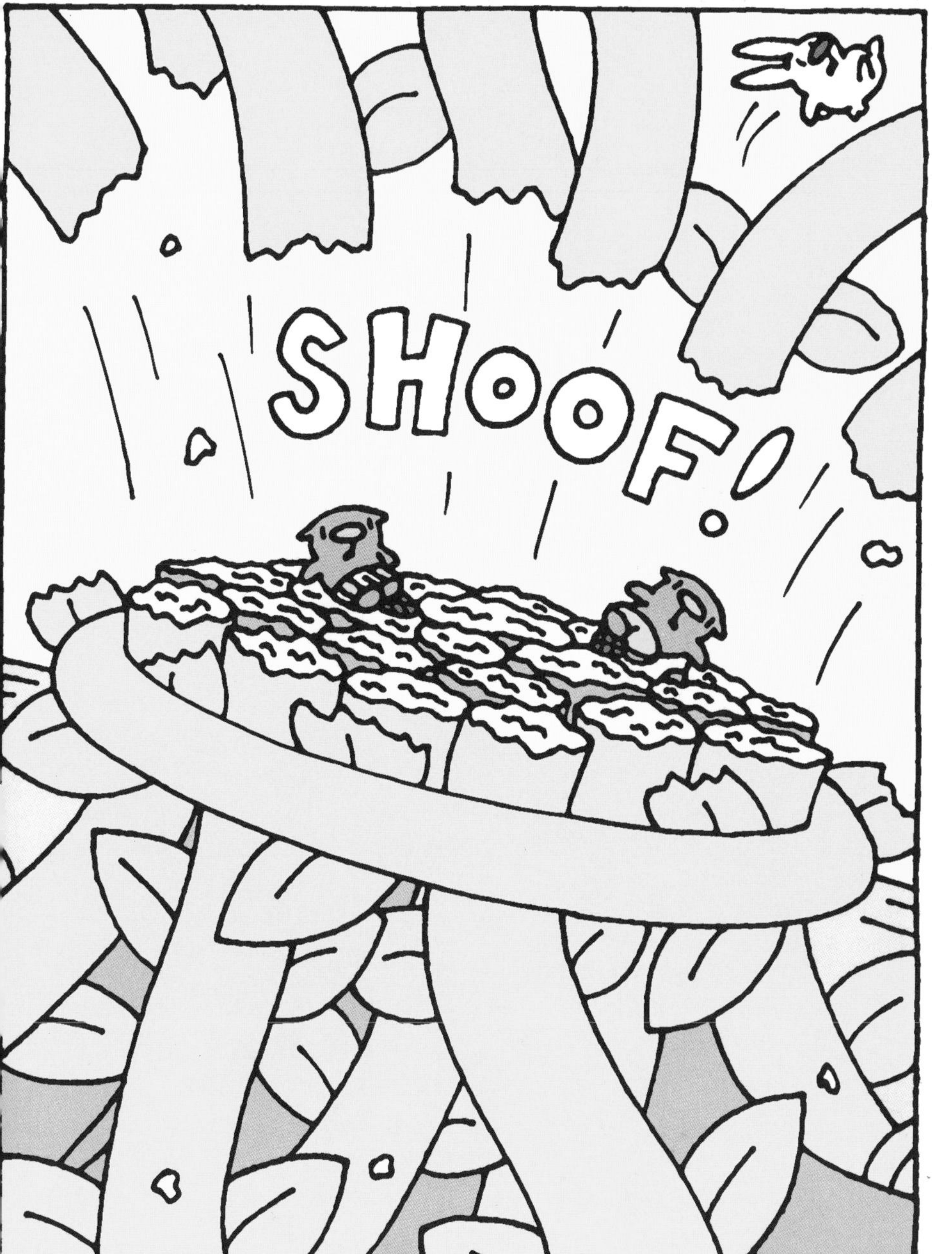
SHOOF!

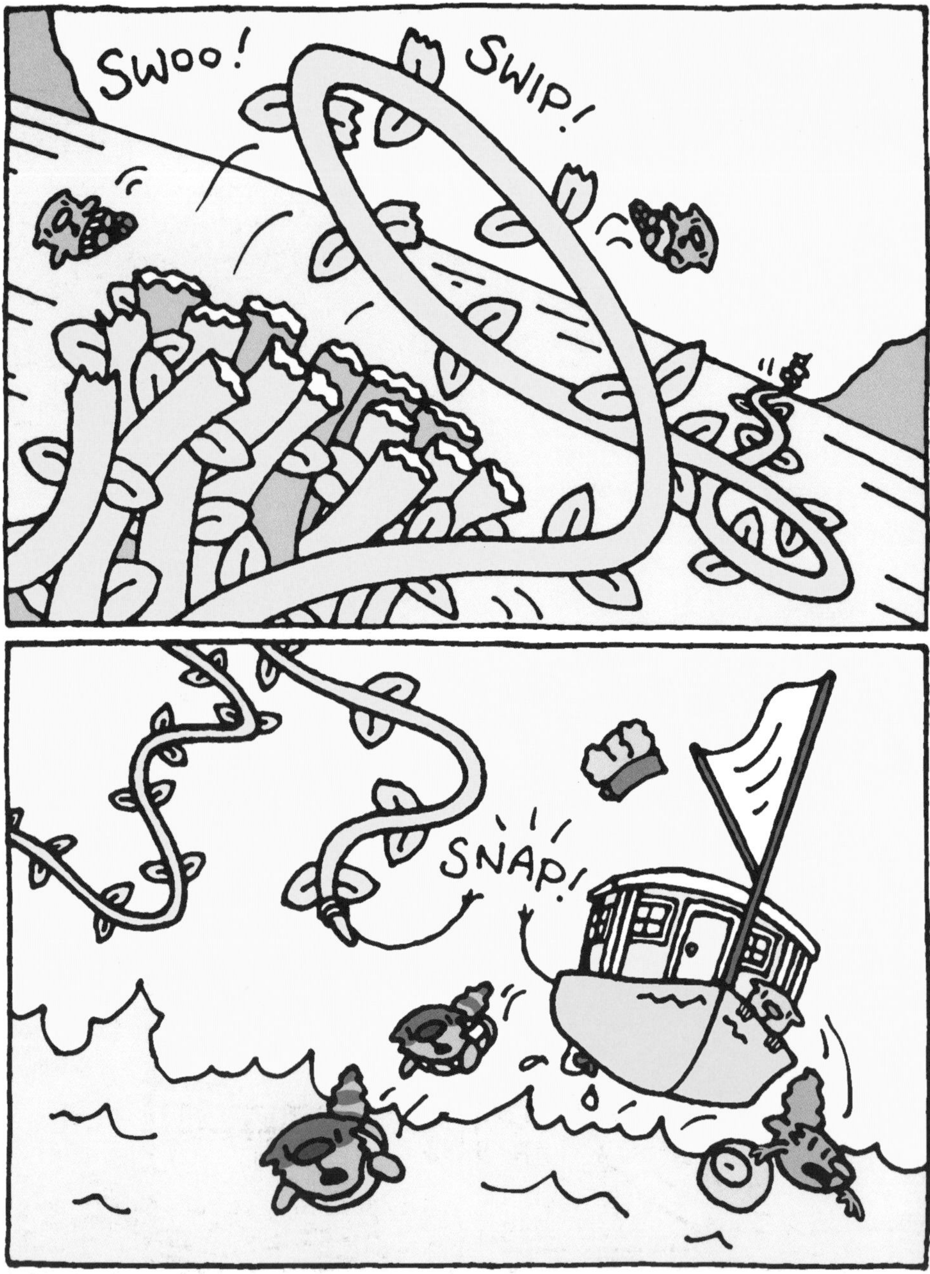
SWOO!
SWIP!
SNAP!

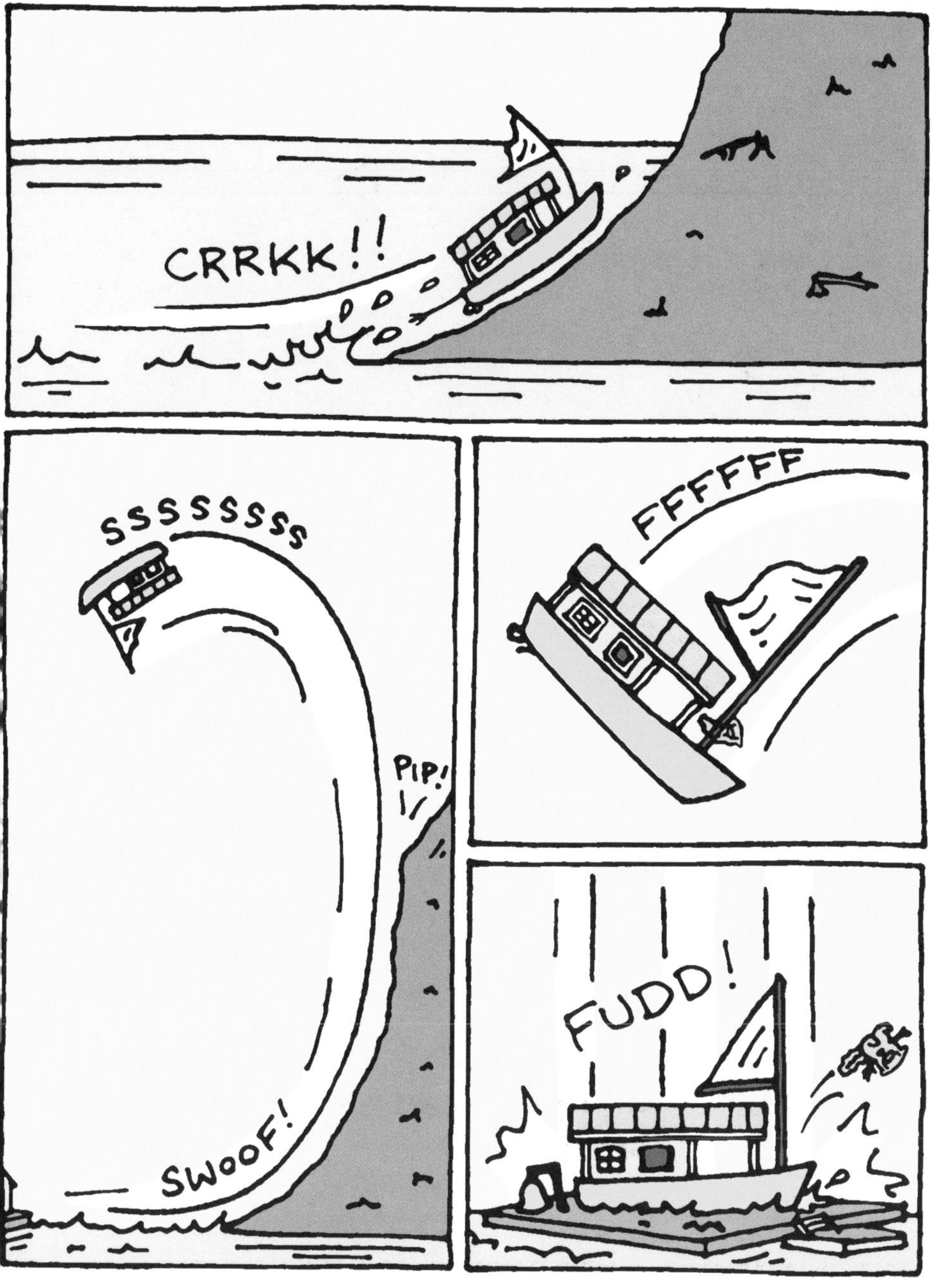
CRRKK!!
SSSSSSSS
PIP!
SWOOF!
FFFFFF
FUDD!

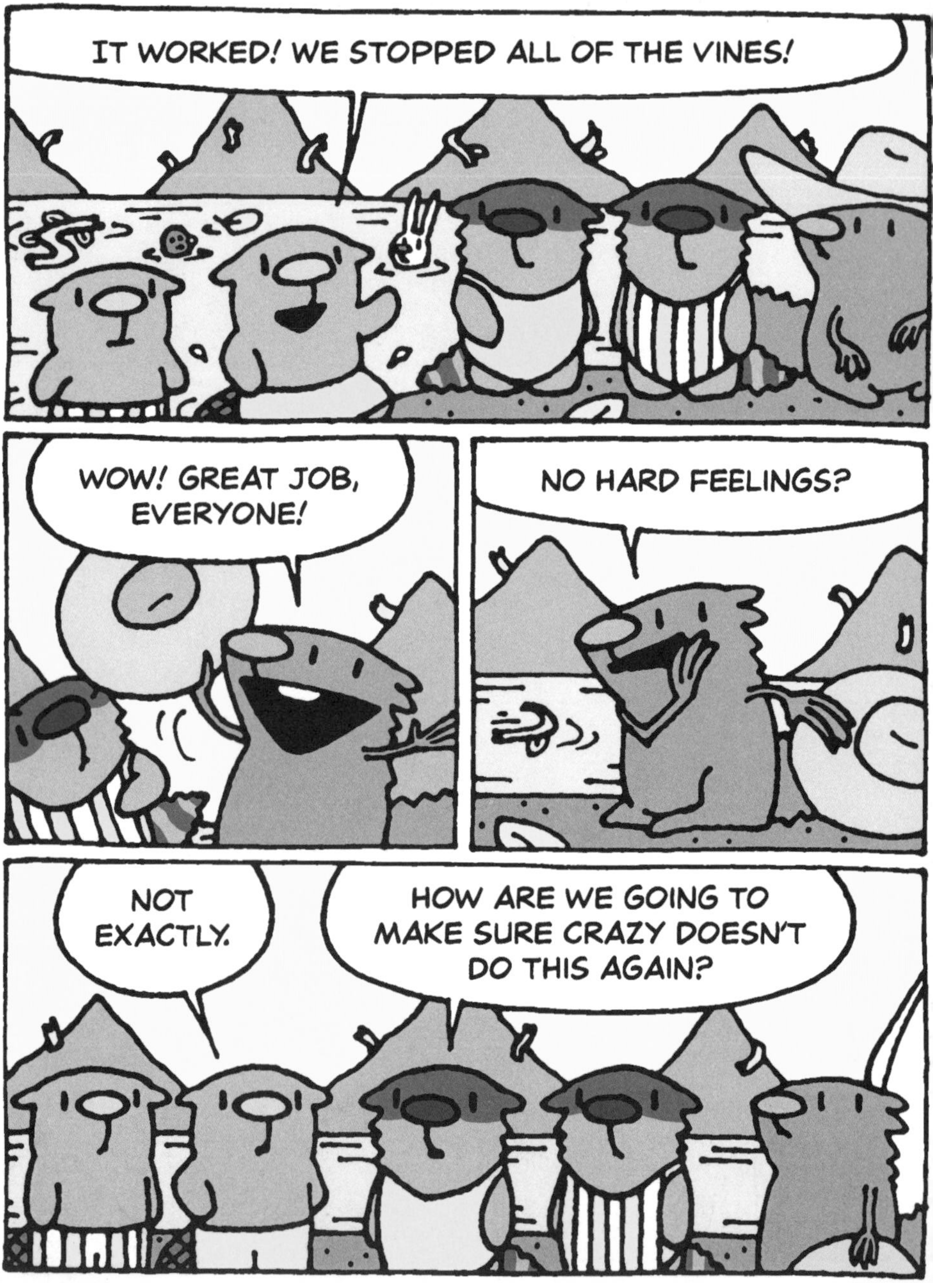
IT WORKED! WE STOPPED ALL OF THE VINES!
WOW! GREAT JOB, EVERYONE!
NO HARD FEELINGS?
NOT EXACTLY.
HOW ARE WE GOING TO MAKE SURE CRAZY DOESN'T DO THIS AGAIN?

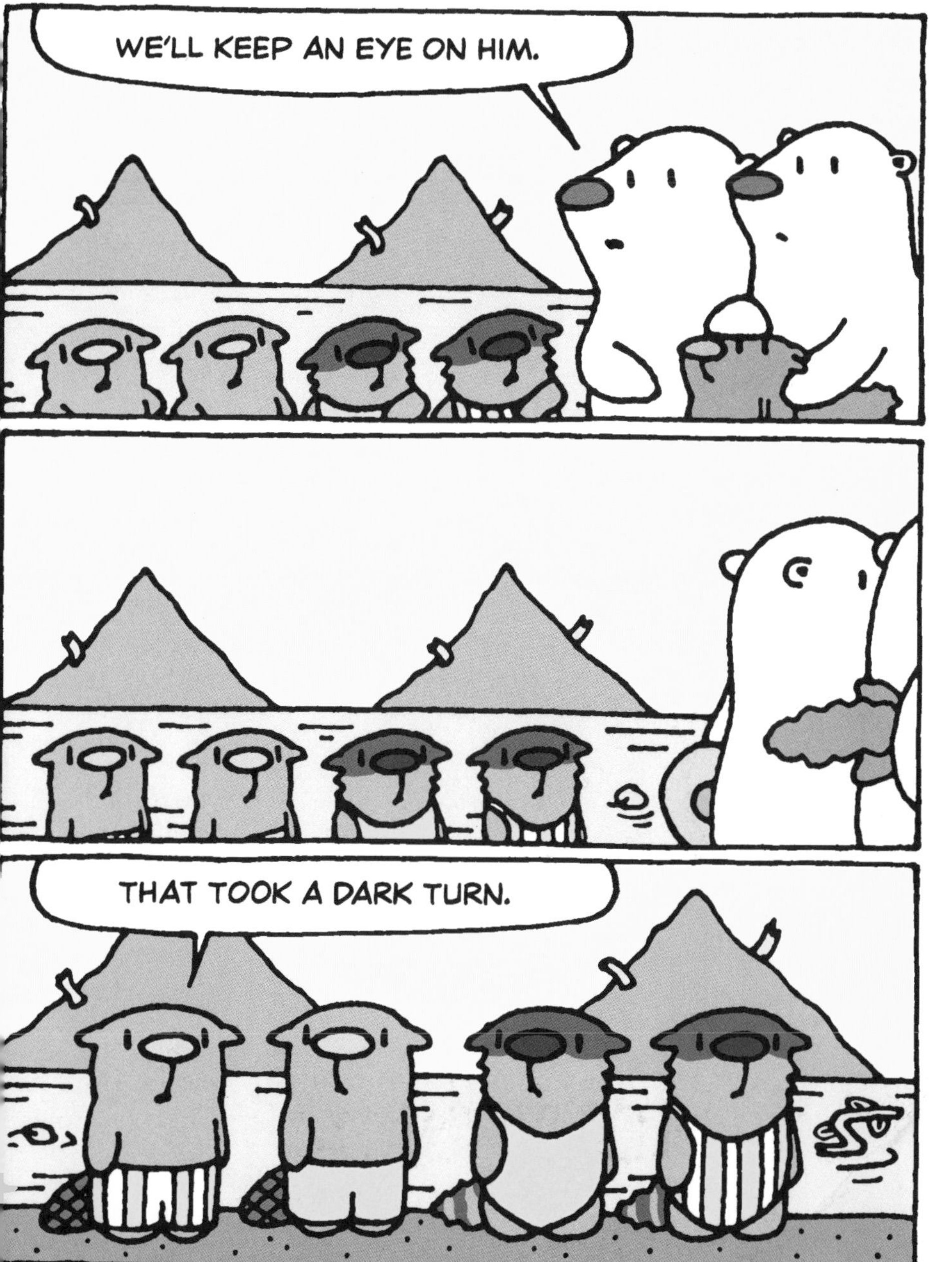
WE'LL KEEP AN EYE ON HIM.
THAT TOOK A DARK TURN.

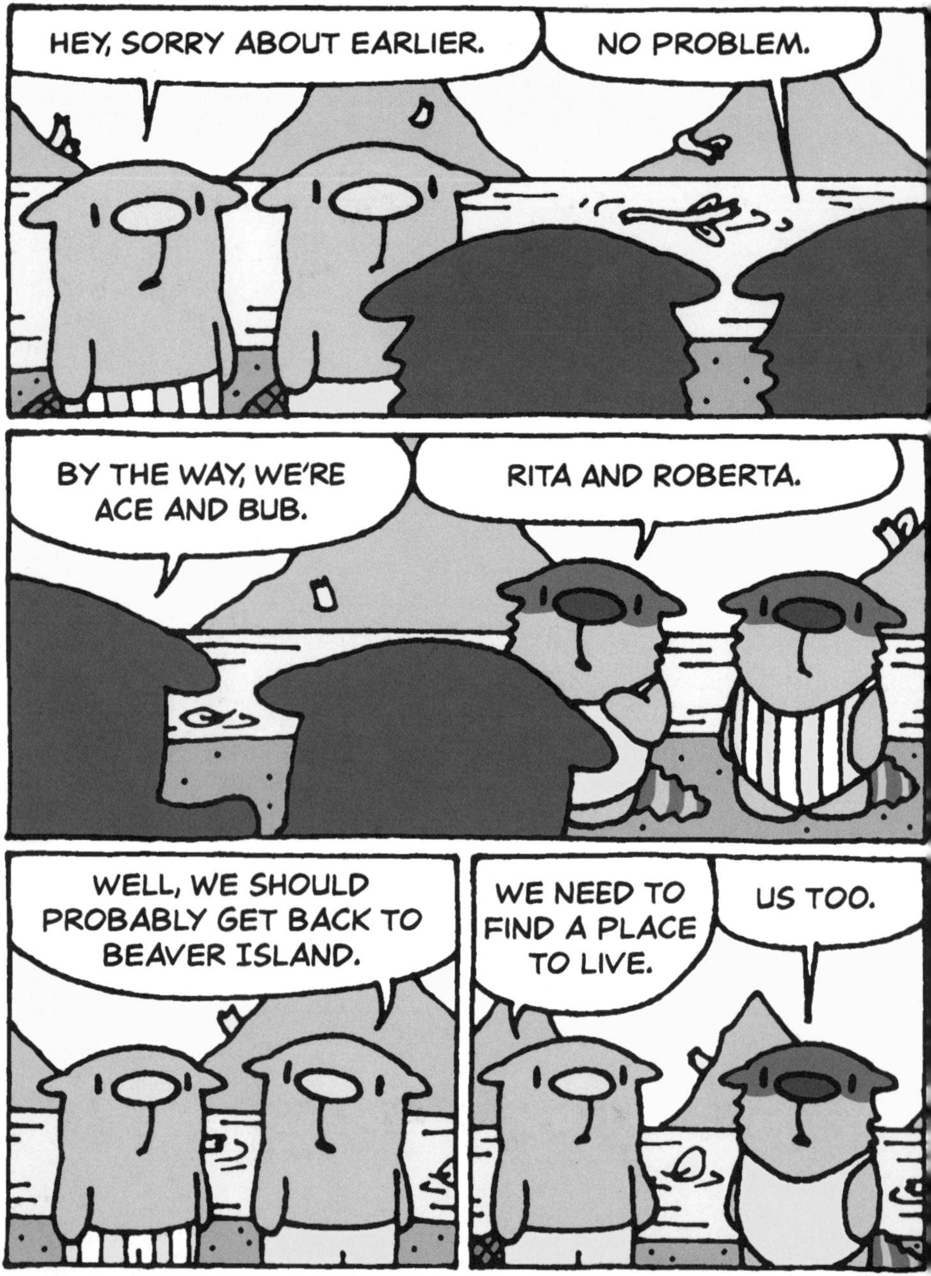
HEY, SORRY ABOUT EARLIER.
NO PROBLEM.
BY THE WAY, WE'RE ACE AND BUB.
RITA AND ROBERTA.
WELL, WE SHOULD PROBABLY GET BACK TO BEAVER ISLAND.
WE NEED TO FIND A PLACE TO LIVE.
US TOO.

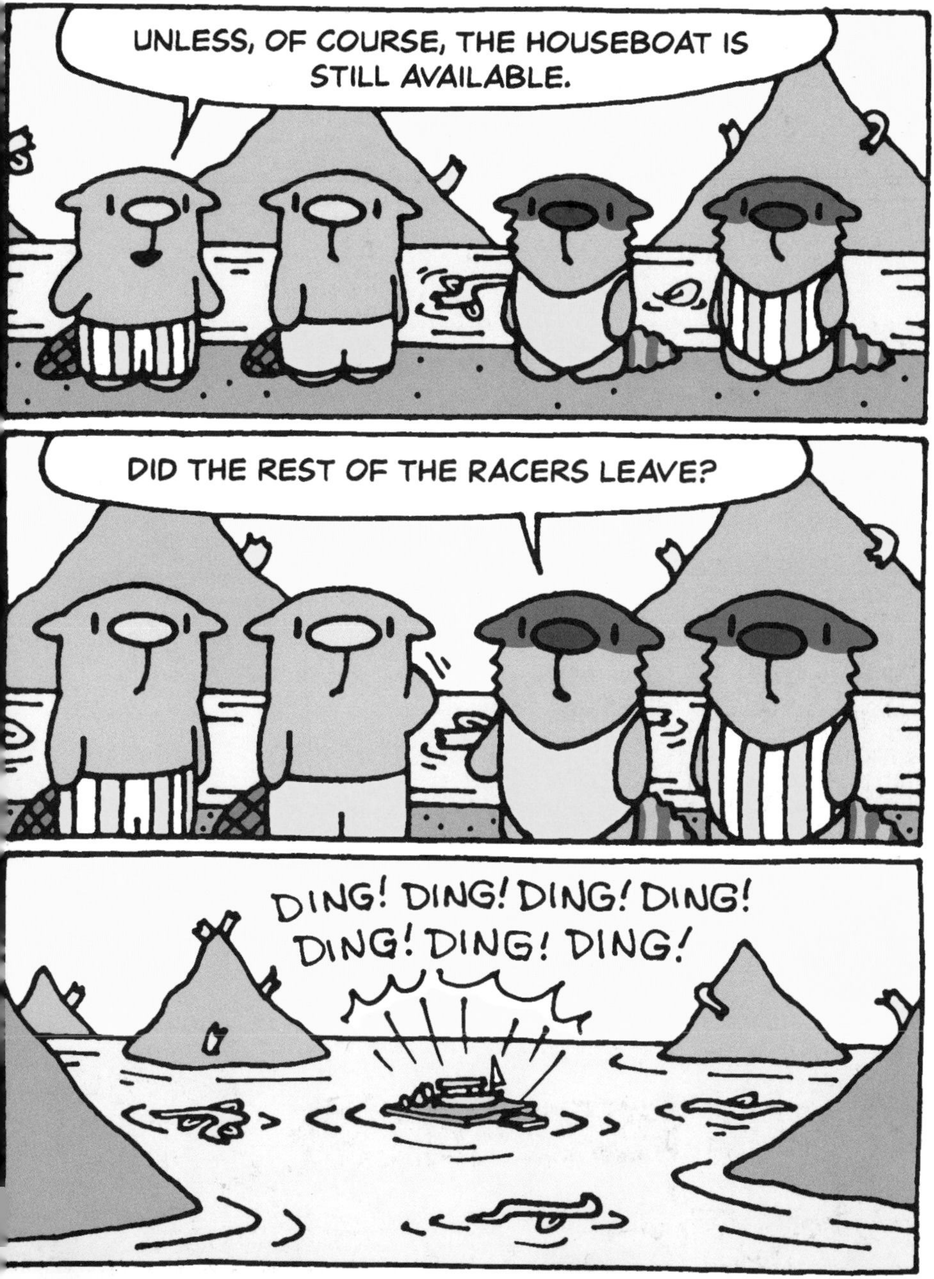
UNLESS, OF COURSE, THE HOUSEBOAT IS STILL AVAILABLE.
DID THE REST OF THE RACERS LEAVE?
DING! DING! DING! DING! DING! DING! DING!

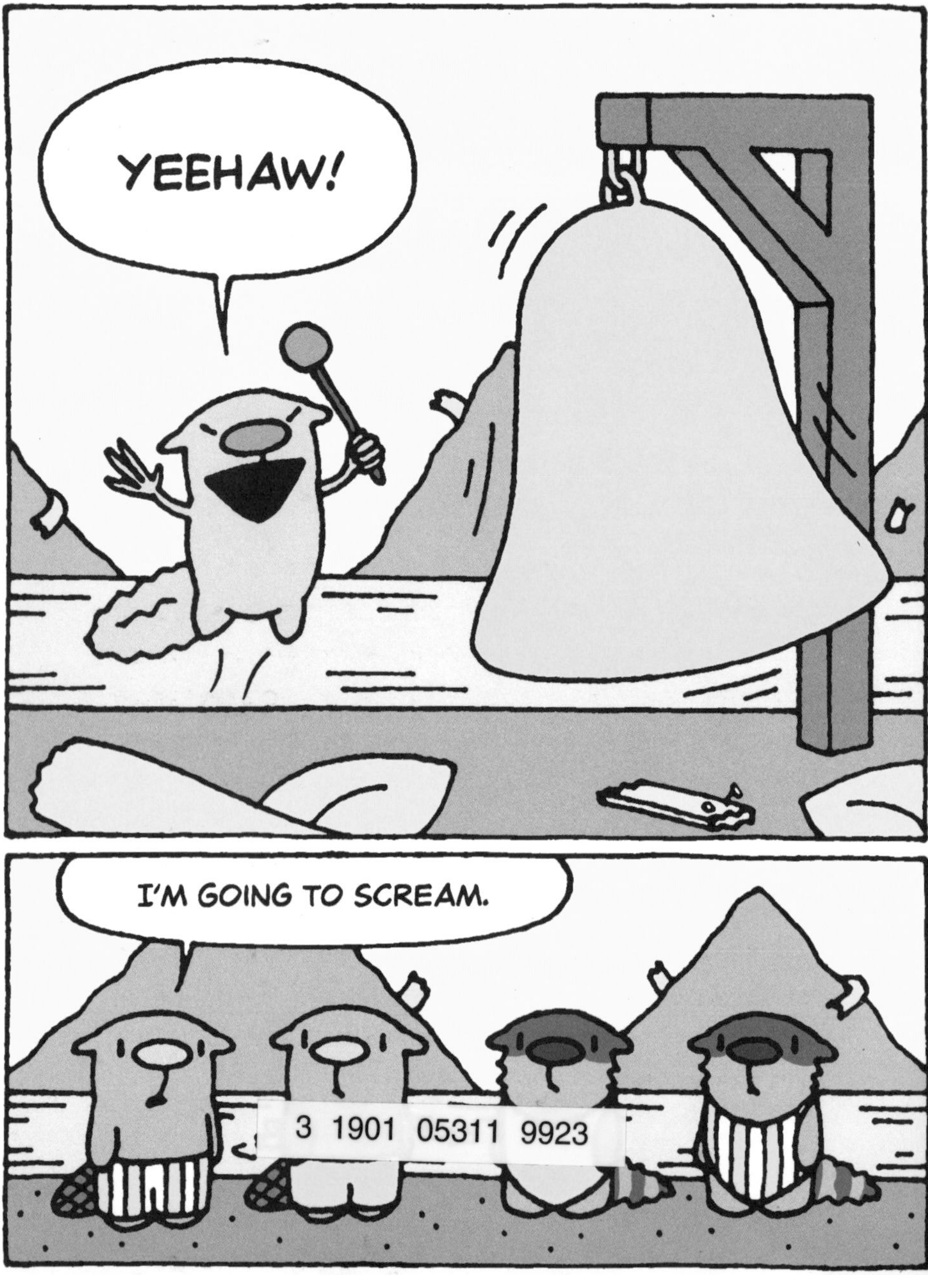
YEEHAW!
I'M GOING TO SCREAM.